PRAISE FOR J.R. SEEGER'S MIKE4 SERIES

"Seeger has crafted a fast-paced narrative which carries the reader to multiple hotspots during WWII... This book may be fictional, but the accuracy and attention to detail yields a fine overview of the extraordinary contributions of a heretofore under-appreciated wartime agency."

ANN TODD, author of *OSS Operation Black Mail: One Woman's Covert War Against the Imperial Japanese Army*

"Seeger quickly immerses the reader into the world and missions of the OSS, our nation's first special operations and intelligence organization. The writing, the 'feel,' and behaviors of the characters are authentic, with plenty here to engage both the veteran operator, as well as the casual reader interested in better understanding the actions [and] courage of our OSS heroes."

LTG (RETIRED) JOHN MULHOLLAND, former Deputy Commander, US Special Operations Command and former Commander, US Army Special Operation Command

"[Seeger] introduces us to the complexities of the war behind the lines across the globe. He clearly knows his stuff; the combat scenes are vivid, the tactics nuanced and sophisticated, with a host of political problems lurking in the background."

COL (RETIRED) NICHOLAS REYNOLDS, author of *Ernest Hemingway: Writer, Sailor, Soldier, Spy* and *Basra, Baghdad, and Beyond: The United States Marine Corps in the Second Iraq War*

"If you like good tales of the shadowy, often hard-edged world of counter-terrorism, read Mike4! Written by a veteran of 'the community,' it will teach while it entertains."

GENERAL STANLEY MCCHRYSTAL, author of *My Share of the Task: A Memoir* and *Team of Teams: New Rules of Engagement for a Complex World*

A Playground for Ambition

Readers are encouraged to go to www.MissionPointPress.com to contact the author or to find information on how to buy this book in bulk at a discounted rate.

Published by Mission Point Press
2554 Chandler Rd.
Traverse City, MI 49696
(231) 421-9513
www.MissionPointPress.com

ISBN: 978-1-958363-04-1
Library of Congress Control Number: 2022909777

Printed in the United States of America

A Playground for Ambition

J.R. Seeger

book 7 in the   MIKE4 series

A nation can survive its fools, and even the ambitious.
But it cannot survive treason from within.
— Marcus Tullius Cicero

SOMETHING SUPER USEFUL

10 January 2012 – Human Intelligence Collection Unit Headquarters, Camp Ederle, Italy

S ue O'Connell sat in her office, gazing at the face of her watch for at least the fourth time since lunch. The minutes crept along at a painfully slow pace toward the end of the workday at 1800hrs.

It wasn't that Sue didn't have work to fill her day. There were intelligence reports to read, finance accountings to review and approve, and even the travel schedules for the HICU collectors who were deployed around the Central Command area of responsibility that ran from East Africa to the Pakistan-India border. Plenty of work to do. But nothing seemed interesting or challenging enough to focus her mind.

Sue was sitting in a repurposed warehouse near the airfield at Camp Ederle, Italy. The sign at the gate said the warehouse was headquarters of Regional Logistics Support Unit or RLSU. Few at Camp Ederle knew it was anything but an office for a bunch of supply geeks. In fact, it was the HQ of the best tactical intelligence collection arm in the US military's Special Operations Forces. Sue was grumbling over a cup of black tea as she sat at an olive-drab Army desk next to an olive-drab three-drawer filing cabinet with a large, black combination lock. The furnishings were remnants from the Cold War, stamped with national stock numbers identifying them as property of the United States Army. She looked at the brown paper files on her desk and the ancient laptop computer. All property of the United States Army.

The entire room reminded her of her first years in the conventional Army assigned to the 18th Airborne Corps. Those were not good memories. She had been a newly minted military intelligence officer building operational analysis for the Balkans, and her days were occupied by briefings, PowerPoints and darkened windowless rooms with rows of computer terminals. Sue understood that experience had represented the real Army, while SOF was small, eccentric and … special. She just never thought that she would move up the chain of command in SOF and find herself back behind a green Army desk, waiting for the end of the day.

The HICU command sergeant major, Jim Massoni, often reminded Sue that this was the life troop leaders endured. Their troops did the active "fun" stuff, and the leaders were left with the paperwork. He also regularly reminded Sue that since she was the senior warrant officer inside HICU, she had to keep up appearances by wearing the standard camouflage uniform and boots. When she went outside the HICU building, she wore an issued Gore-Tex camouflage jacket and her maroon beret. Massoni wore the same outfit with a green beret based on his time with US Army Special Forces.

It wasn't as if the uniform was uncomfortable. It was simply that Sue had grown used to living in civilian clothes and modified hiking boots with a left boot specially made for her below-the-knee prosthetic. Mostly, she chafed at the fact that she had returned to office life rather than field life. She looked at her watch again. Another five minutes had passed.

Sighing heavily, she picked up one of the files on her desk and was forcing herself to open it, when the voice of Sarah Billings pierced her mental gloom: "Hey, Boss. How about some tea and lies?"

Sue looked up at her friend and co-worker. No matter what the circumstance, Billings lived up to her nickname of "Flash," always seeming full of enthusiasm. Sue wished she could exhibit the same attitude, but lately she had difficulty putting on a happy face at work. As she stood up from her desk and headed into the open area where coffee and tea were brewed, she dead-panned: "Why not? Are you going to start telling lies, or shall I?"

Flash smirked. "Every time I try to tell you a Flash adventure story, you say 'no thanks.'"

"Well, that's because it almost always ends up with some story of a one-night stand with a man."

Flash seemed taken aback, momentarily. "Would you be more comfortable if it was a one-night stand with a woman?"

Sue laughed for the first time all day. "No, that would not make me more comfortable."

Flash was already at the coffee station pouring coffee into a bright red coffee mug with a yellow lightning bolt across the front. She handed Sue the tea mug. A gift from Massoni with an image of a one-legged pirate saying "Aaargh." Sue dropped a tea bag into the cup and filled it with boiling water. She took a spoon from a drawer, scooped a dollop from a honey jar and stirred it into her mug. Flash was already sitting at the picnic table that served as their official lunch room. Sue pulled up a chair and said, "Lies?"

Flash said, "How about explaining to me why you have become Madame Grumpy these past few weeks."

Sue shook her head. "When Colonel Smith asked me to be his executive officer in 2009, I thought it might be an interesting but temporary change from my job as an agent handler and intelligence collector. Instead of hunting terrorists and recruiting human sources to assist in that hunt, I would be Smith's deputy, helping to manage the deployed handlers as well as the analysts here in HICU. Just an interlude. A break from travel, and then back to work. Temp-O-Rary!"

Both women knew the story well. HICU's leader, Col. Jed Smith, was severely wounded in an ambush while conducting an intelligence operation in Bahrain. From his hospital bed, he had tasked Sue with serving as executive officer and leading the team while he recovered. Everyone assumed that Smith would soon be back on the job.

Flash nodded. "Yeah. Well, we both know that's not how it turned out."

Instead, Smith's injuries made it impossible for him to continue the overseas deployment. He accepted an assignment to SOF head-quarters at Ft. Bragg, North Carolina, where the joint operations staff in SOF command had a separate compartmented office that managed all human intelligence collection missions across the entire command.

"I get why they wanted him back there," Sue said. "It is a rare opportunity for a trained collector to be in charge of the intelligence collector missions. I also understand why the colonel took the job. It was the same reason I chose to become a collector after my wound. I wanted to stay in the fight. Clearly, Smith does as well."

Flash said, "I get it. Smith's new job was good for SOF and good for HICU. Just not so good for Sue O'Connell, world traveler and super spy. Hey, eventually they are going to find an officer qualified to take the job. In the meantime, you are doing a pretty darn good imitation of Smith, including the grumpiness."

"Oh, thanks."

"Hey, I'm always here for you, sister."

"Except . . . "

"OK, except when I'm not. And in this case, I think it's definitely time for you to put on your big girl Ranger panties and stop being Madame Grumpy."

Sue looked down into her tea, hoping somehow it would offer an answer. She was responsible for managing the activities of two dozen HICU field agents. It could be a life-and-death responsibility. Despite her own discontent, she knew she had to focus on the challenges ahead.

Before Sue arrived at HICU in 2006, there were only ten agent handlers spread out from the Eastern Mediterranean to Pakistan. Sue and her six HICU colleagues arrived after training at the CIA training facility known as the Farm, and they provided a needed boost to the program. Now there were twenty-four collectors based throughout the eastern hemisphere — the primary SOF terrorist hunting grounds. Only one of the HICU team, Sandy Tealor, had a two-year permanent assignment. He had moved wife and family into the Bahrain military compound maintained by the US Navy Fifth Fleet. Otherwise, the HICU team were espionage nomads.

Sue's first assignment had been in Cyprus and her subsequent assignments had been a mix of Afghanistan and Iraq, the two war zones with the largest complement of SOF operators in the global war on terror. Sue's life had been one of regular travel working alone or with another HICU colleague and, often enough, with members of the CIA known in SOF parlance as "OGA" standing for the other government agency. That operational pace prevented much in the way of social life with her HICU colleagues or with anyone in Camp Ederle. Like Sue, her colleagues were on the same carousel of six-month deployment followed by two weeks leave, three weeks training and another six-month deployment. While it was exhausting, it was also challenging and it allowed her complete independence of action.

Now, Sue was responsible for the operational activities of all the HICU collectors, whether operating in buddy teams or as singletons. When she looked over at the white board on the wall across from her desk, Sue could see photos of each of the HICU members and where they were assigned. There were notations on the specific unit and/or embassy they were supporting and when they were expected to return to Camp Ederle. Some of these men were friends she had known since the Farm and some were just faces of men and women who had arrived, received a basic presentation from Sue and Massoni, completed location-specific training, and quickly left for a war zone or some SOF location that few civilians in the United States would even recognize on a map. Of the twenty-four, there were only two other female collectors at HICU, one deployed to Nairobi and one to Mosel in Iraq.

Sue looked up from her tea and said, "Look, the biggest challenge we are still facing is the one that we faced back in 2009. Our sources are still disappearing. Not as often, but still often enough to make SOF and Department of Defense counterintelligence ask questions about our operations. In the last three months, an Afghan source disappeared and one of our Iraqi reporting sources was killed in an ambush. It is not right. We destroyed the hub of cyber hackers targeting SOF operations back in 2009. How are terrorist organizations or third country security services still finding our sources? Are there flaws in our tradecraft giving away our meetings? Is there a double agent somewhere in the system? Is there another cyber operation revealing their secrets? It keeps me up at night, Flash."

Flash said, "Hey, you, Massoni and I have pushed the collectors every time they return home. I haven't seen any flaws in their trade-craft. The short answer for now is there doesn't seem to be any way that our operators in the field are the problem."

"So, what is the problem?"

Massoni's voice came from behind Sue's back. "Are you solving REAL SUE's problems behind my back?"

Sue said, "You know I hate it when you call the unit REAL SUE instead of just using the initials RLSU."

"Really, boss? I didn't know."

Flash choked on her coffee as Massoni pulled up a chair. He'd obviously been listening for more than a moment.

"Here's the deal, boss. You know what I think. The problem is somewhere upstream, somewhere inside SOF headquarters. We have told Smith what we think, and he said he is working on it. In the meantime, we just have to keep our teams safe and sound."

Sue tried to divert the conversation back to her own problem: "Surely there must be a senior officer qualified to take command? Hell, I would be happy to hand this mess over to a junior officer. Just somebody so I can focus back on my trade."

Massoni's response came with a shrug. "Look, boss. You are in charge until you aren't in charge. That's the way it is. After two years, surely you have to know that you just need to embrace the suck."

He took a sip from his coffee mug, looked up and said to no one in particular, "Who made this stuff? And what do you call it? It certainly isn't coffee!"

Massoni walked over to the sink and emptied his mug, then came back to the table and sat down. "When I became a sergeant major, my chief mentor at sergeant major academy told me my days of being a cool guy were over. Well, I guess he was right, mostly. Last year you were promoted to Chief Warrant Officer 5. After the promotion, you were reassigned from executive officer to acting commander. Well, you are acting all right and as your sergeant major, I'm here to tell you to stop acting and just take charge. You need to recognize there are going to be fewer and fewer days left in your time in service where you get to be a cool cat. Warrant officers get to be cool cats far longer than the rest of us, that is the purpose of the warrant officer cadre. Still, there always comes a time when the Army wants you to be a leader and a teacher rather than a full-time doer. So, you have to get your satisfaction from making sure our folks are well supported in the field and the team back here at REAL SUE are productive and happy. And, by the way, that is a darn important job. Especially since we haven't figured out who is killing our assets. So, just RTFU, do the job and stop whining."

Sue knew that when Massoni used jargon from his time in the Ranger Regiment — like RTFU, which meant "ruck the fuck up" — he was drawing a line in the sand that she did not want to cross.

Sue decided to change tack: "Did that advice work for you, Jim?"

Massoni smiled and said, "Nope. I still hate it that I can't be out in the field. But that speech is what I'm paid to tell you. Now, get back to work, boss. I got an email from Smith. He says you are behind in your paperwork and he wants to know why. He also wants to know why we still haven't found the hole in our security."

Sue walked back into her office. She knew Massoni was right. It was time for her to stop moaning and just take charge. If the command didn't like her actions, they would make that clear. If they did like her actions, they would leave her alone. In the meantime, she accepted there were some positive aspects to her current job. She oversaw a very productive team. She had the authority to make sure the team got as much support as she could give them. She had no direct supervisor looking over her shoulder and she had Massoni to make sure she didn't do anything stupid. Flash and the rest of the analytic staff at HICU were top notch and they did most of the heavy lifting when it came to providing support to the collectors in the field. Her communications and support officer, Master Sergeant Marconi, was great at providing whatever was needed and, usually having something on the shelf before it was needed.

An hour later, Sue looked at her watch and started fidgeting with the red and blue 24hr bezel. 1630hrs. Ninety more minutes before she could go to the gym and be certain she wouldn't be called back into the office for a call from Smith or one of her field collectors. There was another reason to look at the watch. It was a gift from her boyfriend, Jasper Derry.

Over the past year, she started a serious relationship with a man, something that hadn't happened since she had joined SOF. Sue's relationship with Chief Warrant Officer Jasper Derry began during a work trip in 2009. Sue and Flash worked briefly with Derry on a counterintelligence investigation of a cyberattack on DoD networks. The relationship expanded over the Christmas holidays in 2009 when Jasper came to visit Sue and her family in what they commonly referred to as the Potomac River house, an old farmhouse near Washington, DC, which was the legacy of Sue's grandfather. The relationship took time to develop, with Derry in California and Sue in Italy. In 2011, Derry requested a transfer from California to the large counterintelligence office in the US Army Europe headquarters in Heidelberg.

Sue found many things to like about Jasper Derry. He had been forced to give up a Green Beret after a serious injury in Iraq. Like Sue, he chose to stay in service by transferring into the military intelligence world, specifically as a counterintelligence investigator. As near as Sue could tell, Derry was a committed investigator. He didn't talk much about his work, but there were plenty of investigations for Derry in the USAEUR area of responsibility that included all of NATO. These investigations focused on physical and cyber threats from Russia, Iran and China. Though they were busy with their own work, the two wounded warriors managed to spend at least one weekend a quarter together. Sometimes in Germany, sometimes in Italy and sometimes in another European venue.

The United States Army in Europe was small compared to its size during the Cold War, but the US Department of Defense Military Welfare and Recreation facilities in the region remained in place. There were always more opportunities than time to enjoy something fun whether it was hiking, skiing, white-water rafting or even learning to fly. During these trips together, their relationship started slowly. That was Sue's choice. She had not had a physical relationship with a man since she lost her left leg below the knee. For the first time since that injury in Afghanistan, she was willing to share her good days and bad days with someone special. Sue had to admit that staying in one place for two years had made this possible. Sue and Derry used their personal time to explore Northern Italy in her Fiat 500 that she purchased when HICU moved from Ft. Bragg to Camp Ederle. They met in different locations to explore Europe and their relationship grew.

What would happen next with Derry was anyone's guess, but for now, it was good enough. Sue was definitely serious and, at the end of their last ski trip, Derry showed he was as well. For once, they were at a lodge near Innsbruck, Austria, instead of an MWR facility in Germany. It had been a wonderful weekend and they were going their separate ways the next morning. Sue would take the train south to Vincenza. Derry said he had to start a work trip in Southern Germany. After dinner, Derry presented Sue with a large emerald green box. Inside was a stainless-steel Rolex GMT Master with a red and blue bezel. A serious tool watch and certainly the most expensive watch Sue had ever worn. Sue knew it had cost Derry at least two full paychecks, possibly more. She said, "Jasper, what is this all about?"

Derry's response was, "You have said more than once you needed a GMT watch so that you could track two time zones and stop waking your mom up in the middle of the night. And, you told me you had men and women deployed all over the Middle East and South Asia. I figured it was time for you to ditch that old Seiko diver and wear a watch that would help you keep track of different time zones. It's not much bigger than your Seiko and I figured you deserved a real watch, not one you bought at the PX."

As she slid the watch bracelet on, she realized he had sized it perfectly for her wrist. She said, "It is an expensive piece."

"Yup. But you are worth it. And I want you to wear it like you stole it. It isn't a precious thing. It is a tool watch."

Sue knew it was precious for so many other reasons. She cried that night before they went to their room. She cried again the next morning when they packed and said farewell. At that point, Sue felt that she might have found the man who could be her mate for life. If her mom and dad found love while serving in the trade, why not her? She thought about that the entire time on the train and this afternoon she was thinking about it again. She decided she would call Derry before she went to the gym. She looked down at the watch. The GMT hand was set to Greenwich Mean Time, known as Zulu time in military speak. That way, she could do a quick bit of math whether adding hours when she was focusing on HICU deployed officers or subtracting hours if trying to sort out when to call her mom. She knew Derry was on the same time zone as Camp Ederle, so no math was required.

Her daydreaming was interrupted as her office door crashed against the plywood wall and nearly knocked over the bookcase that held dozens of boxed up files. Flash followed the door as she ran into Sue's office. Flash was in her established office attire: head to foot in black. Black trainers. Black sweats. Black-framed reading glasses pushed into her short, jet-black hair and a large black G-shock watch on her wrist. Sue said, "Flash, I don't need any more paperwork. Please tell me you aren't adding to my suffering." Flash smiled. Her white teeth and pale blue eyes were the opposite of her black attire. "Still grumpy, eh. I guess there is no pleasing you."

Flash paused for a second and added, "Boss."

Sue said, "Now I know why Smith periodically threw stuff at Massoni. I don't have anything soft available. Fair warning."

"Hey, remember, you are now the boss and have to put up with us simple troops slaving away on the ramparts of democracy."

Sue looked around at her desk for something to toss at Flash. Nothing soft came to hand, so she just growled. "There is nothing simple about you, Flash. Nothing at all."

Flash dropped the playful banter. "I just came in to tell you I found out something super useful regarding that Russian private military contractor that has been in the center of our CI work for the past four years."

Sue thought about the PMC named SWORDFISH, which had twice attacked HICU operations. The company seemed to operate on its own rules. Not exactly working for Moscow, but certainly aligned with Russian strategic goals. It was a mercenary unit claiming to be a private security company. The attacks in Afghanistan argued they were much more. Sue was convinced that SWORDFISH had something to do with the ambush that nearly killed Smith though she couldn't prove it. None of the collection requirements issued by SOF offered any reason for her to task Sandy to get more information on SWORDFISH when he was already busy rebuilding his counter-terrorism intelligence network, which had been affected by multiple disappearances and one death.

In the past year, the Russian PMC had surfaced in dozens of HICU reports focused on Syria, Iraq, Afghanistan and even the Horn of Africa. Luckily, there hadn't been another confrontation like the one that Sue, Flash and their CIA counterpart Jamie Schenk had in Northern Afghanistan in 2009. Sue remained convinced it was only a matter of time before there was another gunfight between the merce-naries and the US intelligence operators on the ground somewhere. Either SOF or CIA units would eventually run into SWORDFISH and it was likely to be deadly.

Sue was most definitely interested in Flash's new information. She said, "What's new on the SWORDFISH front?"

"Two things, fearless leader." Sue scowled and Flash took a moment to enjoy Sue's discomfort. "First, it turns out the SWORD-FISH leadership is made up of very nasty people."

"That is supposed to surprise me?"

"No, I mean very nasty people as in a couple of them are listed on the Hague Tribunal for war crimes in Yugoslavia."

This did surprise Sue. When she served with the 18th Airborne Corps in the mid-1990s, she did a tour in the former Yugoslavia. The men wanted for war crimes in that civil war were all locals, Serbs, Croats or Bosnians. In fact, part of the UN peacemaking force included Russians. She said, "So, they are Serbs, or Croats, or Bosnians or Albanians or … what?"

"Nope. Most are Russians to be sure. The one guy I'm talking about is an ethnic Russian who joined one of the Serbian militias. Bad dude."

"OK, that might explain the attitude of shoot first and ask questions later. Interesting, but how does that matter to us?"

"Now comes the really important part!" Flash waved her hands like some carnival magician. "It turns out SOF J2 has identified that one of those cats is traveling to Germany with a small security entourage. It looks like a work trip to expand their business model outside of supporting the Russian Federation."

The intelligence shop at SOF headquarters, the J2, had formal and informal links to the entire US intelligence community. Sue was sure that if the J2 said there were SWORDFISH travelers coming to Germany, there definitely were SWORDFISH travelers coming to Germany. That could mean trouble, but it also presented a collection opportunity that could not be missed. She said, "Where?"

Before Sue framed a more detailed question, Flash continued, "A private aircraft flying from Moscow to Frankfurt in two days. Manifest says one Viktor Alexander Shemkovich is a passenger. And, according to SOF, Shemkovich is an alias for a war criminal named Marko Vladich. Russian father, Serbian mother. Raised in the Soviet Union. Trained as a special operator for the Soviet and eventually Russian Ministry of Interior. Now, chief operating officer for SWORDFISH."

"What else does SOF headquarters say?"

"They said: 'Go find out what he is going to be doing in Germany.' It looks like REAL SUE has a new mission. Now, isn't that great?!"

Even as she winced at the use of REAL SUE as the monicker for the unit, Sue thought about the opportunity. She said, "And, you know, we don't have anyone we can spare to support a new tasking except..."

"Flash!" Flash did a quick bow.

"And her partner in crime, Sue O'Connell."

At that point, Massoni walked in and said, "If you think you are leaving me behind, you can forget about it."

Sue said, "Were you eavesdropping, Sergeant Major?"

Massoni offered with his most sincere voice, "It is the mission of a sergeant major to know everything, all the time. How else can I complete that mission if I don't listen to all conversations? Especially conversations between my boss, that's you Sue, and my team, that's you, Flash."

Sue nodded. "So, who watches the shop when we are gone?"

Flash and Massoni looked at each other. Finally, Massoni said, "We are the shop. The shop is wherever we are. I will get with Marconi. He will figure out how we can work in Germany. I am sure that will be easy."

Flash said, "Sergeant Major, wasn't it you who told me once that everything is easy..."

Massoni competed the sentence, "Until you do it." He smiled his most sinister smile and said, "Yup, but Marconi is good. He will accomplish this simple task for his best friend, the unit sergeant major." He turned to Sue and said, "You now have the ball, Boss. We need to run with it. Of course, first you need to figure out who we will work with in Germany. After all, we don't have anyone in Germany, so we don't have any human sources there."

Massoni paused for a moment. He raised his index finger of his right hand and said, "It seems to me you have some connections. Perhaps, a certain CI officer in Heidelberg? I'll bet he has some sources on the ground. If only we could reach out to him."

Sue blushed and Flash laughed out loud.

A DRIVE IN THE COUNTRYSIDE

12 January 2012 — Hyatt Regency Hotel, Reston, VA

Barbara O'Connell sat in the ground floor lounge of her hotel, watching cars pull up, deliver guests and then drive away. A mix of snow and sleet flew diagonally across the windows as if the Northern Virginia winter was trying to decide if it would deliver a storm or just a threat of a storm. One of the few things that Barbara disliked about the mid-Atlantic states was winter. It never seemed to decide. Would it be snow? Sleet? Ice? Rain? When she worked at CIA headquarters, she never knew in January if she should wear a parka or a rain coat. Ultimately, she decided the best answer was to wear one and keep the other in the car. Those days were long past. Retired now, she lived in Western New York, where there was no confusion about winter weather. From the middle of December to middle of March, it was always wise to wear a parka and snow boots no matter what the forecasters said.

As she watched and waited, she was nursing a mid-morning cup of Earl Grey tea. When she and her husband, Peter, were assigned to headquarters, they lived in Reston and commuted together every day from their modest home not far from this hotel. They would drive along the back roads of Northern Virginia to CIA headquarters in their Jeep Cherokee, grumbling about the early morning commute and enjoying the evening travels home along a heavily wooded route that paralleled the Potomac River.

Life in the CIA in the 1990s was hectic. Eastern Europe was free from Soviet domination. After 1991, the Soviet Union ceased to exist, and a number of former Soviet 'republics' splintered off from Russia to become new independent states. Meanwhile, Iran and Hizballah continued to target American and Israeli interests in the Middle East, Europe and even South America.

As a senior CIA officer with Persian language skills and survival Arabic, Barbara served as a senior Counterterrorism Center case officer roving Europe and the Middle East. She found and developed new sources to provide leads in the hunt for Iranian networks and for a new set of Sunni extremists who followed a hard-line Islamic dogma. Barbara didn't know it at the time, but her work in the mid-90s built a foundation for the CIA understanding of al-Qaida and, most especially, the AQ leader, Usama Bin Laden. While she traveled, Peter served as a senior headquarters manager inside the CIA Central Eurasian Division. After years in the field and having served multiple tours inside "the Bloc" as it was called in the 1980s, he now managed headquarters support for the stations in the former Soviet republics along the southern tier of Russia.

Though Barbara didn't know it at the time, Peter was involved in a complex counterintelligence operation which would eventually result in his death.

As Barbara took a sip of her tea, she wondered whether anything she or her husband had done was worth it. Though decades had passed, the Russians were still adversaries, the Chinese were becoming adversaries and even after the death of Bin Laden, al-Qaida and its various offshoots were still threatening. Barbara's children were still in the game and still risking their lives. Sue was serving as an intelligence officer in the US Special Operations Forces. Bill was a special agent in the FBI in Washington, DC. She knew that the people inside Russia who had poisoned her husband were all dead at the hands of their own countrymen. But it still was a bitter, confusing tale that she had trouble understanding.

In the past few years, Barbara had been working as a freelance investigator for an international law firm, Stearns and Mandeville, under the direction of her old friend, Beth Parsons. Beth retired as an ambassador the same time Barbara left the Agency. While Barbara had attempted unsuccessfully to live a quiet retired life, Beth had taken on a new career as a worldwide troubleshooter for Stearns and Mandeville. As a retired ambassador with a law degree from Georgetown University, Beth was an ideal addition to a firm that worked on international legal wrangles of one sort or another for US-based multinational corporations. In exchange, the firm periodically took on work that Beth found interesting and important.

According to the brief call Barbara received two days ago, Beth was on one of those investigations and she wanted Barbara's help. Barbara enjoyed working with Beth and felt she owed her for some of the support Beth provided in the last decade as she uncovered the final remnants of the strange tale of the counterintelligence and vendetta that killed her father-in-law, her husband, and her last lover. Plus, Stearns and Mandeville paid well. Very well.

Beth Parsons's arrival ended Barbara's dour musing. Barbara knew Beth favored Maserati and Jaguar sports cars for her personal ride, but today was a business trip. She arrived in an ebony black Range Rover that Barbara assumed cost more than her cottage in Chautauqua, New York. The sleek sport utility vehicle pulled under the shelter of the main hotel entrance. A very fit, very well-dressed middle-aged man stepped out from the driver's side of the vehicle, walked around the right rear door, opened it and helped Beth as she stepped down to the curb. Barbara noticed the Rover was armor plated. Probably not noticeable to passersby, but Barbara had ridden in enough up-armored cars to know that it took more than a little effort to open a fully armored door with armored glass. The driver had used just enough body leverage to reveal the door was more than it seemed.

Barbara watched as Beth spoke briefly in the driver's ear. He returned to the vehicle and drove off, leaving Beth Parsons at the entrance to the lobby. She strode in as if she owned the entire hotel. Beth was dressed in a calf length, navy-blue wool coat with corresponding navy-blue calf length leather boots. She completed the ensemble with turquoise silk scarf and a turquoise wool beret. Barbara felt significantly under-dressed whenever she met Beth. She was wearing her standard winter business attire of forest green wool slacks and a white, wool rollneck sweater. A Barbour waxed-cotton field coat and brown ankle-high hiking boots completed her outfit. Barbara often referred to herself as a "mere, wretched federal pensioner" and she no longer had any reason to impress anyone. Comfort remained the primary goal, fashion be damned.

Beth finished her scan of the lobby and started walking toward Barbara. She held out both hands and said, "Dear, it has been too long. I am so glad to see you."

Barbara closed the distance and gave Beth a hug. Both women were in their 60s and both kept fit in different ways. Barbara focused on walking and yoga. Her body was supple. Beth clearly had some sort of trainer and a commitment to fitness. As Barbara hugged her, through the layers of wool, she could feel the muscular athlete inside the fashion statement.

Beth said, "I wonder if you wouldn't mind going for a drive with me?"

"Your car or mine?"

"Are you still driving that old Rover?"

"Yes."

"How about we go in mine? I think it is a bit more comfortable and Richard can do the driving for us so we can have our … chat."

Barbara nodded and, as she looked over Beth's shoulder, she could see the Range Rover was back in position at the entrance, four-way flashers illuminating some snowflakes. The Northern Virginia weather had decided: it was going to be a winter day. The driver was dressed in a black leather bomber jacket and black jeans. He was standing by the rear passenger door waiting for them and, again only Barbara probably noticed, conducting a periodic scan of anyone who came near him or the Range Rover.

Barbara said, "Let's go before your driver finds something troublesome in Reston."

Beth laughed and said, "He is very good at what he does, but not exactly a low-key personality."

"You need to tell me why you are suddenly traveling in an up-armored vehicle with a guy who looks like he just retired from the SEALs."

Beth shook her head. "Please don't say that too loud. Richard retired from an Army SOF unit and hates it when people call him a SEAL. He thinks the current bout of press on Naval Special Warfare is improper even if they did get the nod to kill bin Laden. He says Army SOF insists on maintaining their standards as quiet professionals no matter how high profile the target. I've tried to engage him on the subject. He just clams up."

Barbara smiled and said, "Well, let's see if we can team up and elicit something besides yes ma'am, no ma'am."

Beth laughed and said, "Good luck with that."

After they loaded into the Range Rover, Beth did quick introductions. "Richard, this is my friend Barbara O'Connell. Barbara, this is my minder, Richard Smith. At least that's what he says is his last name."

As Richard gently pulled away from the hotel and quickly entered the westbound lanes of the Dulles Toll Road, he said, "Smith is a good English name, and it happens to be my name."

Barbara smiled and said, "Sure. Well, good to meet you, Richard Smith."

"Likewise." The Rover may have been armored, but it accelerated quickly and they had a very smooth drive as they headed west toward the eastern border of the Shenandoah Valley. Beth pulled down a table between them, opened a thermos of coffee and offered Barbara a tin that revealed two fresh croissants. The interior of the Rover filled with the smell of the coffee and the buttery pastries. Beth leaned toward the driver's headrest and said, "Richard, some coffee?"

"No Ma'am. I'm good to go. Coffee and some water up front."

Beth looked at Barbara as if to say, "I told you so."

Barbara decided it would be up to her to start the conversation. She said, "Beth, this is all good and I am fond of fresh pastries, but why a car meeting? I mean, I understand the firm might want some privacy, but this just seems over the top to me."

Beth stopped drinking her coffee and said to Barbara, "Dear, of all the people who work for the firm, surely you understand the importance of security."

"Security indeed. Armored vehicle. Armed professional... no offense, Richard."

"None taken, Ma'am."

Beth smiled and said, "Well, this new project has some strange little kinks to it and the firm just figured it would be good to start with high security. We can always back down on security if we figure out it isn't needed."

Richard said, "If we look organized ... "

Barbara completed the saying, "We might even be organized."

Richard smirked and said, "Exactly."

Barbara continued, "OK, we both know that some of my work has been a little unconventional."

Beth said, "Like hunting a Russian assassin on the Adriatic Coast?"

Richard added, "And wasn't there some story about a gunfight at an airfield as a Russian spy escaped?"

Beth continued, "Or a gunfight where you had the gun and the other guy had a hand grenade?"

"Now that is a story I want to hear," Richard interjected with a low whistle.

"OK, you two," Barbara laughed. "I surrender. It does seem that O'Connells have a reputation for playing with fire."

Beth nodded, "Barbara, drink your coffee and eat your pastry while I tell you a story."

NOT EXACTLY A BEDTIME STORY

B eth started her story. "This isn't exactly a bedtime story. It is more of a nightmare that we are trying to end for an American family. It starts at the end of World War II and the OSS."

Before Beth could continue, Richard said, "As all good adventure stories begin."

Beth smiled and said, "It seems Richard has decided that he and I are going to right a wrong like characters out of a novel."

Barbara nodded, "Well, it's not as if we haven't tried over the last thirty-some years."

Beth put down her coffee cup. "If you two heroes will let me continue."

Barbara raised her hands in mock surrender and Richard said, "Sorry, Ma'am." Barbara noted he didn't sound contrite.

"So, along with the atrocities committed by the Nazis during the war, one of the things that the Nazi leadership did was loot occupied Europe. They had already stolen all the valuables from their own Jewish population and once the greater Reich included the Nazi-occupied portions of Europe, they expanded their criminal enterprise to include valuables from museums, libraries, churches and, of course, private mansions. The owners of the valuables were often lucky to get out alive with only the clothes on their back." Beth paused to drink her coffee.

"The OSS created the Art Looting Investigative Unit in late 1944 and it conducted extensive investigations using classic human source intelligence collection methods and detailed research in cultural archives in the US and the UK. The Nazis worked hard to cover their tracks in occupied Europe, but they couldn't destroy the academic research from the 1930s universities in the US and the UK. As allied troops started to push back the German Army, the ALIU started working in Europe to find these art treasures and return them." Beth took another sip of coffee. "One of the members of that outfit was Jackson Stearns, the founder of Stearns and Mandeville. And, one of his most junior investigators was a young Army Air Corps pilot named Parsons."

"Didn't you tell me your dad flew in B24s in the war?"

"He did indeed. He was wounded during the raids over Ploesti, Romania. Bailed out and eventually repatriated through an escape and evasion route set up by the OSS. When he got back to England, his wounds prevented him from returning to the 8th Air Force, so he asked to work with the OSS. While he recovered from his injuries stateside, he worked for ALIU in DC until it was disbanded in 1946."

"So, you have deep roots in this one."

"For a change, it looks like my connections are the ones that make this a vendetta."

Barbara took a sip of the rich coffee Beth had served, and thought for a moment about the vendetta that the Beroslav family had with her family that caused so much heartache. It all started in a forest in Southern France in 1944 when Peter O'Connell Sr., killed a Russian spy named Beroslav. It continued with the murder of her father-in-law, and ended in Pakistan in 2009 with the death of the last of the Beroslavs. It reminded her of the saying attributed sometimes to Confucius and sometimes to Socrates: *Before you embark on a journey of revenge, dig two graves.*

The Range Rover was quiet for a few moments as they passed the exit for Middleburg and headed into the hills of the front range of the Shenandoah. The mix of sleet and snow transitioned to just snow, and the slap of the windshield wipers across the armored glass was the only sound in the vehicle. Richard had turned on the lights as well as the large Hella driving lights in the Range Rover. In the blue glow from the instrument panel, Barbara could just see Richard's right cheek and ear. For the first time, she noticed a deep scar running along his temple and ending at his earlobe. For some reason, this observation made her feel more secure in his presence. As her good friend and Special Forces Sergeant Major Max Creeter used to say, "This is a guy who has seen the elephant." That memory of Max, who died in her arms from a sniper's bullet, came out of the darkness of her mind. She shook her head to bring her mind back to the present. She said, "So we are going after Nazi loot?"

"Indeed, we are, Barbara. Our firm has had a family as a client since the 1950s. The Mayerhaus family came to Jackson Stearns when he first started as a lawyer working in Baltimore. Bernard and Sara Mayerhaus were Austrian Jews who escaped the Nazis, fleeing first to France and then to the US after 1940 when the Nazis occupied France. Bernard was an electrical engineer and started working almost immediately in a defense plant building Liberty Ships. Sara raised their two children in a refugee ghetto in Baltimore. Somehow, around 1942, the US Navy came to realize that Bernard was a genius in electrical engineering and they grabbed him from the Bethlehem-Fairfield Shipyard and sent him down to the Naval Torpedo Station in Alexandria. By the end of the war, he was a senior civilian engineer for the US Navy. He moved the family to Alexandria and they all became citizens in the 1950s.

"While they treasured their new life in America, Bernard and Sara missed their home in Vienna. After the war, Bernard traveled to Germany and Austria as part of a Naval Intelligence effort to identify any German engineering research that might give the US Navy an edge in the Cold War. The Navy and Army Air Corps were focused on what were called at the time 'super weapons' including German missiles, jet engines and torpedoes. The Russians were doing the same thing in their occupation zones, hauling entire factories back to the Soviet Union. Bernard tried to visit his old neighborhood in Vienna to see if there was anything left of his family belongings. What he encountered was a strong anti-Semitic attitude. All of his old neighbors were gone and the current residents were not interested in talking to what they saw as an American Jew from the occupation force. Bernard returned to the US brokenhearted at the loss of family heirlooms and a small art collection that he and Sara acquired in the 1930s. That collection included impressionist and more avant-garde paintings from the Bauhaus era."

Barbara looked out the side window of the Rover as she listened. The snow obscured just about everything beyond the headlight beams. She wondered how many of these sorts of émigré stories were part of the fabric of modern America. It had always been immigrants that made America strong. Peter's father was second-generation Irish and her grandparents were a mix of Poles, Hungarians, and Germans who fled Europe in the 1920s and 1930s.

Beth interrupted her musing. "I don't know how the Mayerhaus family found Jackson Stearns but they did and he took on their case. There are plenty of twists and turns in this story but we have been working for the Mayerhaus estate, now in its third generation of Americans, since 1956. Bernard started a small engineering firm that became very large working on high-end electronics for the US Navy. His children and now his grandchildren spend their time and money on multiple charities in the greater Washington area. One of Bernard's grandchildren is with the State Department and I expect will one day be an ambassador. Another is in a law firm in New York. In short, it is a classic American success story and our firm has worked on multiple projects for them over the years."

After taking a small bite from her croissant, Beth continued. "Now, back to the matter at hand. Last year, I received a note from one of the firm's research assistants. As you know, I've been involved in the firm's legal work in Eastern Europe and in the independent states of the former Soviet Union. The assistant was working on an entirely different project related to land ownership in Western Ukraine when she found a reference to Russian oligarchs trying to acquire valuable European art that has not been on the market for years. The oligarchs were using their connections with the Russian security services to find retired members of the German Stasi who might have kept records on former Nazis residing in East Germany, Poland and Hungary."

Barbara thought for a moment and said, "It seems like a real stretch."

"Yes. A cold trail, but one that ended up uncovering leads to the Mayerhaus case. Bernard listed four paintings that he thought were the most valuable in their collection. There were two from the Hungarian Bauhaus painter, Lazlo Moholy-Nagy, one by a Russian impressionist named Valentin Serov, and one by the Russian impressionist Vladimir Baranov-Rossine. At the time, Bernard and Sara bought paintings that were not considered important and the artists were only just starting to be famous. So, they were not paintings that were going to end up with a senior Nazi leader. Especially since Nazi leadership held a poor opinion of avant-garde art. It was considered... decadent. Of course, local functionaries would have been allowed free rein on any of these sorts of goods and we think the oligarchs were tracking down some of the more valuable acquisitions from that time."

Barbara nodded and asked, "What are these paintings worth today?"

Beth took a sip from her coffee. Her burgundy lipstick left a trail on the hot ceramic mug. She leaned back against the leather headrest of her seat. She closed her eyes for a moment and then said, "Honestly, we have no idea. We are involved because it is a lost legacy that the estate wants recovered. What our researchers have determined is these three painters are now central to our understanding of early 20th century art in Central Europe. The paintings themselves are totally unknown and they are small. According to Bernard and Sara's notes, they were all about 50cm by 65cm. Our best guess is that the four paintings at auction could be worth as much as three to five million."

Barbara almost spilled her coffee. She had little background in fine art so she had no way to measure value. She had expected the paintings would be worth tens of thousands of dollars. This was clearly a real treasure hunt. "Three to five million dollars?"

"No, dear. Three to five million Euros. At most, about six million dollars."

Beth continued, "Austria was partitioned during the immediate post-war period. Vienna was a divided, occupied city just like Berlin with American, British, French and Soviet sectors. Vienna was deep inside the Soviet sector of occupied Austria and the NKVD and the KGB had huge presence in the city. By the time Austria was allowed its independence in 1955, the intelligence networks of the KGB were extensive."

Barbara nodded, "Now you are getting into my area of expertise. I remember talking to Peter's father about the early Cold War days in Europe. It was definitely spy versus spy. Those early operations were far more violent than anyone in America ever knew. Peter's mother was probably killed in one of those operations in Berlin. Peter's dad never gave up hope that he would find the perpetrators."

From the front of the truck, Richard said, "Did he?"

Barbara puzzled over the question. "Did he what?"

"Find the perpetrators?"

Barbara shook her head and thought about the events that led up to her father-in-law's death by an assassin's bullet. Murdered in the Chautauqua house where she now lived. "No, Richard. The perpetrators found him and killed him."

"Early Cold War stuff, eh?"

"No, Richard. Twenty-first century stuff. Old vendettas last a long time."

Richard shook his head.

Barbara continued, "Well, I know from my Peter's work in the 90s that the KGB set up several front companies in Vienna. The objective was to move funds from the former USSR into bank accounts that could be used both personally and professionally. This was part of the beginning of the oligarch network." She paused and then said, "If the oligarchs want these paintings, it is going to be hard to prevent them from getting them if we don't know where they are today."

Richard slowed down as the weather continued to grow more serious. The highway to their front was empty of cars and two inches of newly fallen snow covered the road from shoulder to shoulder.

Beth looked up at the snow beating against the windshield and said, "Richard, I think we need to head back into the city."

"Yes, Ma'am. I will turn us around as soon as I can and head back toward Reston."

Beth turned to Barbara and continued her story, "Now this is where it gets interesting. Last month, my research assistant found a lead to the paintings in Odessa in Ukraine. When we reached out to the German art dealer managing the sale, he said he had taken the paintings on consignment, contingent upon verification of their authenticity. The paintings arrived last week. According to one of our investigators, one set of interested parties are owners of a Russian private military contractor based in St. Petersburg."

Barbara said, "PMCs are modern mercenaries. Mercenaries have an unsavory reputation and any company working with them could be in legal jeopardy. That I understand, but what does it have to do with the Mayerhaus case?"

Beth said, "The query had to do with different art auctions in Dusseldorf and Frankfurt. The investigator identified one of the auctioneers. He did confirm that the paintings were sourced originally to a family in Vienna."

"Mercenaries and art auctions? No wonder we are holding a car meeting. This might get interesting. So, what's the plan?"

"First, we need to get over to Germany. So far, we have no proof that these are the Mayerhaus paintings. After that, we must figure out how to recover their property and avoid a long legal battle. I think you and I might need some specialized assistance, so I have already reached out to Longstreet and his pals. They are in Germany right now working with one of our other clients. The auctioneer is in Bad Homburg which is near ... "

Barbara whispered, "Frankfurt. I know Bad Homburg."

"Sorry, dear. I forgot about your operation in Germany."

Barbara had worked several years earlier with Beth and with Jake Longstreet's team from *Condottieri Malatesta* in the hunt for a hired assassin who turned out to be a distant cousin of her husband. During that operation, she had confided about the murder of one of her assets in the park at Bad Homburg in the 1990s. It had been the first time that she had lost an agent. Over twenty years later, she still blamed herself for his death. Barbara decided to change the subject. She said, "Are these two cases linked?"

Beth said, "I don't see how, but I do know that Longstreet's team is most worried about protecting our client's IP from either Russian or Chinese intelligence collection. Now, are Russian oligarchs interested in art auctions also interested in tech theft? It seems a stretch."

Richard piped up from the driver's seat, "Not to me."

Beth shook her head. "Richard faced Russian mercenaries in a little-known skirmish in North Africa. He holds a grudge."

Barbara said, "Well, so do I."

Beth said, "And that's why you are both going with me to Frankfurt. How soon can you pack your bags?"

This time it was Barbara who smiled, "What makes you think I didn't pack them before I came down to Reston?"

LOOKING FOR TROUBLE?

Bill O'Connell looked across the dinner table at his mother. "Really? You need to get involved in hunting Nazis? Russian spies weren't enough?"

Barbara looked to her right at Bill's fiancée, Molly Hansen. "And when are you guys going to get married?"

Molly smirked and said, "You know changing the subject isn't going to stop him."

Barbara said, "I am his mother. I don't think I need to justify my actions."

Bill decided he would try one more time. "Do I need to get out the cuffs?"

"Bill, you could try to cuff me, but I suspect you wouldn't succeed. I've had KGB ruffians try that much to their regret."

Molly's mouth dropped open. "When did that happen?"

"Molly, one interrogation at a time if you please. Now, the work with Beth Parsons is really a simple research project in Germany. We find out as much as we can about the paintings and then Beth's firm does the rest."

Molly shook her head. "I don't suppose a simple B&E would be part of the project?"

Barbara laughed. It had been a nice, simple dinner at Bill's townhouse in Georgetown. The townhouse was another bit of her father-in-law Peter O'Connell's legacy. Purchased in the 1960s, renovated in the 1970s, the townhouse was now worth more than everything Barbara owned. Still, it made an easy commute for Bill to the Wash-

ington FBI Field Office where he worked as a special agent in counterintelligence. Molly was the senior agent in the Gang Task Force in
the same field office. The meal had been a simple pasta puttanesca
that she whipped up for her son and his fiancée before they got home.
Their only job had been to bring home some fresh bread and a bottle
of red wine. They accomplished that without drama and Barbara
had done the rest.

Barbara realized that she could have avoided this conversation,
but recently she tried as hard as she could to avoid lying to her children. She turned to Molly and said, "Breaking and entering is not in
my tool kit ... anymore."

Bill had resigned himself to accepting his mother's newest foray
into international law. He begrudgingly offered, "That's only because
Beth Parsons has someone else doing that part of the job."

"Not so, my dear son. The auction house is a client. Well, at least a
collaborator. They are going to open their warehouse for us to inspect
the pieces. They are Germans after all, and they don't want anything
linking their firm to a 20th century dark past. And, as an auction
house, their reputation is more important than any sale."

"And when the Russians come visiting?"

"That's when we call the LKA."

Molly was not convinced that Barbara would call the German
Landeskriminalamt, the state police, before she tried to do harm to Russian intruders. After all, she had watched FBI video of one of Barbara's misadventures and participated in another at what was supposed
to be a quiet holiday dinner. She said, "Make sure you have them on
speed dial."

"Count on it."

Bill asked, "Seriously, do you think these paintings were stolen
from the Mayerhaus family?"

"Bill, I have no idea. Beth's team seems to think so, but she won't
know until she sees the paintings. There are other possibilities. They
could be some other paintings by these artists or they could be forgeries."

"And Beth wants you there because ... ?"

"I'm good company."

Molly almost choked on the last sip of wine that she was drinking. She recovered and said in her best Texas drawl, "Yup, Ma'am. You are definitely good company."

All Bill could do at that point was ask, "Anyone for coffee and dessert?"

THE SERGEANT MAJOR NETWORK

"L et me get this straight," said the man behind the desk. "You intend to hunt a Russian mercenary in Germany on Commander SOF authorities, and you want me to help?"

Massoni smiled a Cheshire cat smile. Before he could respond, Flash said, "Exactly! I knew you would be all in on this one." She looked at Sue and said, "Didn't I tell you that Derry would be all in?"

Sue was speechless. She could see her boyfriend was uncomfortable with the entire project and more than a little peeved that she might be using his access and their growing relationship as leverage for an SOF mission that was entirely outside the bounds of his job description. Sue had two years in this relationship. She was cautious when she talked about the HICU team or any of the HICU missions, but it had been impossible to avoid sharing some work information, especially when their holidays were interrupted periodically by calls from Massoni or from Derry's supervisor, LTC Joe Banfield. Sue knew Derry had all the clearances needed but did not have that last step: need to know. It had been a source of tension for the first few months. Eventually, Sue had made up her mind to share some things about work but not others. Most of the secrets she offered were hardly secret. After all, the information she provided about her own deployments or the deployments of members of HICU were supported by orders issued by US Army Europe. Still, she wondered how many secrets over the years her parents kept from each other.

Adding to this complex web of secrecy balanced against trust, Sue and Derry had been slow to reveal the enduring physical and emotional scars from their respective war wounds. When Sue first met Jasper Derry back at his old post at Fort Ord, she could see his arms held burn scars. He was cautious at first to reveal that those burns covered a good portion of his torso and down his left leg. It took months to build trust and physicality so that Sue saw the entire damage that an IED had wrought on her boyfriend. Once they both revealed their scars, it was as if it they were made for each other. It was the first physical relationship she had since her injury and it was passionate in ways that Sue never thought would ever happen again. Since Derry was reassigned to Germany, Sue had grown used to having a man who knew precisely how she felt about her wounds, about the nightmares, and the burden of keeping it secret from everyone but her mother. Now, that emotional intimacy seemed to be at risk over this simple operation.

Massoni came to the rescue. He said, "Chief, I know this is more than a little irregular. And, you know that we are following the directions of our three-star. Before we came here, I sent a P4 message to the USAEUR CSM. I pointed out that this was a fast-moving operation, and I needed his advice and his boss's concurrence. I did get both before we came to you."

Flash laughed out loud while Sue contemplated what had just happened. Massoni used his connections inside the command sergeant major network to smooth over any troubles they might have. To do so, he sent a direct addressed email, known in the Army as a P4 or "personal for" to the most senior Army NCO in the entire theatre asking for top cover on the operation. Sue wasn't surprised that Massoni knew the US Army Europe command sergeant major, but she was slightly miffed that he hadn't told her before they arrived at the CI Shop at Campbell Barracks. She had spent time planning how they were going to do the job but hadn't spent any effort figuring out how to get the permission to do it. Once again, Massoni taught her a lesson on how the Army worked.

Derry said, "Well, Sergeant Major, I suspect I will get instructions sooner or later, so I am at your service. What do you need?"

Massoni smiled and said, "You need to help my boss." He pointed to Sue.

Sue finally regained her composure and said, "Jasper, we need some surveillance capability and, ideally, some reporting assets that might know where our targets are going. Once we have their identities confirmed and we have them fixed in place, we will work through you to have them detained by the Germans as persons indicted for war crimes. We have details on when they are going to arrive in Germany. We have no idea why they are coming here or who they will contact."

Derry smiled and said, "Oh, well why didn't you say so in the first place?"

It was Massoni's turn to laugh out loud.

14 January 2012 — Campbell Barracks

The next morning, Derry walked into the small office he had arranged for his colleagues. While it was easy enough to get approval for space once the USAEUR command sergeant major instructed the Campbell Barracks support officer to make it happen, the reality was there was little available space on post. They ended up opening a storeroom, little more than a large closet, for the HICU team. He found three OD green folding tables and six chairs in one of the military CONEX containers nearby. The rest had been up to them. The HICU team brought in three large rolling plastic boxes, the ubiquitous water- and dust-resistant PELICAN cases used in every theatre by every military unit. They opened the lids on the cases and started the process of creating a HICU Forward Operating Base in Heidelberg. Massoni told Derry, politely of course, to get lost and he did so.

After giving the team a full 18 hours to set up, move into their quarters on post and do whatever sort of morning PT that SOF operators did, Derry knocked on the door at 0830hrs. He had coffee and a fresh German coffee cake from the local bakery. Once he heard Massoni shout "Enter!" he opened the door. Derry was surprised by the transformation. Every available space was in use.

The three cases were stacked in the far corner and served as a storage space for various pieces of currently unused kit as well as flat space for a small coffee maker. The tables were set up along the length of the room with three sets of computers all linked together by what appeared to Derry as a rat's nest of wires culminating at the far table in a small printer and a large, humming alternate power source plugged into the wall socket. All three computers had yellow cables running to a separate yellow box sitting on that last table. The box had a single cable running to a wall port linking the HICU computers to the Army secure network.

Flash was the first person visible. She was in a set of black sweats and, peeking out from under the table, a set of black high-top trainers. She had her own table with three different screens linked to one keyboard. Her fingers were flying between the keyboard and wireless mouse. She was wearing headphones that were funneling exceptionally loud music into her ears. She peered over the middle screen and shouted, "SNACKS!"

Sitting at the second table, Massoni and Derry's girlfriend (at least that was what he thought) Sue O'Connell were working on two laptop computers. They were both wearing Army woodland camouflage uniforms with name tags and US Army over the chest pockets and the US Army Special Operations Command Spearhead Insignia on their left sleeves. Derry could see they were wearing very highly polished jump boots. He wondered if that was Massoni's decision or if they were trying to "fit in" at Campbell Barracks. He knew their old-school uniforms and bloused jump boots would stand out if they left their closet and walked around Campbell Barracks proper. Perhaps, that was the point after all. He was pleased to see Sue was still wearing his gift. It was a man's watch, but it worked well on Sue's left arm.

Sue seemed to be reading HICU communications, while Massoni's actions would be best described as "fiddling" with something on his laptop. They looked up and said their greetings in normal voices. Derry said, "I brought coffee and cake."

Flash reached over the middle screen and snatched the bag from his hand. She said, "I WILL TAKE THE CAKE." Massoni seemed totally disinterested, but he stood up and reached over to pull down Flash's headphones.

He said, "No need to shout."

A barely chastised Flash said, "Sorry, Sergeant Major." Flash turned to Derry and said, "The sergeant major is grumpy because this travel laptop is not configured the same way as his computer back at REAL SUE. He is like a fish trying to ride a bicycle."

Massoni grumbled, "And they didn't bring my coffee for the coffee pot. I have had to drink something they say is coffee but is only brown water."

Sue shook her head and said, "It is a real treat working with you two." Sue stood up, stretched and walked around the table toward Derry, trying not to limp after sitting in a metal folding chair for nearly two hours. She smiled and said, "Thanks for the breakfast treat."

Derry wasn't sure how to handle this strange mix of military formality and personal relationship, so he opted for formality. "No problem, Sue. I know you are busy, but the command received an email today saying there were some OGA folks coming down from Frankfurt. They want to have a meeting with you. Commander's conference room at 1000hrs."

Massoni finally stood up and stretched. Sue looked over at him. Jim Massoni had been part of her military family for years. Before he was the HICU sergeant major, he had been a team sergeant major in Sue's first SOF unit, Surveillance and Reconnaissance. Known simply as S&R, the team served as the "find and fix" part of the SOF mission to "find, fix, and finish" terrorist networks. He was more than just a sergeant major to Sue; he was like a protective elder brother. She knew that if Massoni was on your team, you were certain to be safe. At just under six feet tall, Massoni had shoulders and arms that looked like he could bend iron bars. His legs were thick cords barely restrained in his fatigue trousers. Years ago, when she first saw him in PT shorts, his legs seemed impossibly thick muscles covered in scars. He had never revealed where and when he got the scars, but Sue was sure they were from some sort of encounter with shrapnel. Since Massoni had served in combat with both Special Forces and the Ranger Regiment, it was entirely possible that it was multiple altercations with shrapnel. Massoni in uniform was impressive; Massoni in PT shorts and a T-shirt was terrifying.

Massoni said, "Thanks, Chief. Of course, it's way too late for breakfast since we have been working for nearly three hours, but I know it's the thought that counts. What I want to know is who squealed to the Klingons to let them know we were here."

Derry flushed. He said, "That was me, Sergeant Major. I work closely with the OGA offices in Frankfurt and Munich. Honestly, I can't afford to get sideways with them. They needed to know if we were going to start hunting the Russians in Germany."

Massoni growled a low rumble. Flash took over and, through a mouthful of German coffee cake, said, "He doesn't hold a grudge ... much."

Sue decided both for Derry's sake and to avoid the classic back-and-forth that was part of the relationship between Flash and Massoni, she would say something, anything. The only thing she could come up with was, "Who is going to attend?"

Derry seemed relieved that he could provide a fact-based answer rather than some opinion. He said, "On the OGA side, for sure it is the chief of base in Frankfurt. Neal Bascomb. Good guy, great German language, served in SF back in the day when 10th was in Bad Tolz. He is our ally. However, base headquarters also said they are expecting three including one VIP from CIA Headquarters. I don't know their names. On our side, it will be the G2 and his sergeant major and all of you."

Sue looked at Derry and said, "Not you?"

Derry shook his head. "Not invited."

Massoni thought for a minute. He wasn't worried in the least on how the Klingons felt about HICU, but he was determined to look the part for the senior USAEUR intelligence officer, certainly a general officer, and a USAEUR sergeant major. He looked at his watch. It was an old Marathon general purpose watch issued twenty years ago. Black face, tritium luminous hands and markers, wrapped around his large forearm by a black, single pass nylon strap. Covered with dings and scratches from years of combat and more parachute jumps than he could remember. He turned his gaze on Flash in her sweats and asked in his most polite sergeant major voice, "Flash, did you bring a proper uniform?"

Flash looked at Massoni and responded like a recalcitrant child, "Yes, Sergeant Major. I did bring a uniform. I even brought boots and a beret!" Now it was Flash's turn to look at her watch, the ubiquitous G-shock worn by over half the Army and nearly every SOF operator in combat. She shook her head, shut off her computer, stood up and ran out the door to shower and change.

Derry looked at the two remaining HICU operators and said to no one in particular, "Was it something I said?"

Commander's conference room, Campbell Barracks

As Sue walked into the USAEUR commander's conference room, she realized that military conference rooms had changed little in nearly twenty years of service. Long faux-wood table — probably a plywood composite — twelve feet long, four foot wide, two inches thick. Multiple triangular pods spaced every three feet to serve as both speakers and microphones when the conference room was being used for secure video-teleconferences. Twelve black composite rolling office chairs spaced along the table. In front of each chair was a small white pad with the USAEUR logo embossed on top, a pencil, a plastic glass, and a bottle of water. Twenty straight-backed chairs lined along both walls. A large screen at the end of the table opposite the commander's chair. In the corner to the right of the commander was a separate workstation for the communications officer who would be managing either the teleconference or whatever PowerPoint slide show might be part of the meeting.

The only difference Sue could see was that the USAEUR commander's room had slightly newer furniture, a bigger LED screen and amenities, at least water. In combat theatres, the seniors manufactured similar environments, usually in inflatable structures and usually with wires running along the floors which offered trip risks to Sue's prosthetic. No risk here as she noticed the dark blue carpet was also new.

Sue went over to the wall to take a chair when Massoni grabbed her elbow and said, "Sue, you sit at the table today. You are the HICU commander after all."

"Acting commander."

Flash added "So, act like it," as she and Massoni sat along the wall behind Sue.

They were fifteen minutes early which, in Massoni sergeant major parlance, was right on time. The next to arrive was the communications NCO who walked over to his workstation and started to boot up the computer and turn on the LED screen. Flash walked over to him with a flash drive and said, "When the time comes for our part of the presentation, here is our side."

"Yes, Ma'am. I think you are number two in the agenda, so I will put your stuff in the queue."

Flash nodded. She had spent so little time in the conventional army, she always had some trouble with protocol. She was a chief warrant officer, so that meant this young NCO was correct in calling her ma'am. It just didn't quite fit her mental image of the Flash, super cyber hero.

Flash sat down next to Massoni, Sue swiveled her chair to see them. Flash gave her a smile and a thumbs up. Massoni nodded.

The next to arrive was Derry's OGA counterpart, Neal Bascomb. Bascomb was in his mid-40s, balding with a full, greying beard. Sue noted he was fit — always a positive sign for SOF operators who lived in a world of nothing but super-fit personnel — and was wearing a dark wool suit and carrying a khaki trench coat under his left arm.

He sat down at the table across from Sue. That left the six chairs empty at the head of the table. The G2, his sergeant major and the three mystery guests from CIA headquarters would fill five of them. Sue had expected Bascomb to be carrying a briefcase filled with material for the meeting. It was his turf after all and, according to Derry, the reason for this coordination meeting. The fact that he had no material suggested the briefing would be coming from the CIA headquarters gurus.

Sue worried that might mean a classic OGA briefing that would start so far in the past that it might as well begin with the preamble, "First the earth cooled, then the oceans were formed." At least it wouldn't be a briefing with hundreds of PowerPoint slides like most military command briefings. She settled into her chair awaiting the boredom to begin. She was glad that she had followed TDY rule number one before the meeting: always pee when you can.

A MEETING OF THE MINDS

The meeting was nothing like what she anticipated.

An army lieutenant colonel walked in and announced, "Ladies and gentlemen, the commanding general." Everyone in the room stood up. As the tall, grey-haired man walked into the room, Sue glanced at Massoni. He just shrugged. The general walked around the room and shook hands with everyone before sitting down. It took a moment for Sue to recover from the fact that the commander of US Army Europe was now hosting the meeting. She regained her composure as she sat down and watched the rest of the CG's entourage walk in. The USAEUR command sergeant major was next. She noticed he wore master parachutist wings, a combat infantryman badge, a pathfinder badge, a set of HALO wings. This man was someone from SOF. No wonder Massoni had the connection. Next was the USAEUR G2. Sue had wondered if she would recognize this military intelligence brigadier general from her time in MI at 18th Airborne Corps. Absolutely not. The G2 had a Ranger tab riding over his USAEUR patch on his left shoulder. He had a set of pilot wings and jump wings bracketing his name tag. His last name was Chancellor. As he turned to sit down, she noticed on his right shoulder he was wearing the 75th Ranger Regiment scroll as his combat patch. Sue thought to herself, here is an ally to be sure.

The real surprise guests came next.

Patty Dentmann was living proof that physical stature had very little influence on charisma. She walked into a room full of men in uniform who were at least a foot taller and that meant absolutely nothing to her. They realized that and responded favorably. Sue had seen this before when she served with Dentmann in Cyprus. At that time, Dentmann was the Chief of Station in Nicosia and Sue was the HICU agent handler based in Akrotiri. When Dentmann worked with other seniors, whether British general officers, British special operators, or senior US officers, it was always the same. She took no guff from any of them, offered respect and expected the same. Why Dentmann was in Heidelberg was beyond Sue.

Next was an Army officer Sue did recognize. Jedidiah Smith walked slowly into the room. He was thinner and paler than she expected so many months after he returned to active duty, but he was still the same officer who ran HICU until wounded in Bahrain two years ago. Sue hadn't seen Smith in uniform for years. She noticed he was in the current digital grey/blue Army Combat Uniform and jungle boots, typical of SOF units in the field. His tan beret was tucked into the left cargo pocket of his trousers. More importantly, she noticed that he was no longer Colonel Smith, but now Brigadier General Smith. Whether it was his new assignment or his past record or the influence of commanding general SOF didn't matter. He was now a general officer and she needed to remember that when she talked to him. Well-deserved was all Sue could think.

The final character in this list of guests was probably the most unexpected of all. Following Smith was a bear of a man dressed in a somber, navy suit, white shirt and blue tie with what appeared to have a design of small white parachutes. Sue remembered the tie as one worn by her mentor and best friend of her mother, Max Creeter. For a brief moment, Sue wondered if it was some sort of club tie. It seemed hard to imagine that Creeter and Jamie Schenk would be members of the same club.

Sue had worked alongside Jamie Schenk in more than one war zone, but she had never seen him in a tie or a suit. Yet, there he was looking as uncomfortable in the suit as she was in a room full of general officers. What he didn't appear to be was uncomfortable with the company he was keeping. What in the world was he doing in Heidelberg? Before Sue could ponder the meaning of any of this, the CG spoke.

"I want to thank you all for coming here today. I know this is a complicated story and an evolving mission, but I wanted to have a clear understanding of what was happening and what would happen as we move forward on this operation with the CIA. I especially want to thank Ms. Dentmann for flying in from Washington to attend the meeting. It isn't often that I get to host my counterpart here in central Germany. Patty, thanks for coming."

Dentmann said, "General, thanks for the invitation. It is a treat to get out from the hazards of Washington bureaucracy and get back to work with a great partner. I suspect I have you to thank for inviting Brigadier General Smith to this meeting. I think the insight from the SOF J3X will be exceptionally important."

The CG said, "Patty, I don't think I have met the third member of your party."

"General, Jamie Schenk may play a critical piece in this effort. He is my referent for all things military. He has multiple tours in war zones in the last decade. We brought him home to take on this and other special projects. Let's just say he has a way of solving problems that is … unconventional. That sort of problem solver is not common in our headquarters. He splits his time between my front office in the European Division and my field stations. He has access to headquarters resources central to the program."

"Welcome, Mr. Schenk. Patty, do I need to make any introductions between all of you and the folks on the other side of the table?"

Dentmann laughed out loud while Smith and Shenk smirked. "General, we have all worked together several times in the past. I think we can say we *know* the crew across the table."

"Then, let's get started. G2, why don't you get the ball rolling."

The screen at the end of the table opened with the SWORD-FISH logo followed by a series of photos of SWORDFISH personnel working in Central Asia, Syria, and Libya. Chancellor offered details as the photos progressed. "The purpose of this meeting is to discuss the private military contracting company known as SWORDFISH. SWORDFISH is nominally responsible for physical security for Russian Federation government and corporate facilities worldwide. While we cannot be certain precisely when this PMC incorporated, the first intelligence community reporting comes from a DIA report in 1998. The directors of SWORDFISH are all retired military officers or former members of the USSR security service, the KGB." The screen displayed eight photographs of men in uniform.

The G2 paused for a moment for everyone in the room to see the photos of the SWORDFISH leadership. He continued, "SWORD-FISH headquarters is in St. Petersburg with a subordinate office in Moscow. They have offices in every nation in the former Soviet Union except for Ukraine and Georgia. They also have smaller offices in six African countries, four countries in South America and two in Southeast Asia. Most important to this meeting, SWORDFISH has offices in Leipzig, Vienna, and Belgrade." The screen first showed a map of all the locations and then switched to a map of Europe with smaller pictures of office buildings in the locations in Germany, Austria and Serbia.

"Over the past five years, DIA and Army G2 have reported on SWORDFISH paramilitary operations in Libya and Syria. CIA has reported the PMC operating in the Central African Republic and in Angola and, in the Western Hemisphere, in Venezuela and Cuba. In each of these reports, SWORDFISH employees have been involved in both their overt mission of corporate security and covert missions providing military training and participation in combat or state-security missions. Some ground photography from Libya shows SWORDFISH logos on Toyota Hi-Lux vehicles armed with heavy machine guns and Soviet-era BRDM armored cars. The intelligence community assessment is SWORDFISH is an informal arm of the GRU with exceptionally close ties to the Russian special forces. Of course, another part of SWORDFISH seems to be involved in cyber operations against US and UK military installations, most especially, special operations installations. I understand our colleagues from

HICU have some experience in that part of the SWORDFISH enterprise and will speak to that later in the briefing."

The G2 looked directly at Sue to confirm his last comment. Sue nodded in what she hoped was a deferential nod. Sue had come from the conventional Army before going through selection and transitioning to SOF. It had been years since she was in a conventional briefing with senior Army officers. Even the SOF commander had a way of running a meeting that felt inclusive and where rank was not important. What was important was what you knew and what you could do for the mission. Sue wasn't entirely sure how the USAEUR commander or his G2 would feel about hearing from a chief warrant officer, even if she was now wearing the CW5 rank, the highest rank in the warrant-officer cadre. Also, she had planned on having Flash do most of the talking. How that would work was anyone's guess.

The screen shifted to what was clearly a surveillance photograph taken with a long lens from the parking lot at a private airfield. There were four men coming out of the airport terminal and walking toward two black Mercedes Gelandewagen SUVs. The G2 said, "These are surveillance photos taken yesterday. The four men in the frame include two SWORDFISH travelers, Viktor Alexander Shemkovich and Georg Stanislaw Chesnik, and two individuals traveling on Russian diplomatic passports, Michel Istorik and Alexander Payalshik. Istorik and Payalshik are known GRU aliases." The G2 paused for a drink of water from the bottle in front of him and said, "Not terrific aliases. Istorik means historian and Payalshik means plumber in Russian. It's as if they weren't even trying to be ... diplomatic." Sue heard Massoni's low growl behind her. She hoped he would be patient.

"The vehicles were registered to the SWORDFISH office in Leipzig. The team we had on the airport did not follow them. When the SWORDFISH vehicles left the airport, they were followed by a surveillance team that we believe belongs to the German BFV. Our team is not known to the Germans, and they chose to break contact at that point." The G2 turned to Dentmann and said, "I believe our Agency colleague can take up the story from there."

Sue heard Flash fidget in her chair. She had expected to be the next speaker. Sue now realized that HICU might not have any speaking role in this briefing. That was just fine with her because it was clear that this was a far more complicated tale than she had expected.

Patty Dentmann stood up. She might be a cat's whisker over five feet tall, but she now had the attention of everyone in the room. "Next slide, please." The NCO delivered a slide with another surveillance photograph taken in a European city. Two men were walking down the street in front of a storefront with a small sign saying *TABAC*. From the shop marquees and the street signs, it was in either Germany or Austria. Dentmann said, "Last year, one of our officers in Vienna recruited a source reporting on Russian oligarch activities in the city. Russian oligarch funds have flowed into Vienna and London since the collapse of the USSR. We have been tracking those funds since the mid-1990s. They were originally KGB funds dispatched just before the collapse of the USSR. However, over the past three years, we saw a significant change in funds going into German banks. We tasked Berlin station to find out why. Next slide please."

Another rattle of keys and a new slide opened. This time an expanded image of one of the men in the previous photograph. Dentmann continued, "As you can see from this enhanced photo, this is Chesnik from SWORDFISH. The second individual in the photograph has not been identified."

Dentmann continued, "We know from other reporting that SWORDFISH is interested in a small German-American firm based in the suburbs of Frankfurt. *Sternbild GMBH*, is a collaboration between a German engineering firm and a US software firm based in the greater DC area. They are designing a cutting-edge capability for micro-satellites that will focus on identifying and, ideally, eliminating the level of space junk that is in orbit around the earth. Next slide, please."

The screen displayed a digitally created image of the earth with what looked like a white cloud over the Northern Hemisphere. Dentmann continued, "This is a best-guess simulation of the level of space junk up there just waiting to crash into something important: Remnants of old satellites, old rocket bodies tumbling through space and debris from previous crashes. The Air Force and IC have been worried about this for years. Our large communications and reconnaissance satellites are at risk from a random strike. The International Space Station has had several close calls. Since these pieces range in size from peas to pies and are travelling at over 10,000 miles per hour, you can see why we are worried."

Dentmann paused just long enough to make sure everyone in the room was listening. "Right now, *Sternbild* GMBH may have one of the best solutions for at least predicting the hazards and, over time, possibly even eliminating them. Next slide, please."

The screen displayed an engineering production clean room. Men dressed in white surrounded a device on the work stand that looked like a silver tube about four meters long with a diameter of a meter. At one end of the tube was a metal umbrella-like object on a spindle that projected about two meters from the tube. "This is a commercial program that we have identified under the code name GINGER-HAWK. I don't want to go into science that I don't understand." Sue was glad Dentmann passed on discussing rocket science. She was a liberal arts major who was easily lost in any discussion that involved calculus or engineering.

Dentmann continued, "This prototype will be launched soon. Once in orbit, it will use navigational software to identify an orbit that has a high probability of space debris. Onboard sensors using laser imaging detection and ranging or LIDAR will track the individual objects in the debris field. Once objects have been identified, GINGERHAWK uses small pulse engines to match the course and speed of the debris. The collector has a relatively weak electro-magnet that draws the object into the grasp of its titanium alloy umbrella. In the vacuum of space and given the LIDAR seeker technology, GINGERHAWK will keep that object in its grasp with the electro-magnet. I understand that if it did not have this capability, the electro-magnet would have to be powered by far more batteries that would make GINGERHAWK ten times the size. After the umbrella is completely covered with debris, the umbrella mechanism closes and GINGERHAWK will use small control rockets to set a re-entry course which takes the debris back to earth. The basic technology is well-established but the blend of this software and technology is unique. The key new feature of the *Sternbild* design is in the autonomous hunting software designed to find the debris."

Dentmann paused again. This time she took a drink of water from the bottle in front of her. She continued, "The Intelligence Community, the Department of Defense, and even the German Ministry of Defense have all tried to gain some degree of financial control over the project. So far, the German and American engineering and software teams have rebuffed all approaches. They haven't been aggressive in their refusal. Instead, they have simply rebuffed government investment. They may believe they will make a fortune with the commercial satellite industry once they have a proof of concept. Of course, that fortune will only happen if they are independent of any state-run organization. We still don't know who is funding GINGER-HAWK. If it is Russian or Chinese funding then that is troublesome. If SWORDFISH is somehow involved, and using the KGB/SVR funds they pulled from banks in Vienna, then it is a serious threat — whether or not the *Sternbild* team are aware of the link."

Dentmann looked directly at the general at the head of the table and said, "After all, GINGERHAWK could just as easily be reverse engineered into a very sophisticated and very deniable anti-satellite weapon."

Dentmann sat down and nodded to Smith. As Smith stood up, Sue had to admit that Patty Dentmann knew precisely how to engage an audience.

Smith spoke directly to the Commanding General. "Sir, our dominance in the counterterrorism fight in Iraq and Afghanistan and, honestly, all over CENTCOM, is based in part on our situational awareness. And our SA is based on speed in our communications network and our ability to synchronize all source intelligence. That speed is supported entirely on satellite communications from the tactical to the strategic. If any adversary was able to retrofit GINGERHAWK so that they destroyed our established satellite network, it would be devastating. SOF command is working with DARPA to design micro-sats that could serve a new system and would work to unify allied communications. I know you have been briefed on our plan to launch the prototype this summer using your theatre and NATO SOF as the test bed." Smith paused and took a drink of water.

"But, we are at least two years away from full deployment of a satellite network that would serve as a redundant system for all NATO forces in EUCOM. In any future conventional conflict, our ability to win against adversaries in Europe and in Asia will be based as much on this sort of information dominance as the skills of our troops and the sophistication of our weapons. The collective concern SOF, DIA, and CIA have is that the Russians are designing small, equally sophisticated anti-satellite weapons designed to significantly reduce our advantage. If the Russians acquire this autonomous hunting software on the GINGERHAWK prototype, they would be able to neutralize both our current and any future systems. We must know if the Russians are focused on this small company in your AOR. If they are, we must do our best to prevent any operation."

The CG nodded and said, "I understand why it is important, Jed. The question is what can we do about these civilians and, in the case of USAEUR, how can we help? After all, as near as I can tell from the debriefing so far, we have suspected Russian intelligence officers traveling in Germany on legitimate passports and legitimate visas. In the case of SWORDFISH, we have a company registered in Germany. This is not an environment where we can capture and interrogate suspects when we want to do so. I know SOF has become the premier manhunters in CENTCOM, but in EUCOM we have to live with the fact that we are guests of our NATO allies and we have to work inside their legal systems."

Smith looked at the General and said, "Sir, we fully recognize the structure of our relationship here in Europe and, most especially, in Germany. And, we also understand that a counterintelligence investigation with our German counterparts would be the ideal answer under normal circumstances. However, these are not normal circumstances. These are not Russian intelligence officers permanently assigned to Russian diplomatic facilities. Instead, we have Russian intelligence officers traveling under commercial cover on legitimate visas with legitimate work that they accomplish for their German business clients as well as clients in Austria and Serbia. We do have an angle that we can use to engage the Germans that will have nothing to do with SWORDFISH proper." Smith paused for a moment, took a drink of water and said, "The angle is based on work that the Humint Intelligence Collection Unit identified this week." Smith looked over at Sue as if to say "over to you!"

Sue wasn't prepared to say anything at this point. She wasn't entirely certain what Smith intended for her to say in the briefing. Sue realized the longer she paused, the more likely she would demonstrate to the commanding general that she wasn't up to whatever plan Dentmann and Smith had in mind. She looked at the commanding general and thought to herself, "Stall while you think of something important to say." Sue stood up and started to stall hoping something important would come to mind.

"Sir, I'm not sure how much you know about HICU. We were created in 2005 by the SOF commander to handle human sources providing critical SA for the SOF mission to find, fix and finish the CT threat. We are often partnered with another SOF unit known simply as Surveillance and Reconnaissance that is our stand-alone physical surveillance capability. We started in a compound at Ft. Bragg and transitioned into your AOR in 2008. We are currently based in Camp Ederle in Northern Italy, working out of a warehouse on post. We have twenty-four collectors based in ten different countries in both CENTCOM and AFRICOM areas of responsibility." Sue could see she was losing the general and that was not a good thing. She felt a small pinch from behind her. She looked over to see Flash pointing a thumb directly at her own chest. Sue had no idea what Flash might say, but she was certain she had nothing more to say. "Sir, the specific angle that we are here to pursue is based on research conducted by Chief Billings, our senior analyst at HICU."

Flash stood up and looked beyond the general toward the communications NCO. She said, "Please load our presentation." As he worked the computer terminal, Flash began her briefing. "Sir, as

General Smith stated, one part of the success SOF has is situational awareness. That success has been based on our understanding that terrorist networks are dynamic and our team has to consider the total network before we determine the right adversary in the right place at the right time so we can design a finish operation." Flash looked over her shoulder at the screen. It showed a grainy photo of the SWORDFISH warehouse outside Dushanbe. Flash continued, "In 2009, we conducted a series of joint operations with the CIA to disrupt a SWORDFISH cyber hacking operation of DoD and, specifically, SOF networks. The initial investigation started at the DoD language facility in Monterey and that investigation coupled with an FBI operation in Northern Virginia led us to the data center in Dushanbe managed by SWORDFISH. Slide 6, please."

Sue was pleased that Flash saved her. She was also amazed at the level of confidence that her colleague demonstrated in front of the most senior officer in theatre.

"This slide shows a photograph of the SWORDFISH target Shemkovich. Next slide, please." The next picture was a long-range surveillance photo of what looked to be a heavily armed mercenary platoon dismounting from a Russian cargo truck. Based on the equipment, it looked to Sue like the photo was taken in the 1990s. Flash continued, "Sir, please note the individual in the lead of this company. This photo is of Marko Vladich, a Serbian militia leader who is a person indicted for war crimes by the Hague Tribunal. Slide 7, please." The screen changed to a side-by-side set of photographs, one of Shemkovich and one of Vladich. It was clear from the comparison that they were one person. "Sir, Shemkovich is a Russian national but has a Serbian parent. We do not have any details on whether Shemokovich was working as an independent, as a Russian special operations officer or as a SWORDFISH employee when he was in Croatia. What we do know is Shemkovich aka Vladich is a PIFWC." Flash paused for a moment to make certain the comparison was clear.

She continued, "Of course, we would have to build a more robust case with additional ground photography and confirmation from the Croatians, but once we do so, we could be very confident that this individual could be detained, if not arrested, by the German National Police on the INTERPOL Red Notice issued by The Hague Tribunal. HICU has already worked with Croatian military intelligence in a different disruption operation in 2008, so we have an established liaison relationship with them. At the very least, once we have the full package, it should delay if not disrupt any activities that Shemkovich aka Vladich and his colleagues intend to conduct in Germany. Thank you, sir." Flash sat down. As she did, Sue heard Flash let out a very deep exhale as if she had been holding her breath the entire briefing. Flash might have appeared confident, but she had been very nervous throughout the presentation.

The general looked at his G2 and asked, "Bill, what do you think?"

"Sir, we both served in the Balkans. We both know how vicious the Serbian militias were and how few of these criminals have been brought to justice. Even if this didn't include a threat to the entire DoD communications network, I would push for our support to this project." The G2 smiled at his guests and said, "Of course, I don't know precisely what sort of support they would want from us."

For the first time, the Frankfurt chief of base spoke. Bascomb looked directly at the commanding general and said, "Sir, I think the only thing we need at present is your approval to move forward. I understand from my chief and Jed that between SOF and the Agency, we have the necessary resources in theatre to conduct the operation. We have a blanket approval from the ambassador to pursue any/all PIFWCs so long as we partner with the Germans. If we are successful in building the necessary target package, then we would ask that your headquarters work with the ambassador and take the information to the Germans to initiate action. The most important point is that we start working on this today because the SWORDFISH team has a few days' head start and we need to conduct our operation before they are successful in stealing, or perhaps, buying the data from *Sternbild*."

Smith said, "Sir, we will keep you and Bill informed the entire way. My CG has instructed me to stay here until the project is completed, one way or the other. I have a small team of three — a communicator and two analysts — who have traveled with me and would serve as your SOF direct communications link. I will be in regular communications with the HICU team and with Neal. SOF also has a strong working relationship with the German counterterrorism force known as GSG9. When needed, I am confident they will have the necessary authority to conduct any operations in Germany. In short, I believe we can make this happen and I absolutely believe we have to make this happen."

Dentmann finished the presentation by stating, "General, this has the potential for being a significant win in three areas: a counterintelligence operation preventing tech theft, an opportunity to bring a war criminal to justice and, finally, an opportunity to work with our German counterparts on a compatible target."

The commanding general nodded. He looked at his command sergeant major. The sergeant major nodded. He then stood up and said, "Ladies and gentlemen, make it happen. I won't waste your time any more in this briefing. I believe you have plenty of work to do and sitting here briefing a general is only slowing you down. Bill will keep me in the loop. Good luck to you all." Everyone in the room stood up as the commanding general and his sergeant major left the room. Sue wasn't entirely certain, but she thought his sergeant major winked at Massoni.

Massoni leaned over to Sue and said, "As you know, everything is easy … "

Sue completed the sentence, "Until you do it. Jim, that's what I'm trying to figure out. What do we do next?"

Massoni smiled and said, "I reckon Jed and the EUR Chief already have the plan. All we must do is execute."

Flash leaned in and said, "Did I do ok?"

Massoni laughed. "If you mean did you save Sue's ass, yes you did great. If you mean did you make us look brilliant, the answer is absolutely."

Sue turned to Flash and said, "I'll hug you later."

Flash nodded. "I certainly hope so."

THREE D CHESS

S mith walked over to the HICU team. He said, "If we have to work with pirates, I suppose working with you three is about as good as it gets."

Massoni said, "Sir, when exactly were you going to tell us that you are now a flag grade officer?"

Smith said, "Does that mean you will give me more respect?"

Massoni laughed and said, "It's not in the sergeant major contract, sir. You get the same amount of respect you always received from me."

Smith nodded and said, "Dandy." He turned to Sue and Flash and said, "Well done. I apologize for not giving you some of the details in advance, but we still haven't sorted out what communications are compromised and what are secure. And, since you are living in a USAEUR space, we figured it was best not to send the material. You did very well ... considering."

Sue said, "Thanks to Flash."

Flash added, "Once again, thanks to Flash."

Dentmann and Jamie joined the group. It appeared that Bascomb had been dispatched by Patty Dentmann to accomplish some immediate task. Dentmann said, "O'Connell, you are like gum on my shoe. Every time I think I have cleaned you off my responsibility list, there you are."

"At least this time, I wasn't wired to a bomb in the trunk of a car."

Jamie said, "Don't get me started on how many times you have forced me out of my home."

Dentmann turned serious. "I know this is a lovely reunion, but we need to get cracking on this project. Here is what Jed and I agreed. First, you move from your spaces to a stand-alone space we maintain in Wiesbaden. It is small but it is secure. Pack up your stuff and be ready to leave this afternoon. Jamie will drive you to your new digs."

Smith said, "And, don't say anything to Derry. He is not read in on the project and he doesn't have the need to know."

Sue said, "If we don't have Derry involved, what local resources do we have?" She tried to make the question not sound like a complaint, but it didn't come out quite right.

Smith said, "O'Connell, that part of the equation has been handled between Patty and yours truly. Derry does not have the need to know. Clear?"

Based on Smith's tone of voice and his use of her last name, she realized Smith was not asking her, he was ordering her to keep her lover, Jasper Derry, out of the loop. Given the fact that Smith and Massoni were so close and given the likelihood that Patty Dentmann and her mother were in contact, it meant that everyone in the equation knew Sue and Jasper were in a relationship. That might be the reason why they wanted Derry out of the loop. Or, it might simply be a case of need to know. She said, "Check, sir."

Jamie said, "Hey, don't look so glum. You have me to keep you entertained!"

Flash asked, "And what exactly do you do now for the CIA?"

Jamie said, "I fix things. You would be surprised how easily the right man applying a screwdriver in the right place can fix broken parts."

Massoni smiled and said, "Like you did in Salvador?"

"With your help, Jim. Don't forget, it was with your help." Jamie looked at the HICU team and said, "Get hot on packing up. We don't have a lot of time to spare. I have a Mercedes Sprinter van ready to go. It won't take long on the A5, but we need to get to work today. Seriously, we need to be working right now on this project."

Massoni looked at the two warrant officers and said, "We have our orders, let's get going."

As the HICU team left the briefing room, the USAEUR G2 walked back in. He approached Smith and said, "Do you think O'Connell will follow orders?"

Smith nodded, "More or less. When it comes to compartmentation, more. When it comes to avoiding trouble, far less."

Dentmann said, "Gentlemen, this is a game of three-dimensional chess. We have many moving parts and each move affects more than one playing surface. If O'Connell doesn't follow instructions right now, we are sunk. If she doesn't follow instructions later, we can fix her mistakes." Dentmann turned to Jamie and said, "Jamie, work your magic and make sure she follows instructions now."

Jamie was almost out of the conference room when he spoke, "Always the easy jobs. Thanks, Boss. I will see you on the other side of the Atlantic when we are done."

Dentmann laughed hard which ended with a snort. She said to Smith, "He is a very good plumber."

The G2 looked up and said, "Plumber?"

Smith said, "He fixes leaks."

ON THE ROAD AGAIN

Sue's mind was spinning from the briefing. The HICU team had come to Germany a day earlier with hopes of bringing a war criminal to justice and disrupting a shadowy organization linked to Russia. Now, suddenly, they were tasked with keeping anti-satellite technology out of the hands of America's adversaries — an assignment so critical that it required a briefing with the top US general in Europe.

And how were they supposed to do the new job without engaging Jasper? After all, her team was from a HUMINT office and, right now, they had no human sources on site that would help do the job. As a CI officer, Jasper Derry would have a network of informants operating in and around military bases in Europe. When Flash delivered her brief, Sue could imagine exploiting that network to get ground photography while either she or Flash headed to Croatia to confirm the identity of Shemkovich/Vladich. Now, she wasn't sure what they were going to do. Also, she was more than a little miffed that Smith and Dentmann had decided to cut Jasper out of the loop. What in the world was so secret that they couldn't include a senior Army CI investigator? He already knew their target, so what was the point?

As Sue was mulling this over, a silver Mercedes Sprinter van pulled up to the three HICU operators. The electric window on the driver's side rolled down unleashing the sounds of 1970s rock and roll. Jamie's head appeared and he said, "Hey, how about a lift?"

Massoni said, "Schenk, have you grown soft? We only have a quarter mile to walk to our new digs."

Jamie's smile under his large moustache broadened. "Not anymore. We've already worked out your move to another location. Smith sent some of his minions to pick up your kit from your closet on post and put the kit in the van. My job is to get you and your kit over to my safe house. So, unless you want me to hand you a GPS point on a map and let you walk, I think you should hop in."

Massoni could smell some sort of Smith intervention in this equation and decided that it was best for him to lead his two warrant officers into the van. He looked at Sue and Flash and said, "Who wants to ride shotgun?"

Flash was already running around the front of the car as she said, "Got it!"

Massoni turned to Sue and said, "Boss, the principal always rides in the right rear." Sue nodded and walked around to the right rear door. Massoni had already jumped in behind Jamie.

Sue found her current level of emotion curious. For months, she had grumbled about having to make decisions on everything from HICU operators' travel accounting to their deployment schedules. Suddenly, she was back in a world where she was being told what to do and when to do it. Why in the world was she angry now? As she got into the vehicle, she realized that she had grown used to being the boss and sliding back into the role of operator seemed almost like a demotion. Sue shook her head to clear her thoughts as she jumped into the cacophony of Jamie's music. She said, "Hey, can we talk while you drive?"

Jamie looked over his shoulder as he put the van in gear. "WHAT?" He smiled and shut off the sound system. "OK, so what do you want to talk about? The Dada art movement in Europe? Confucian philosophy? The maximum effective range of a .50 caliber machine gun?"

Sue couldn't help herself. She started to laugh as they drove through the main gate and onto a German highway. "OK, wise guy. When exactly are you going to tell us what Smith and Dentmann have in mind?"

"Well, I am not exactly in their confidence ... "

Massoni said, "Here's the deal. Let's start with why you are in

Europe. After that, you can cough up what you know or I'm choking you right now."

Flash said, "Hey, we are now on a German autobahn traveling at light speed in a van driven by this madman. How about we stop arguing and let him concentrate on getting us to wherever he is taking us? Whatdya think?"

"Thank you," said Jamie. "Now, we can either listen to my playlist or we can talk nice about what's going on. O'Connell, your choice. I don't really care what Massoni wants."

Massoni was reaching over the headrest to rap Jamie in the head when Sue grabbed his arm. "Working with you guys is going to be special, I can see that already."

Flash said, "Hey, it's always a party with Jamie around. And, we are on the road again!"

Jamie smiled and said, "I always liked you, Flash."

Flash said, "Prove it, big guy."

Sue could see Jamie blush around the collar of his white shirt. Before she could say anything, Jamie started relating his side of the story.

SPECIAL DUTIES

As Jamie negotiated the traffic northbound on the A5, he started relating his end of the story. Sue noticed that Jamie's driving style in Germany was far less aggressive than her previous experiences with him in Iraq and Afghanistan. He even stayed in the far-right lane of the autobahn, the lane usually reserved for heavy trucks and Europeans driving cars that were not built for the high speeds of the German highways. Jamie was splitting his concentration on driving and storytelling. As Flash pointed out later, that was probably a good thing because driving on the autobahn was a full-time job.

"So, after we finished off the raid on the SWORDFISH communications network in Tajikistan, headquarters decided that, once again, Hurricane O'Connell had blown my work to smithereens."

"That was not my fault."

Massoni and Flash spoke at the same time, "She always says that."

Jamie nodded, "I know. In fact, at the same time there was also a move to concentrate the Agency work into a small number of locations that were totally focused on al-Qaida in Afghanistan. Northern Afghanistan was not considered critical to those needs. We packed up the classified stuff and turned over the entire kit and kaboodle to the Tomahawks."

Massoni said, "I'll bet they were not real pleased."

Jamie nodded, "Who would be pleased when Jamie leaves?"

Massoni said, "I can name a couple of thousand..."

Jamie shrugged and said, "Well, the Tomahawks are Hazara

Shia. They are used to being left in the lurch. At least we gave them training, equipment, a very nice safe house, an equally nice barracks, and bushel baskets of dough. We even left our trucks. It was time for them to take charge of their own area. They knew what needed to be accomplished. Our collection capabilities were useful to them, but honestly, they were always more comfortable with their standard ways of intelligence collection. Basically, direct observation and infor- mants. I hope they make it. Given the history of Afghanistan and the ethnic animosities, I'm not real confident they will."

Massoni said, "We are not always the most reliable allies."

Jamie nodded. He went quiet as he drove along the autobahn.

Flash said, "Before we get all morose and pull over for a little cry, I want to know the rest of the story. How did you end up involved in this operation?"

Jamie said, "When they pulled me out of northern Afghanistan, I figured it was back to Langley for some sort of job or possibly the Farm to teach."

Massoni said, "Exactly what sort of Klingon skills did you think they would let you teach?"

"Hey, I'm a smart guy."

Flash smiled and said, "You are a blunt implement."

Jamie smiled. "I take that as a compliment."

"My point exactly."

"OK, so back to my story. Somehow, a genius in headquarters found out that I was a 10th Special Forces guy who had tested at 3/3 German when I came on board at the Agency."

Sue wasn't surprised that the Agency had tested Jamie's language skills when he came on board. She was surprised that he tested at 3/3 which meant he had both speaking and reading comprehension in German at the operational level. Few special operators, Sue included, maintained their foreign language skills after years of rotating in and out of Afghanistan and Iraq. The only way that made sense to Sue was if Jamie had been a very fluent German speaker before 9/11. She said, "Those are amazing numbers."

"Yup. Haven't I been saying I'm an amazing guy?"

Massoni said, "OK. I will wait until we are out of the vehicle to pat you on the back."

"Thank you."

Flash poked Jamie in the ribs. It felt like she had poked her fingers into a concrete wall. "Will you get on with the story?"

"Sure. So, I'm back in headquarters. I'm turning in our kit from Afghanistan and making sure my guys get their pay and new jobs sorted. Then, I get a note. Report to the European Division front office. I had to get directions to find the darn place. Anyhow, I get there and Dentmann herself greets me. She takes me into her office and tries to give me coffee. I explain I am a tea drinker. She says, 'Just like Sue O'Connell.' I realize up front that things are not going to go well for me."

"Dentmann was the COS in my first assignment."

"Yeah, she said. Dentmann tells me she needs someone for special duties in her division. She points out that she grew up in the Agency chasing bad guys in the Middle East before she ended up in the Eastern Med chasing ... well, other sorts of bad guys. She has great officers who are good at conventional espionage, but right now, there are some irregular operations that need to be accomplished and she asks me to create a small unit of players who work just for her."

Jamie paused as two large German sedans blasted by the van and swerved back into his lane. They disappeared over a hill on the autobahn and were not seen again.

"There are plenty of folks in the Counterterrorism Center who can do these sorts of jobs, but their bosses over there have them working all over the world. Dentmann wants her own team and she wants me to run it. Anyhow, she tells me she needs a guy to set up a small outfit inside her front office. Special Projects Staff. I didn't have a job and, as you probably know, Dentmann is not someone who takes no for an answer. I say yes. Her admin staff move me from the paramilitary side of the outfit to her division. They give me a closet next to the copy machine, wire in a computer terminal and tell me to start reading into the division reporting. Basically, they tell me to wait until Dentmann has sorted out what she wants to do with me."

"Boring?"

"Nope. There are two different gyms in the headquarters building, two different coffee shops and a huge library. Plus, a language school that I used part time for a few months. Finally, Dentmann calls me into her office and tells me I am heading to Wiesbaden on a long term TDY."

"And here we are."

"Yup."

"And that's the story?" Flash asked, sounding doubtful.

"Mostly."

Sue said, "Mostly?"

"Well, all I can tell you right now until we get to our new digs. I want to save some of the story for the surprise."

Flash offered in her most sweet voice, "I love surprises."

"Wait until you see this one. I guarantee you are going to love it."

Massoni said, "Another tragic tale from Schenk. I almost believe it." Massoni caught Schenk's look in the mirror. It said simply, "I have more to tell you ... later." So, Massoni let it go.

Flash was not about to let it go. She asked, "How in the world did you hear about our effort against these creeps from SWORDFISH?"

Jamie smiled, looked at Flash and said, "OGA sees all, knows all, and reveals little."

Massoni said, "Keep your eyes on the road and off my troops!"

"Yes, Sergeant Major."

Sue spent the rest of the drive sulking about everything related to this change of mission. She had been excited about working in Germany with Derry and what she now considered "her team." Instead, this simple mission had become a larger, more complex, multi-agency team, and for some reason, Jasper Derry was no longer included. Sue had worked on teams of this sort in the past. It almost always meant receiving instructions that offered little in the way of flexibility and plenty of oversight. Worse still, it didn't look like she was going to get a chance to explain to Derry what was happening. She resolved to give Derry a call when they arrived at the still undisclosed destination to explain that she was going to be unavailable for a few days. It seemed the least she could do after roping him into the operation at the beginning.

Jamie exited the A5 just as it entered the ring road around Frankfurt. He pulled the Mercedes into the westbound lane of another German autobahn, marked A66, and followed signs toward Wiesbaden. He slowed down as he joined the A66 and said to no one in particular, "The traffic police are wicked here. It's 100km or less even though the highway is designed for higher speeds. Cameras and motorcycle police all along this stretch."

Flash nodded. "So, are we headed to Wiesbaden?"

Massoni offered, "Or some small town on the Rhine?"

Jamie smiled and said, "Yes."

Flash wouldn't let it go. "Wiesbaden or the Rhine?"

"Neither. Or, perhaps, both."

Sue finally turned her grumpiness on Jamie and said, "Stop with the Klingon shit, will ya?"

Massoni looked over at Sue. He hadn't heard that tone from Sue in years. He wasn't entirely sure what was going on in her head, but it didn't look or sound good.

Jamie said, "We have a safe house in Schierstein just outside Wiesbaden. It is located on a set of docks used for years for barge traffic on the Rhine. Satisfied?"

Sue continued to sulk. Massoni was not pleased. He shared another look into the rearview mirror and saw Jamie's eyes. They were both thinking the same thing: "What is going on?"

Flash decided to change the subject. "You been here before?"

"I've been here for just a month setting up Dentmann's end of this project." He looked into the rearview mirror at Sue and said, "Before you ask, our side of the project had nothing to do with the SWORDFISH creeps, or at least it didn't before you found the link. We had local source reporting that there was both Russian and Chinese interest in the space-junk device, so we brought in a couple of special teams to look at the possible threats. That's the origin of Project GINGERHAWK. Of course, once we heard from Smith, it only seemed to make sense to roll your effort into GINGERHAWK. Let's not forget, I have a grudge against the SWORDFISH guys too."

The vehicle was quiet for the rest of the drive until Jamie exited A66, entered the local traffic pattern in Schierstein and drove into the warehouse district near the Rhine. He pulled into the driveway of what appeared to be a poorly maintained set of workshops protected by a metal fence. As he pulled up to the gate, two men dressed in German sky-blue coveralls opened the gate and let them in. Jamie smiled as he pulled up to the larger of the two workshops. He shut off the van and said, "Welcome to your new home!"

As she got out of the van, Flash looked around at the exterior of two old brick buildings illustrated with multiple years of faded graffiti. A rusted corrugated-metal fence surrounded the compound.

"Swell," was all she said.

15 January 2012 — somewhere over the Atlantic

B arbara O'Connell was not used to this sort of travel. During her years in the CIA, she had only traveled once in first class on a commercial aircraft and never in a Gulfstream 5 private jet. When Beth told her they were going to travel "in style," she assumed that Stearns and Mandeville were going to pay for first-class tickets. Instead, Beth, Richard and Barbara were sitting in leather seats around an oak table in a private jet. Beth explained that the firm had a time share with a business-jet company. The company regularly traded "space available" seats in exchange for legal advice on parking locations and fueling at foreign private airfields. Beth told Barbara that this aircraft was headed to Europe to pick up some high-tech investors headed back to the US and the jet company was more than willing to offer seats on what would otherwise be an empty leg of the flight. Barbara didn't believe a word of what her friend said, but she wasn't about to complain.

They had no departure hassles at the private side of Dulles Airport, and if she understood correctly, they would face no immigration hassles at the private parking location at Frankfurt. And, since the G5 had a top speed of 0.8 Mach or 500 knots traveling at 40,000 feet, they would be in Germany in about six and half hours, almost two hours faster than a commercial flight. Plus, they weren't flying the typical night flight route. That meant they could work on the project without interruption throughout the flight. The only limitation was they had to live with a packed lunch, bottled water, and coffee from the aircraft coffee maker. Richard served them lunch and then sat down as they went over the plan.

Barbara said, "I still don't quite understand why you wanted me along."

Richard put down his ceramic coffee cup, smirked and said, "We like your company."

"There is that, Barbara. We do like your company and your flexibility to jump on a plane with no notice." Barbara could see Beth had more to say, so she waited patiently to hear the rest of the story. Sometimes, silence was a useful weapon.

"So, we just might need someone with a background in intelligence to sort out what, if anything, is going on with the auction. The auction house has had several inquiries about the paintings. They seem legitimate, but there are questions about the man in possession of the paintings, Friedrich Altmayer. He runs an antique shop in Sachsenhausen and another in Vienna. Both shops might be legit, they might not. We just don't know. I have warned Longstreet and the boys that we might need some assistance. With you and Richard along, I figured we can handle just about anything short of combat."

Barbara said, "I thought we might use the LKA for that sort of thing."

"Well, we might. But I have found European Union protocol is ... cumbersome. We often help clients in Europe to resolve issues before they feel obligated to call the police. It seems to me you did something similar both when we worked together in Greece and then did a bit of piracy over the Dalmatian coast."

Barbara raised both hands in mock surrender. "I get it. Sometimes, we need to think out of the box."

Richard nodded and said, "And, sometimes it takes special effort to ... resolve situations."

Beth laughed and said, "And you are both really good problem solvers in your own ... special ways."

Beth stood up, stretched and walked to the back of the aircraft to the women's bathroom. Barbara decided it was time to find out more about her companion. She offered a simple question as an opening gambit. "Richard, you have any experience in this sort of recovery operation?"

He smiled and said, "I've done some personnel recovery operations when I was in my old unit."

"Do tell!"

Richard looked down at his coffee cup and said, "I suppose my unit stuff is still pretty sensitive. So, let's just say, there was a kidnapping of a US diplomat in Croatia when we were working PIFWCs. Serbian bad boys grabbed one of ours and disappeared into the hills in the Serbian enclave in Albania. Back in those days, we didn't have the intelligence or the technology we use today in Afghanistan or Iraq. It was a short-fuse operation because the Serbian militia was threatening to send the diplomat back in pieces if the USG didn't stop bombing their military headquarters."

Richard paused. Barbara wasn't sure if he was simply pausing for effect or if he didn't intend to continue. She looked at him and said, "Give it up!"

"Well, we did know the location of some of their bases on the Croatian-Serbian border. So, we just visited one of those, grabbed one of their leaders, and offered a trade. They were convinced we might do some permanent harm to their guy if we didn't get our guy back safe. It wasn't exactly … "

"Diplomatic?" Beth's voice intruded. The aircraft noise and Beth's athletic stride had allowed her to appear behind them before they knew she was listening.

Richard smiled and said, "I guess there were some folks in Washington who were a bit miffed."

Beth laughed and said, "Miffed? Yeah, I guess that's one way of putting it."

Barbara could see she wasn't going to get much more from Richard, so she switched the focus to Beth. "What exactly are we going to do?

I'm certainly not an expert in modern European art and, no offense Richard, I doubt Richard is either."

"It is a pretty simple process. I have loaded data from the ALIU on my laptop. Some is from the National Archives, some from boxes of material from my dad's records. It will take a bit of time to dig through that, but once we do a deep dive on what the OSS found and match it with the material we have from the Mayerhaus family, including black and white photos of their living room taken just before the Anschluss and before they had to flee Austria, we should have a pretty good understanding of what we are looking for and how we can approach the auction house. I think if we divide up that work, we will be ready to work by tomorrow afternoon. We have another two hours before we touch down in Frankfurt."

She placed the paper file in front of Richard. "You need to look at the ALIU records." Beth handed one of the laptops over to Barbara. "You need to look at the work my researcher did on the other bidders. See if anything tells us whether they will pose additional problems for us. And I will use this laptop to compare details of the art from the Mayerhaus file against the art catalog prepared by the Frankfurt auction house. I suspect we will need to continue this work later in the hotel, but we can get started."

Barbara looked up from the laptop and said, "Anyone need more tea or coffee?"

PANOPTICON

The sun had set. Winter darkness in Central Europe was dramatic. By the time Jamie had shut off the lights of the van, Sue realized the grey, cloudy sky had shifted almost immediately to blue-grey night. Her recent visits to Germany had been personal and evenings had been spent either in a pub near a fire or in some cozy Bavarian hotel with Jasper Derry. The cold Rhine-River wind that rushed across her face as she walked to the door of the OGA safe house was a stark reminder that this was a work trip and Derry was not invited. Once again, Sue decided that once she was settled, she needed to call Derry.

Jamie opened a steel door on the side of the corrugated steel structure. They walked into a small six-by-six-foot room with a small desk on one side of the room with a sign-in sheet on a clipboard. On the other side of the room were thirty small cabinets in five columns with six rows. Ten of the cabinets were open and had small keys fitted in the locks. The rest were closed. Jamie pointed to the cabinets and said, "This is where we store our mobile phones and any other tech that emanates a signal or can store data. Flash, I know you have more than the rest of these folks, so feel free to take two of the lockboxes."

Flash stuck out her tongue and began to fish into pockets of her jacket and her ruck. Jamie had been correct. When she was done, there were two cabinets full of two mobile phones, a series of flash drives, and two e-tablets. Sue took her phone out of her pocket and put it in the cabinet with her tablet. Massoni took out what looked like an antique flip phone and tossed it into the cabinet. As he did, he remarked, "I'm not going to waste my time locking this up. If your team wants to steal it or do some sort of modification, I say go for it. At REAL SUE, Marconi says it barely serves as a phone."

Jamie shook his head. "If that's the way you think, I hope we don't blow your mind in the PANOPTICON."

Massoni said, "Wasn't that a 1970s kung fu movie?"

Flash said, "Jim, that's *The Octagon.* The panopticon was a British prison design."

Jamie smiled. As he opened the second, hardened door using both a cipher lock and what appeared to Sue to be a fingerprint reader, Jamie said, "Welcome to the PANOPTICON."

The first thing Sue noticed was she had to step up into the room. It was a classic "box within a box" secure compartmented information facility or SCIF. The exterior walls of the building were separated by an air gap into the plexiglass walls of the SCIF. Those walls were curved even though the exterior walls were square. There was a two-foot air gap between the exterior walls of the building and the interior walls of the PANOPTICON. A series of LED lamps lighted the room in a slightly blue glow. As she looked up, she realized that the regular lights were paired with LED red lamps which she supposed would be used to avoid the loss of night vision. There were fifteen manned computer workstations distributed along the curves of the room. Ten men and five women dressed in jeans, work shirts and black or navy-blue fleece jackets. Another five empty stations completed the circle of computers along the walls. Sue noticed two of the empty stations were marked with blue masking tape "FOR HICU." Their location was at what might be considered the nine o'clock position on the curve. In the center of the SCIF was a slightly raised platform with three separate workstations looking out over the SCIF. One was manned, the other two empty. Except for the five unmanned stations, the screens glowed a soft blue and the individuals at the workstations were focused on what seemed to be live surveillance feeds. Behind the central station was another, smaller polymer box with a mirrored reflective surface.

All the personnel except for the individual working at the center platform were wearing full headsets and microphones. Airflow was controlled through a series of vents that had special screens. Sue wondered if the vent screens were designed to prevent dust or disrupt electronic emanation. There was a quiet hum from both generators and the fans designed to keep the computers cool. It was all quite 1970s spy-movie stuff. More like what a super villain might have in his lair than either an OGA or SOF location.

Flash couldn't help herself. "So, Klingon. Did you design this yourself or did you have help from some comic book?"

Jamie smiled and said, "The PANOPTICON has been here for years. It is a US-UK partnership initially set up during the Cold War and maintained ever since. It was initially a backup to the Wiesbaden facility when they were flying AQUATONE over the Eastern Block."

Sue shook her head and said, "AQUATONE?"

Massoni said, "Sorry, Sue. Well before your time. CIA U2 reconnaissance flights. Wiesbaden airfield was one of the headquarters for the flights."

Jamie continued as if he had not been interrupted. "It has been part of our counterterrorism operations in Europe since 9/11. Basically, a forward operating base for both HUMINT and technical operations targeting al-Qaida. Once we realized that AQ talent spotters and support agents were based in Germany, the focus changed."

Sue finally caught up after daydreaming a bit about super villains. "No German participation?"

"Sue, it's not that the Germans aren't great allies. The problem is the German privacy laws and the European laws are very strict about surveillance operations. Folks far smarter and far more senior than me decided years ago to design this operation as espionage rather than a liaison CT mission. We periodically provide the data to the Germans, usually the *Bundesamt für Verfassungsschutz*."

Massoni laughed and said, "Easy for you to say."

"While you were struggling with Chinese, 10th Group decided I needed German. So, yes. It is easy for me to say." Jamie paused again. "The BfV is the German CI and CT service. It is the German version of the British Security Service. Germans are more than willing to accept the fact that we get data in ways they can't. So long as we don't spy on German citizens, it's all good."

Flash smirked and said, "And you wouldn't spy on Germans."

Jamie said, "Actually, the answer to that is PANOPTICON doesn't spy on Germans. If the BfV wants to look at German domestic terrorism, that's their business. Right now, we are not interested in anything but foreigners temporarily resident in Germany or foreign travelers. They might be protected by EU regulations, but ... " Jamie shrugged his shoulders.

Sue said, "Are you tracking our targets?"

Jamie nodded. "Turns out that SWORDFISH is high on the list of several US and UK intelligence organizations. That's because they seem willing to help just about any terrorist willing to pay for the help. We will talk about that later." Jamie turned to Sue and said, "It seems to me you learned that lesson about Russians in Cyprus."

Sue nodded. During her work there, she had uncovered a Russian company selling components of explosively formed projectiles to al-Qaida and Hizballah. They simply sold the devices to the highest bidder.

Flash said, "Klingon, how long have you been tracking SWORD-FISH?"

"If you mean here, I suppose they have been tracking them since Sue uncovered the Russian connection in Dushanbe. As you know, I just got here." Jamie smirked and it was clear to the three SOF operators that he intended to stick to that story even if it wasn't entirely true.

"I will let you do your own introductions. We are about to have a shift change ... "

A gentle, computer-generated voice announced, "The time is 1600hrs Zulu. 1700hrs in Central Europe. Shift change in thirty minutes. Light change begins in 5, 4, 3, 2, 1." A small tone sounded and the interior lights shifted to red light.

Jamie said, "The new team is already on site in our quarters. I will show you to yours."

Massoni said, "Are we the only SOF unit here?"

"Nope. There is another team here. I suspect you have heard of them. The MIKEs."

Sue snapped to attention as if she had been hit with an electric shock. The MIKEs were the S&R team that was her first introduction to SOF. After her initial selection, she joined a surveillance team that used the callsigns MIKE 1-8. The team leader, MIKE6, was Bill Jameson. As near to a surrogate father as Sue had. MIKE5 had been the callsign for Jim Massoni before he shifted to HICU. Her callsign had been MIKE4. "Why are the MIKEs here?"

Flash decided to give Jamie a break. "Try to keep up, Sue. We are hunting SWORDFISH guys. We need surveillance specialists. The MIKEs are the best in SOF. Full stop."

Jamie nodded. "We also have my own surveillance team here. Their callsigns are Lambda 1-8. Of course, I call them the Black Sheep."

Massoni groaned as Jamie broke out into full laughter. "Finally, we have a four-man Brit team here as well. Callsign Dorset. Now, let's get you settled in your quarters. My Black Sheep already moved your kit into your rooms."

After a tour of the rest of the compound that included quarters for up to fifty and a garage filled with a dozen European cars and two radio vans, they settled into a cafeteria-style meal prepared by an Army chef and four enlisted men. Given the shift work, Jamie pointed out that the cafeteria served six meals a day at 0300, 0700, 1100, 1500, 1900, and 2300hrs. As the newly arrived HICU team sat down with Jamie, Sue could hear both British and American accents as well as a table of personnel speaking English with distinctive Eastern European accents. They all sported several days growth of beard and clothes better suited for a construction site than a warehouse of spies. Sue asked, "Who are those guys."

"Those are my Black Sheep. They are precisely what they sound like: recent immigrants to the US, recruited by yours truly to work as a surveillance team for Europe Division. They are a mix of Poles, Hungarians and Croats. Their only common language is English. They all served in their own military units — either intelligence or special forces. They all served with US or UK SOF in Afghanistan. Now, they work for me. They know how to fit in. They certainly look the part of foreign laborers working on European Union visas."

Flash said, "Where do the Brits come from?"

"Mostly UKSF intel shops though we have two analysts from 5."

"Men or women?"

"Yes. Flash, go find out for yourself. It is that pair sitting together over there." Jamie tilted his head to the right.

Flash said, "Maybe later. I always wanted to work with the British Security Service. They have a great reputation in network analysis." Sue nodded. She knew BSS, also known colloquially by its World War II name MI5, had been exceptionally good at targeting both the IRA and left-wing terrorists targeting British troops stationed in Northern Germany during the Cold War.

"Yup. And Sue, I know you will recognize the guys at the table directly behind you. Just in case we need some muscle, I asked 10th Group for four guys. They said they could only come as a 12-man detachment. We don't have that sort of bunk space. I said I hope I don't need a full detachment of shooters. I need some guys who can deliver "selective violence." I thought I was being clear and kind to my old Group. Instead, 10th Group said no dice. After I got over my rejection," Jamie looked skyward and did his best to look hurt. After a brief pause, he continued, "I discussed the point with the folks from 5, they put me in touch with the guys down in Poole. Less than a week later, I got four SBS guys who were more than happy to be away from Southern Iraq and away from their headquarters. They are Dorset 6 and 1,2,3."

Sue looked over her shoulder and saw four very familiar faces:

George, Brian, Mac and the very large operator known as Dozer. She served with them in Cyprus and in Syria on previous CT operations. They were sitting at a long table with what appeared to be the UK contingent. She relaxed a bit. Perhaps this would be a good gig after all. She still needed to contact Jasper, but at least she would be amongst friends and her military family. She said, "Where are the MIKEs?"

"Keeping the mid-watch on our two SWORDFISH creeps and three other creeps that are staying in a rental house on the Rhine in Bingen. They are off shift at 2200hrs when the Brits take over. If you can stay awake, you can have coffee with them when they have dinner at 2300hrs. The Black Sheep pick up at 0600hrs."

Flash looked over at Massoni. He nodded. He grabbed Sue's coffee cup and his own and walked over to the coffee pot. He said over his shoulder, "Your coffee is crap."

Jamie raised his mug and said, "Drink tea, then."

Massoni growled.

An hour later, Sue was standing outside the sleeping quarters wing of the safe house. It was cold and a mix of sleet and rain had just started to bounce off the macadam driveway. Sue was wearing everything she had that could be called outerwear: long underwear, jeans and a long sleeve undershirt, a sweater, a fleece jacket, and a heavy military Gore-Tex rain parka. She had a black neck gator and a black watch cap. She was cold. Stamping her feet inside her military issued winter boots didn't seem to help keep either leg warm. She was trying to connect to Jasper Derry's mobile phone. She was about to quit trying after three attempts when his voice finally came through the headset she had tucked under her knit cap.

"Derry."

"Jasper, it's Sue."

"Sue, you just disappeared on me. Where the heck are you?"

"At work."

"At work, where? Back in Italy?"

"Nope."

"Not gonna tell me, are you?" It was a question, but Derry made it sound like a statement.

"Not right now."

"No sweat. Are we still in the game on the project we discussed?"

Sue was relieved that Jasper didn't use any target names. She sighed and tried to sound convincing. She hoped her digitized voice didn't reveal the lie. She said, "Not for now."

"OK. How soon can I expect to see you?"

"Don't know."

The voice at the other end started to sound irritated. "So, why did you call?"

"To just hear your voice and apologize for not staying in touch."

"No worries, Sue. I get the mission-comes-first line. I just am a little pissed that you dropped me in some sort of stew and now I'm the one left alone in the pot."

"I will let you know as much as I can as soon as we can see each other face-to-face."

"And when will that be?"

"Maybe later this weekend?"

"So, you are still in Europe?"

Sue decided that it wouldn't compromise anything to answer. She said, "Yes."

"OK. Look forward to it. Keep safe."

"You too, dear." Sue blushed at gushing on the phone like a teenager. She heard Derry hang up.

Sue thought to herself: Well, that went badly. O'Connell, what were you expecting? You couldn't tell him anything and you expected him to just accept the fact that after pulling strings with his command, you have to say something like "sorry, never mind." Sue shook her head and walked back toward her quarters. She looked at the blue-green glow from her new watch. It was approaching 2200hrs. At least she could spend a little time with the MIKEs before she called it a night. That would be a plus in what had been a confusing and emotionally draining day. As she walked in the rain, she said to herself, "Some kind of action hero you are."

The German intercept officer looked up from his computer. He said, "We captured both ends of the conversation."

"Can you geo-locate both?"

"Absolutely."

"Excellent. Place both phones on our target list. Give me details every night on the results of your work."

"Yes sir."

A HOLIDAY IN THE TAUNUS

Richard pulled the rental BMW 750i in front of the entrance to the hotel. Though Barbara preferred to drive, over the last week she had grown comfortable with Richard's driving and, she had to admit, the rather luxurious modes of transportation Beth used to get from one place to another.

Beth and Barbara were riding in the back seat of the car. Beth riding on the right, Barbara riding behind Richard. Beth said, "This will be our base of operations for a few days. I don't honestly know if we are going to need to go to the client's warehouse or if he is going to bring the pieces to us. For certain, we are scheduled to meet him here tomorrow. After that, we will just have to play it by ear." She leaned over and touched Richard on the shoulder. "After you park, come straight through to our suite of rooms on the second floor. According to the email I received, it will be rooms 202-205."

"Check." Richard watched as the hotel staff approached the car. He pulled the trunk release and then got out of the car, walked around the front and opened the door for Beth. She got out and Barbara followed her. Beth turned to the staff, addressed them in formal German. They nodded and took the suitcases out of the open trunk and then followed Beth and Barbara into the hotel.

Barbara had spent a career operating low-profile and that generally meant staying in moderately priced, travelers' hotels near an airport or a train station. The Schlosshotel was none of those things. It was truly a *schloss* — a palace — turned into a five-star hotel and resort that included golf, a spa, and multiple dining halls that were associated with princes of the realm back in the days of Kaiser Wilhelm I and Otto von Bismarck. Barbara tried not to appear too much of a rube as she followed Beth to reception.

The reception desk clerk was dressed in a perfectly cut, bespoke black suit with white shirt and a pale blue tie. He responded immediately to Beth's arrival. He spoke unaccented English as he said, "Madame Ambassador Parsons, it is very good to see you again. I have made all the arrangements you requested, please follow me." He nodded to a young woman dressed in the same uniform as he abandoned his post and led them to the elevator. "We arranged your standard suite with two adjoining rooms for your staff. I assume you have brought Richard along with you, but I have yet to have the pleasure of your colleague." He turned to Barbara and offered a well-manicured hand. "My name is Felix Heingart."

Barbara took the hand and said, "Mrs. Barbara O'Connell."

Felix nodded as they entered the elevator. It was clear that his formal introduction was nothing more than an effort to be polite. He was interested in making sure Beth Parsons was happy. As they rode up the two flights to their rooms, he said, "Madame Ambassador, I have arranged for you to have lunch in the suite at 1400hrs. Will that be satisfactory?"

Beth nodded and said, "Felix, that will be most satisfactory. Have you arranged the meeting room for us?"

"Absolutely. It will be set for four at 1000hrs precisely."

"Excellent. Then the only thing I think we will need is a reservation for dinner tonight in the Victoria."

"Certainly. What time would be convenient?"

"I think early. Perhaps, 2000hrs? After all, we have just flown and will need to rest after dinner."

"I will make it so." He walked ahead of Beth and said, "And here is your suite. The staff will bring your suitcases shortly. Do you want them to help you unpack?"

"Not necessary, Felix. Thank you so much."

"It is our pleasure, Madame Ambassador."

When they were finally alone in the room, Barbara turned to Beth and bowed. "Madame Ambassador."

Beth bowed in return and said, "Mrs. O'Connell." She laughed and said, "I used to use this hotel for major NATO conferences and have arranged multiple meetings here for Stearns and Mandeville. They are good at what they do. Discrete, high-quality service. If it is a little too Old Germany for you, I apologize. I happen to enjoy these little perks to serving for the firm."

"I have no complaints. I just never quite received that treatment when I was on the TDY circuit."

"Sneaking around at night was more your job description than mine, dear."

Barbara smiled and said, "Too true."

At that point, Richard walked into the room with five members of the hotel staff carrying their bags. He identified which bags went where, provided the porters with a small tip in Euros and then joined them in the sitting room of the suite. Barbara was pleased to see that he was equally impressed with the surroundings. "Boss, I'm not sure I can handle these sort of digs again."

Beth smiled. "That's what Barbara just said. I offered to arrange accommodations for her in a pension near the Frankfurt Bahnhof, but we both agreed that it would be an inconvenient commute by *Strassebahn.*"

"Hey, I'm not complaining. Otherwise, I suspect you will just send me back to the airport to wait."

"Unlikely, Richard. We may need your assistance before we are done."

Barbara said, "OK, so now that we are settled, why don't you tell me why we are assuming there might be some sort of trouble."

"It's not as if there is any sign of trouble, Barbara. It's more like a feeling I have about the details we have received from the client. Now, here are some of the complications ... "

Richard smiled. "I personally love it when we have complications."

Barbara nodded. "Me too."

Beth continued, "My only concern is the Russian connection. I don't get it, my firm doesn't get it, and even my contacts at State didn't get it. That's the second deep dive we need to accomplish. We need to know whether we are just facing rich Russians or rich Russians with links to the Russian mafia."

"Or rich Russians with links to the SVR or GRU." Richard was already considering the worst-case scenario.

"And that is why you two are here. I figure with your expertise along with the skills that Longstreet's team brings to the table, we should be prepared for any contingency."

Barbara smiled over her mug of tea. "I'm glad that I am considered your … just in case."

Beth said, "Yup. Just like the fire axe in the hallway behind the sign that says IN CASE OF FIRE, BREAK GLASS."

Richard looked at the two ladies at the table and said, "It wouldn't be the first time I was compared to a blunt instrument."

Beth said, "You and Barbara will be a good team. Now, let's get to work." She pulled out two laptops and a large paper file from the Coach leather satchel sitting next to her chair.

Barbara muttered to herself, "Blunt instruments. Dandy." She figured there was something else in play in this operation.

NOT MUCH GOING ON

Bill Jameson was nursing a cup of tea in the open space that served as the cafeteria for the GINGERHAWK team. It had been a very long, very boring surveillance serial targeting the Russians. The targets went to an office space they had rented for the month and then they went to the house they rented for a month. Jameson had his team in static observation points surrounding all the possible exits for both locations. He had the newest member of the MIKEs, John Bell, conducting electronic surveillance. During the previous rotation cycle, the tech gurus at SOF headquarters in Ft. Bragg added a second seat in the back of their communications van known lovingly as the Magic Bus. That seat, along with a full rack of technical surveillance equipment and computers allowed the team to monitor multiple cellphones and any internet communications from their targets so long as they had the Internet Protocol or IP address.

Given the fact that SWORDFISH was a legitimate private security company authorized to operate in Germany, a small amount of research and Bell had the IP addresses and the mobile phones identified and tracked as soon as the two Russians arrived in Frankfurt. But two days of physical and technical surveillance on the Russians had turned up nothing. Nothing. And that made Jameson angry because he knew the intelligence showed the Russians were up to something.

Sue pulled up a chair across from Jameson. She had her own cup of just-poured tea, the steam rising from the mug. "Hey, Boss. It has been some time."

Jameson looked at his former teammate. She looked older. The beginning of grey hair starting to show. More lines on her face. Darker circles under her eyes. Over a dozen years of continuous war and a serious war wound. He wondered what she was seeing as she looked at him. After all, he had been in the harness nearly thirty years and most of it in SOF. He suspected he looked like a fragile old man. Right now, his brain felt fragile. He smiled and said, "I understand they made you the boss over in HICU. Nice work."

Sue shook her head. "It hasn't been much fun. I'm the acting boss awaiting a commissioned officer to take over. It's all paperwork and time-management stuff. This is the first time I've been on an assignment in nearly two years."

"So why so glum, MIKE4?"

Sue smiled at the use of her old callsign from her days working for Jameson in S&R. "I thought this was going to be a simple collection mission. Street work and then delivering the info to the CG who would give it to the Germans who would take these bad guys off the street. Suddenly, it is a BFD with multiple players including OGA, the Brits and you guys."

Jameson nodded. He honestly hadn't heard the acronym for a big, fucking deal since Jim Massoni left the unit. Clearly, he was rubbing off on Sue. "And you aren't allowed to work with your new beau."

Sue blushed. "Massoni?"

"Of course. Who else but a sergeant major is going to have that sort of information?"

"Do you think I'm being a dope?"

"I think you should stop pouting and get to work. Right now, we don't have crap on these Russians and we are going to need something, some sort of edge if we are going to make some sense out of why we are all involved in this operation."

"So, OGA."

"Yup, Jamie and his OGA team are a good place to start. This is their turf and they wouldn't be involved if they didn't have something to offer. Don't get me wrong, I like to operate as an independent as much as the next guy, but this is a far more complicated story than we have been told. I am not sure what we are looking for or how it's going to end, but we need some traction and I'm hoping OGA can deliver."

"Meanwhile, I should stop whining."

"Hey, plenty of time to start whining when we make some progress. Anyhow, instead of your beau, you have all of us. You should be more like your pal Flash and take the good with the bad. I saw her working on revitalizing her relationship with one of the SBS blokes as well as schmoozing with Jamie. She said it was all about intelligence sharing. I'm thinking ... well, let's just say I'm thinking she might be playing a longer game." Jameson smiled and took a sip from his mug.

"Bill, you have any thoughts on whether there is any hope for a personal relationship in our trade?"

"Are you proposing?"

Sue laughed. Jameson was pleased to see her smile. He continued, "Seriously, I don't see how you can stay in the fight and maintain anything like a steady relationship. OGA folks seem to have a better track record but that's because they tolerate husband-wife teams which is something SOF has trouble understanding and the Army has real trouble accepting. I think you must decide whether you want to stay in the fight or create a new life with a man ... ," Jameson paused, "Or a woman. I'm not here to judge."

Sue reached across the table and punched Jameson in the arm. "Let's not be silly."

"I'm really trying to be serious here. I don't know of anyone in SOF who has a personal relationship with another member of SOF or, for that matter, anyone in the Army. I'm just saying if you really want to have that relationship and you already have your 20 in, you need to retire and get serious. You have to be close to 20, no?"

Sue thought hard before she answered the question. She hadn't even considered retirement. She had almost nineteen years in service. "I want to stay in the fight."

"Then stay in the fight. All of us will be happier if you do."

"When is this going to be over, Bill?"

"You mean fighting terrorists? Beats me. We've both been doing that since before 9/11. I reckon counterterrorism is something we won't ever stop. And then we have other adversaries we haven't even thought about since 9/11. I reckon this is going to be like the Cold War. There were guys who started right after World War II and retired before they saw the end of the USSR. That's your granddad's story, right?"

"Yup. And, in the long run, it was the last pieces of that story that ended up killing him."

"And your dad. And, nearly killing you and your mom as I recall."

"So, the trade never ends. No victory parades."

"Seems like it."

Flash sat down next to Sue and said, "Well, you guys look like you're having a very cheery conversation. Want to share?"

Jameson smiled and said, "We were just solving the world's problems."

Sue nodded. "Well, at least identifying them."

Flash said, "Someone smart once told me that the first step in solving problems was identifying that they were problems."

A voice from a distance said, "That was me, Flash." Jim Massoni walked over with a coffee cup in his hand. He said, "Boss, you need to leave Chief Jameson alone. He needs his rest. He is a geezer after all." Jameson offered Massoni a one-fingered salute. It didn't seem to bother Massoni. "Anyhow, the Klingon has something he wants to show you all and you know how Jamie gets when he doesn't have an audience."

"He gets cranky."

Massoni nodded. "Exactly. And no one wants a cranky Klingon in the house."

They walked across the driveway to the PANOPTICON. An entirely new shift of individuals was watching computer screens and listening to feeds from various telecommunications networks. Jamie was waiting for them in yet another, smaller clear Lexan box on one side of the operations center. They entered and Jamie pulled the door shut and closed what looked like a bulkhead from a World War II submarine. The way the Lexan was prepared, it was possible to see out into the operations center but it was not possible for the ops center folks to see inside. Flash said to Sue, "This is a very cool tool. Some sort of polymer that is cut to diffuse light. Can I get one for REAL SUE?"

Massoni growled, "Not unless you want to share the room with me."

"Yikes. I'm definitely not interested."

As the banter continued, Sue looked around the room. There were six individuals invited. The HICU team, Jamie, a woman and a man who were yet unidentified. Once he closed the door and sat down, Jamie started the briefing.

"First, let me introduce our two analysts. John Seymour is from the Agency. He works with Treasury in the National Counterterrorism Center focusing on terrorism finance."

Seymour was a thin, pale, balding man in his 50s. He was dressed in a starched white button-down collared shirt, black wool trousers and a black cardigan sweater. He had reading glasses perched on his nose. There was a black nylon cord that ran from the glasses around the back of his neck. Seymour was wearing a Naval Academy ring and what looked to Sue to be a very old Omega chronograph on a worn black-leather strap. The watch was far older than Seymour appeared to be. Sue was sufficiently distracted that she wondered if it might be a family heirloom. She cleared her head of the frivolous thought and considered the analyst. He was not exactly the sort of hunter she might have imagined from the Agency, but she knew from previous experience that it did take all kinds of people to hunt terrorists. He looked up from a thick ream of paper he had in front of him and said in a very quiet, very deep voice, "Greetings to you all."

Jamie continued, "Dierdre Macomb is on loan from the British Security Service. Her focus is on the link between international terrorist groups and organized crime from Russia or from China."

Sue had to control herself not to smirk. Macomb was a British version of Flash. Dressed all in black: a heavy black rollneck sweater over black jeans and black leather boots. She had dyed jet-black hair pulled into a severe bun at the nape of her neck and black glasses with bows colored blood red. She was wearing a stainless steel, men's Breitling watch that was too large for her wrist. As she raised her hand to greet everyone, the watch spun around her wrist until the face was on the bottom of her wrist. The watch crystal was the first thing to land on the table with a clunk when she dropped her hand. Sue turned to Flash and whipered, "A long lost sister?"

Flash looked at Sue and said, "What?"

Massoni decided to enter the fray. He said, "John and Dierdre, pay no attention to my colleagues. They were raised by wolves. I am Jim Massoni, the taller of the two chief warrant officers is my boss, Sue O'Connell, and the other warrant is Sarah Billings also known as Flash." Massoni turned to Sue and said, "That's how it's done, Boss."

Flash looked over at the sergeant major and made a face. He made one back.

Jamie said, "So, now that we are all friends, let's get to work. The reason we are in this box inside the box is that this material is only for you folks. It is not on the servers feeding the rest of the team and will not be available except in here and only on paper. I need to ask you to read the material tonight and leave it here. There is a small safe in here where it will be stored. In the meantime, I will ask our new colleagues to make us smarter. Well, except for you, Jim. There is no hope."

Massoni looked at Jamie and said, "*Qu ni de.*"

Macomb laughed and said, "He just said screw you."

Jamie nodded and said, "He taught me that much Mandarin years ago." Jamie paused and said, "How about John starts off."

Seymour continued to speak in a low voice, barely a whisper. It reminded Sue of the Afghan analyst at HICU who everyone called Pluto. She had to strain to hear any briefing he provided. The same was with Seymour. "We were invited into the GINGERHAWK oper- ation because of a joint Agency-BSS operation looking at the way some of the Islamic extremists were funding the purchases of sophis- ticated weapon systems. Whether it was explosively formed pene- trators coming from Iran or some of the newer anti-tank weapons we are seeing in the hands of the Islamic State, we know that these weapons are not cheap, and they are not something that any nation-state just gives away to surrogate forces. So, where does the money come from?" Seymour passed five sheets of paper over to the four US SOF operators.

"These three pie charts cover calendar year 2010. The top chart is for Hizballah, the middle for al-Qaida and the bottom chart is the Islamic State. It turns out that there are multiple financial sources for extremists. The most common are donations, small and large, that come from supporters of the cause. These funds are passed through several different cutouts until they get to bank accounts managed by the extremist leadership. Those donations are identified in green on the pie charts."

Sue looked at the charts. In each case, the green portion of the chart was about 1/3 of the pie. Slightly larger for al-Qaida, slightly smaller for Hizballah.

Seymour continued, "The red section in the graphs represent direct financial support from a state sponsor. We aren't going to go into the details of which states sponsor which terrorist organization. It really doesn't matter for the sake of this briefing, but you can see that in the case of Hizballah it is slightly more than al-Qaida, and both Hizballah and al-Qaida have substantial state sponsorship com-pared to the Islamic State. The blue section of the graphs represents criminal enterprises managed by the terrorist entities. Now, look at the first half of 2011." Seymour passed out a new set of charts.

Sue looked at the charts. In each case, the blue section of the graphs covered nearly two thirds of the chart.

Seymour concluded, "We haven't finished the data for the second half of 2011, but the trend line is even more toward criminal enter-prise."

Macomb took over the briefing. "First, it is important to note that there does not appear to be any significant reduction in the gross amount of funds available. So, the real question becomes what sort of criminal enterprises fund their efforts. The amount of money involved is far more than what you might expect from drug smuggling or extortion. This is real money. Where does it come from?"

Seymour took over the briefing. "We believe that the answer is they are morphing into large scale criminal cartels. The US and UK effort to destroy both al-Qaida and the Islamic State and the Israeli effort to do the same with Hizballah has forced these organizations to go deeper underground into their safe havens and dispersed communities around the world. As they have done so, they have transformed their networks into massive criminal fund-raising operations."

Flash interrupted Seymour and said, "OK, so what does this have to do with our current focus on GINGERHAWK and the Russians from SWORDFISH?"

Macomb looked at her doppelganger. She pulled off her glasses and said, "If you will give us just another minute or two, we will get there." Flash nodded, though it was clear to both Sue and Massoni she hadn't conceded the point yet.

Seymour continued, "We have seen a transition from simple smuggling operations of weapons and sophisticated components to more complicated technology theft. SWORDFISH bank accounts are receiving larger and larger transfers from both Hizballah and al-Qaida, advances if you will, focused on the acquisition of different types of technology. First, it was drone technology, stolen from a California firm and passed to Hizballah. Then it was internet hacking software that was either stolen or purchased from Russia. And now, it seems they are focused on GINGERHAWK. Our data show this is not a Russian or Chinese government effort to steal the plans of the space junk device. Rather, it seems SWORDFISH has been tasked by Hizballah to acquire the entire device. We can only assume Hizballah leadership intends to use the device to attack Israeli and US reconnaissance and communications satellites."

Jamie stepped in. "These assumptions are based in part on very sensitive collection against both the Russians and the Chinese. They already have their own anti-satellite programs that are far more sophisticated than GINGERHAWK. They have no reason to task

SWORDFISH to acquire anything from that program. They might want to collect on the GINGERHAWK program, but it seems unlikely they would steal a device. In this operation, we believe with a fair degree of certainty that SWORDFISH is simply doing this as part of a larger, criminal enterprise."

Flash said, "If that's the case and assuming your data are correct on the growth of terrorists using criminal activity for major funding, it is entirely possible that Hizballah is simply subcontracting SWORDFISH for some other criminal enterprise. They might have no intention of using GINGERHAWK at all, but rather selling the device for a profit to some other crime organization that wants an anti-satellite weapon."

Seymour nodded and said, "And that is why we are so intent on gaining any information we can on the SWORDFISH team here. We assume the current trip is simply a reconnaissance effort. It will take a substantial team to steal the current device located in a warehouse in Sachsenhausen. Shemkovich and Chesnik are seniors at SWORD-FISH. It is very unlikely they are going to be directly involved. So, that is the reason we are so interested in using physical and technical surveillance on their visit. This is one of the reasons why the PANOP-TICON has been engaged so heavily in this project."

Sue nodded. She wasn't entirely certain where this conversation was going, so she decided to ask a hard question to clarify. "Does this mean we are not going to design a program that allows the Germans to arrest Shemkovich as a war criminal?"

Macomb offered a quick answer. "It is too soon to tell."

Flash jumped on Sue's point. "So, if it is too soon to tell, why are we even involved? Sue and Jim run a SOF HUMINT program. I am the senior analyst working Hizballah-Iran targets. We have real day jobs. There doesn't look to be a HUMINT angle here anymore, and even if there was, it no longer looks to me like it has anything to do with SOF." Flash looked over at Sue and Massoni. They were nodding in agreement.

Jamie said, "If I said I just liked working with you ... "

Massoni said, "I would say that was bullshit."

Jamie countered, "And, if I reminded you that, in the meeting we just had at USAEUR headquarters, a certain General Smith just said that he wanted you involved?"

Sue said, "I would want to see that in writing." Massoni and Flash looked at each other and then at Sue as she got up, worked the bulkhead door and walked out of the room. She walked through the ops center and headed out the door.

Massoni looked up at Jamie and said, "I'm not sure what happened here, but I'm going to sort it out." He turned to Flash and asked, "If it's ok by you, I would like to have you continue to work with Jamie's team for a bit. I think there are parts of this story where we can help."

Flash nodded and said, "Sure, Sergeant Major."

With that exchange, Massoni left the room.

Jamie said, "So, alright then. Let's continue."

Massoni finally caught up with Sue in the parking lot between the ops center and the other warehouse buildings used as quarters, maintenance and dining area. Sue was walking fast and Massoni noticed that when she tried to stride out, her limp from the prosthetic was far more pronounced. He suspected that every step she took had to jar the prosthetic and hurt what remained of her lower left leg. It was not exactly a good sign.

He caught up with Sue as she was about to enter the building that held the dining area. "Hey, Boss. What is going on?" Sue was sufficiently angry and distracted that she didn't acknowledge his query. At that point, Massoni decided to revert to his formal sergeant major role. He stepped in front of Sue, preventing her travel into the dining area. He said, "Chief Warrant Officer O'Connell, what precisely are you thinking? You just stormed out of a meeting with a pair of senior analysts and Jamie. Ignoring for a moment your insulting comment regarding Smith, I just wanted you to know that you embarrassed the shit out of Flash and yours truly. As your *command sergeant major*," Massoni paused to ensure his emphasis was clear, "I want to know what is going on in your head?"

Massoni had a long history with Sue O'Connell. He had been the team sergeant major when a young O'Connell finished selection and arrived at S&R. He watched her mature as a surveillance operator in the years up to 9/11 and beyond. He watched her recover from her traumatic amputation from a Jalalabad gunfight and he watched her as she matured as an intelligence collector when she returned to the fight in 2004. Massoni was familiar with "O'Connell firestorms" before, but this was the first time she had blown up in front of an audience that was made up of individuals who were not from Massoni's SOF family. It was not something he intended to happen again. However, she did outrank him and that meant he needed to be careful what he said as he counseled the acting commander of HICU. He said, "How about we go into the dining room and have a cup of tea?"

Sue eventually calmed down and said quietly, "A cup of tea would be nice."

TMI

Sue sat at the table while Massoni went to get their beverages. She knew he was going to fill his white porcelain mug with coffee while he filled her mug with hot water and a bag of Earl Grey tea. He knew her well enough to add a small bit of honey. She watched his back as he worked through the various stops on the coffee and tea station in the dining room. Massoni was just under six feet tall and had shoulders that might easily be described as an axe handle wide. Sue had seen him work out and his strength and endurance were scary. In loose-fitting Army ACUs, he just looked like another guy. Sue knew that wasn't the case. Ranger Regiment. SF Regiment. S&R sergeant major and now HICU sergeant major. Jim Massoni was definitely not just another guy.

She also realized Massoni was right and she owed him an apology and then an apology to everyone inside the soundproof box. That part was easy. The hard part was going to be sorting out how she felt about the entire GINGERHAWK enterprise. Her anger was based on multiple strands of emotion woven together like a tightly wound steel cable. She didn't know how to explain them, or whether anything she might say would make sense. And she certainly didn't know how to pull them apart. As Massoni slowly walked back to the table, making sure he didn't spill either mug, Sue accepted the fact that if anyone other than her mother would understand, it was probably Jim Massoni.

"If I stay here too long, I might become a tea drinker myself. This coffee is totally unacceptable. I will speak to Schenk. Or, better still, whoever is running this mess hall. By the way, I tried to find some chamomile tea, but all they had was black tea." Massoni looked at

Sue hoping that this opening comment might reduce the tension between them.

Sue stuck her tongue out at the comment on chamomile. She said, "Did you add milk to the tea?"

"Milk and honey." Massoni took a sip from his mug, made a face and said, "OK, boss. What's going on and what are you going to do next? Start a civil war? Join the French Foreign Legion? Help the Agency abduct humans for some horrific experiments out at Area 51? What?"

Sue did her best to sort out her various feelings of anger, frustration, sadness, and, she had to admit, self-pity. She knew whining would not fit in this conversation. She started, "I'm just tired of being sorta-kinda the boss of HICU. Either I am the commander, or I am not the commander. And, if I am the commander, I want to see some orders telling me they want me here instead of at Camp Ederle tracking our folks downrange. The discussion of maybe it's this, maybe it's that is not exactly useful."

"Nice speech. So, you want less ambiguity and formal orders? When do you want to be reassigned? I am sure I can talk to Smith and arrange RTU orders."

Massoni's comment hit Sue like a slap in the face. There was nothing more insulting for a member of the Special Operations Forces than to be "returned to unit" — meaning returned to conventional forces. It meant exile. No one in SOF would ever reach out. They would be too busy and the exile no longer had a "need to know" anything about SOF operations. It would also mean that the conventional force commander receiving the exile would suspect the only reason they had returned was due to some catastrophic, albeit secret, failure. It was career death.

Massoni continued. "I know that is not what is going on, Sue. The analysts are saying they think Hizballah or AQ or ISIS are working with SWORDFISH. They don't know. Well, answering questions like that are definitely in our wheelhouse. I suspect there are more than a few things rolling around in your head and you are trying to sort them all out at once. Take it from me, that's not how you solve this. You solve this by attacking pieces of the problem one at a time. Pick one and tell your sergeant major in detail what is going on."

The steam from the mug of tea was making Sue's nose run. The dining area was not well heated and it was a cold January day outside. Sue didn't want Massoni to think she was sniveling, so she reached across the table to a pile of napkins and blew her nose. Hard. It was time to pick a problem and talk. She said, "This is obviously a larger operation than we thought. In my view, it is not a HUMINT collection mission that belongs in our rucksack. It smells like there is more about GINGERHAWK than we are allowed to know. I don't like it."

Massoni nodded. He realized it was time to be the supportive sergeant major rather than the hostile sergeant major. He already knew some of the answers, but wanted Sue to come to the same conclusion. "Let's start with the program we thought we were going to do. Why did we come to Germany in the first place?"

"To collect enough information to get the Germans to detain Shemkovich/Vladich."

"Only that?"

"OK, so I wanted to get out of the office."

"Me too. But only that?"

"OK, so I thought it would be fun to work with Derry."

"Now, we have cut out Derry. You don't like that."

Sue paused. Was that really the cause of her anger? Was it really about her boyfriend Jasper Derry? "I will admit I am a little miffed that we are not working with Derry since he was the one who was supposed to have the agent network we could use."

Massoni laughed out loud. "Miffed? Is that what you call storming out of a conference room? Making us all look like chumps? Because you were … miffed?"

Sue blushed. It was childish and she had no excuse. She wasn't quite ready to accept that was the only reason for her actions. "Once we had no agent network, what was the point?"

"And you don't think Jamie has sources that we can handle with him? You did that in Iraq, you did that in Afghanistan and Pakistan saving Jameson's life, you did that in Tajikistan disrupting SWORD-FISH cyber operations. Why wouldn't we do that here in Germany?"

"We just accept the fact that there are parts of GINGERHAWK that we don't understand?"

Massoni looked at Sue. He had been down this path with other operators in the past. He knew this was a rear-guard action. Sue wasn't quite ready to retreat from her actions, so she was coming up with excuses, lame excuses, to justify her action. He said, "Now you want to debate compartmentation?"

Sue relented. "I am being a punk."

"Yup. You are being a punk. Now, put on your big-boy panties and march back into the SCIF inside a SCIF and apologize to the visiting Klingon and the Brits. The rest of us are used to periodic O'Connell storms, so we don't need apologies. What we do need is your full commitment to do the job. Ideally, there will be an opportunity for O'Connell to be a spy again, but if not, then just do whatever it takes to make this work. We will do the job and move on to the next job wherever it takes us. In case you are interested, it is going to take us back to REAL SUE where you are the boss of all you survey."

"Sergeant Major, please forgive me for embarrassing you."

"Sergeants major don't take anything personally, Boss. That's part of the deal. Day one at the sergeant major academy they tell you up front. It's not about you. Of course, you have to be prepared for some penalty that I will impose…eventually." Massoni smiled. Sue wasn't sure whether he was joking or not. She figured it would play out sometime in the future.

"Check, Sergeant Major. So, shall we go back?"

"Finish your tea and then we will go back. While you are doing so, you need to tell me about Chief Derry. What is he like? What sort of CI work is he doing here in USAEUR? And why would a Green Beret choose to be a wonky CI investigator?"

Sue looked up at Massoni. The playful Massoni had returned. She said, "I like him. He's a wounded warrior as well and he understands me. As to why he didn't stay in the SF Regiment or transfer to a CI shop inside SOF headquarters, I haven't ever asked."

"Too busy doing other ... stuff."

"TMI, Sergeant Major."

"Right, Boss. Too much information." Massoni decided this was neither the time nor the place to continue this conversation. However, it was a conversation that he would have to have sooner rather than later. He stood up and said, "Time to get back to work."

"Right. Eat a bit of crow and get back to work."

"Tasty!"

They walked back into the Lexan box. As the remaining team looked up, Sue blushed slightly and said, "I apologize for my outburst and for walking out of the meeting. It was not about the briefing or your actions. It was about something else related to our previous operations against SWORDFISH." With that, she sat down and said, "Can we restart the conversation before I lost my mind?"

Jamie smiled. "Every once and a while, it is a good thing to lose your mind. Just so long as you find it sooner or later."

Flash mumbled, "This time it was sooner." Flash smiled and then said, "Ooof," as Sue's elbow hit her in the ribs.

Macomb simply said, "Yanks."

Seymour restarted the briefing. "The challenge we are facing at present is that several sensitive sources are reporting a strange network of contacts."

Flash couldn't help herself, "Sensitive sources?"

Jamie said, "Sources that none of us are allowed to know, except John. Just accept compartmentation, Flash. After all, right now we are in a box inside a box inside a box because of the sensitivity of the entire briefing. We are going to get to the reasons, but for now, just chill."

Sue said, "We get compartmentation, Jamie. After all, we have been searching for a leak in our comms for the better part of three years. We realize it could be anyone."

Macomb said, "I think we are closing in on the answer to that question as well."

Seymour looked slightly flustered by the interruptions. Before Sue and Flash could ask Macomb what she was talking about, Seymour said, "May I continue?"

Jamie said, "John, sorry. We have been working on this problem for a while and we are all pretty tired of the dead ends."

Seymour nodded and continued. "As I said, our sources have added additional complications to the question of the role of SWORD-FISH in the larger terrorism threat. We always knew the contractor was an unofficial arm of the Russian GRU and we also knew that the SWORDFISH leadership was more than willing to profit by selling equipment to terrorist and revolutionary organizations. What we didn't know until recently was SWORDFISH also serves as a paramilitary arm of a partnership between the Russian Mafia and Chinese organized crime based in Macao."

Massoni was the one to interrupt this time. "Chinese organized crime or covert operations of the 2PLA?"

Seymour looked at Macomb. She answered, "2PLA is certainly the correct link in China. The 2PLA is their offensive military intelligence organization, the second department of the General Staff of the Peoples' Liberation Army. From the earliest days of the Peoples' Republic, the intelligence arm of the PLA maintained connections with the various criminal gangs. Since the gangs had maintained connections with the Republic of China in Taiwan and the British colony of Hong Kong, the PLA used those connections for intelligence operations. Now that China is fully in charge of both Hong Kong and Macao, they also use the gangs to launder money to offshore organizations. Recently, we have reporting that the 2PLA has used that connection to send money to SWORDFISH. This is a serious problem. It was hard enough understanding the nexus among SWORDFISH, the GRU, and terrorist groups. Now, we have to add 2PLA to the mix."

Flash said, "Allies?"

Seymour said, "More likely SWORDFISH sees all of these connections as clients or potential clients for individual operations."

Sue nodded and said, "So, the fact that two SWORDFISH seniors are in Germany may have nothing or everything to do with GINGERHAWK, and if it does have to do with GINGERHAWK, it might not have anything to do with a Russian intelligence operation or terrorists."

Jamie smiled and said, "Sue, now you have grasped the challenge and why we are throwing resources at this problem." Sue noticed for the first time that everyone in the room except Massoni and herself had coffee mugs or bottled water in front of them. Clearly, while she had been in meltdown with Massoni, they had taken a break. Jamie took a sip from his mug and continued, "And it comes down to why you are here and why HICU is involved. You three have been chasing SWORDFISH for years. Further, Smith tasked HICU over the past year to collect on SWORDFISH and associated terrorist entities. And, since he moved to SOF headquarters, many of the requirements issued to HICU have been based on that collection mandate from the National Command Authority."

As Jamie paused, Sue wondered why he used NCA instead of simply saying the White House since that was what NCA meant. Perhaps because of Macomb? Perhaps to underscore the importance? It really didn't matter. If the White House issued a requirement to SOF Intel and, given Jamie's involvement, the CIA as well, then it was as Massoni might say: a BFD. A big frigging deal.

Sue started to feel even more like a dope for her recent outburst. As a professional and as the daughter and granddaughter of intelligence professionals, she should have known that this sort of assembly of capability was not something based on a whim by some seniors at the Agency or inside the Pentagon. If SWORDFISH was working for the two strategic adversaries of the US and the UK as well as supporting terrorist groups that regularly planned and periodically executed attacks on the US and UK, it was definitely a BFD. She decided to apologize again, "Hey, it's clear I was seriously out of line.

I want you all to know that I will do whatever it takes to help on this project."

Flash said under her breath, "Well, that's a relief." Sue gave her a second elbow shot to the ribs.

Sue continued, "So, what do you want from HICU?"

Seymour said, "We need to add requirements to your collectors who are based in the Gulf and Horn of Africa. It turns out that the PRC funds are being passed through banks in those two regions before ending up in SWORDFISH accounts based in Vienna."

Jamie smiled and said, "And, you and I need to make a trip to Vienna to see a banker."

Flash said, "And what about Massoni and me?"

Jamie said, "If it's all right by Sue, I would like to have you two work with the surveillance teams. Specifically, now that we are all on the same sheet of music regarding our target, it seems to me we need a team other than the folks out there ... " Jamie pointed to the rest of the ops center, "to synchronize the intelligence bits that might make sense to the folks in here." Jamie took another sip from his mug. "Also, it would be good if Flash issued the requirements to the HICU collectors downrange. We have the right connectivity here and I think sooner would be better than later to start the collection." Jamie paused and said, "Sue, is that ok by you?"

Sue recognized that Jamie was trying to make up. She said, "Absolutely."

"So, John has to return to his place inside the hollow mountain where all intelligence goes to die." For the first time, Sue saw Seymour smile. He also gave Jamie a one-fingered salute. Sue realized for the first time that Jamie and Seymour might have history. "Before he goes, he can help Flash design the requirements. Dierdre will work with us until her headquarters realize we have kidnapped her and put her inside our own Faraday cage."

"My pleasure so long as you make proper tea."

Sue nodded and said, "So outside the box, no one knows the big picture?"

Jamie said, "Well, the surveillance teams only know the SWORD-FISH targets. In Germany, only Dentmann and Smith know the full picture."

"Not the USAEUR commander?" Flash asked.

Jamie smiled and said, "Well, sorta-kinda. He knows it is bigger than the GINGERHAWK briefing. The problem is if you brief the USAEUR commander..."

Massoni said, "You have to brief his staff and their staff and pretty soon nothing is secret."

Jamie said, "Let's not forget what Ben Franklin said about secrets: Three people can keep a secret so long as two of them are dead."

Macomb said, "I thought Churchill said that."

Massoni said, "I think Sun Tzu said it before either of those guys."

"I will defer to our China scholar," Jamie said with a laugh. "Even if he is talking out his ass."

This time it was Massoni who gave Jamie the one-fingered salute. As he did that Macomb leaned over to Flash and said, "We do that with two fingers."

"Redundancy is a good thing."

LET THE GAMES BEGIN

They worked well into the night and started again early the next morning. Barbara realized that there would be little chance to enjoy the luxurious amenities in the Schlosshotel. After a working breakfast in the room, it was time to get dressed and move to the conference room in the hotel. When she met Beth in the hallway, Barbara felt underdressed. It was typical of her experience with Beth Parsons. Barbara had packed a formal black wool pantsuit and a white silk blouse which was one of the few business outfits she had remaining in her closet. Black pumps and pearls completed the outfit. In the past, she did not have any reason to wear business clothes even when she was working for Stearns and Mandeville. This was the best she had, so it was the one she wore.

Beth also arrived in a black wool suit, but it was a finely tailored wool jacket and skirt combination that fit her frame perfectly. Under the jacket, Beth wore a turquoise silk blouse and a matching Hermes silk scarf. She was wearing the same leather boots Barbara had seen her wear in Reston. She had a small gold necklace, a matching gold bracelet on one wrist, and on the other arm a gold Cartier tank watch on a turquoise leather band. Beth was carrying the necessary papers and her laptop in her leather purse. She looked like she was ready for some sort of negotiation. Barbara would have had no doubt in the past it might have been world domination.

Richard arrived looking precisely like what he was: Beth's muscle. An almost black, navy-blue suit, black shoes that looked like they could be used for running as easily as ballroom dancing, white shirt, stainless steel Omega watch, and a navy-blue silk tie with small para-chutes as the design. Barbara remembered that the one time she had seen her friend Max Creeter wear a tie, he had worn a similar piece. Longstreet had worn the same tie at Creeter's funeral. It meant some-thing, but this was not the time nor the place to ask.

A hotel senior was waiting at the conference room. He fluttered around Beth for a few moments to make sure "Madame Ambassador" was satisfied, and after promising to personally guide her guest to the room, he disappeared. Richard said, "Well, at least we know we are under the care and feeding of a committed bunch here at the hotel."

Beth pulled a small, black plastic box out of her purse. She touched the single button on the side of the box and then placed it carefully under the conference table against one of the large oak legs. "A little gift from Longstreet and the gang. It is a short-range jammer. Designed to prevent any use of WIFI-enabled surveillance equip-ment. It also jams our phones so that they can't be used as trojan horses by other creeps."

"Just in case," Barbara said with a hint of irony.

Richard said with far more commitment, "Just in case."

There was a gentle knock on the conference room door and the Schlosshotel senior returned. He was followed by a thin man in a black suit, white shirt and black tie. He wore thick, black tortoise-shell glasses and an expression of a perpetual state of worry. The hotel senior said, "Herr Doktor Friedrich Altmayer, Madame Ambas-sador."

Beth nodded and said, "Danke, Jacob."

Barbara thought to herself: let the games begin.

Beth looked to the tea tray at the table and asked, "Herr Altmayer, would you like some coffee?"

Altmayer nodded. Richard immediately reached for the tea tray and poured Almayer a cup from the hotel china. He looked at Bar-bara, she nodded and he poured another. Finally, he added some milk to another cup, poured the coffee and handed it to Beth. He then stepped back from the table and stood near the door. Altmayer seemed to wonder if he should be worried or relieved that Beth had a guard at the door. Beth acknowledged Altmayer's expression and said, "My colleague Richard is simply here to ensure we are not interrupted. My colleague Barbara is here to help me to resolve your concerns."

Barbara thought Altmayer showed less worry at Beth's explanation. Only slightly less worry.

Beth continued, "Herr Altmayer, I want to explain how we intend to help you. I think it is worth explaining the context of our research." Barbara watched Altmayer as Beth spent the next thirty minutes providing a truncated version of what she had revealed on the airplane and reiterated in the hotel room last night. What she revealed to Altmayer could be summarized in two sentences. First, there was a chance that the paintings sitting in his art warehouse were looted by Nazis in the early part of World War II. Second, his firm would not want to be involved in selling stolen art. Once she staked out her position, Beth hinted there was a chance that the Russians were part of a criminal enterprise. With each piece of evidence that Beth presented, Altmayer looked more and more disturbed. He was clearly not a man who expressed concern dramatically. Rather, it seemed to Barbara as Beth's presentation continued, the wrinkles around his eyes and the creases on his brow grew deeper and deeper. Barbara thought: this is not a man who should play poker.

Beth concluded, "What I really need to know is how you acquired these paintings. I think we can all agree the provenance is problematic, but precisely how did your firm acquire the paintings for auction?"

Altmayer looked even more worried than he did when it looked as if the paintings were in the sights of Russian organized crime. He paused for a moment and switched to German for the first time in the conversation. "*Es ist kompliziert.*"

Beth said, "I realize it is complicated, Herr Altmayer. I need you to explain in English why it is complicated." Beth smiled her most terrifying smile. Barbara was never certain when Beth smiled like that if she was just going to kill an adversary or kill him and then eat him. Her lips smiled, but her eyes looked more like the eyes of a leopard than a diplomat.

Altmayer nodded. He rubbed his hands and then took a sip from the coffee. Richard filled his cup. Altmayer rubbed his hands again. "There is a small shop in Vienna that we use to acquire items that come out of the Eastern European states of the former Soviet Union. Primarily Russian icons, some sculpture, and paintings. The problem is that items that arrive have complicated documentation. We have been doing business there since 1994, so nearly twenty years. We have always assumed that the items were sold by private owners who want to be paid in hard currency, sometimes Swiss Francs and sometimes Euros. They also do not want their names on the bill of sale, perhaps for reasons of taxes in their home country. We don't ask any questions since our interlocutor has always been a very reliable provider and has no troubles with the Austrian authorities. I insist we have never, please believe me, never had any concern over the acquisition."

"So, I return to the question, Herr Altmayer. Where did your shop acquire the paintings?"

"*Keine ahnung.*"

"Not good enough, Herr Altmayer. I suspect you have never had a clue regarding the name of the owner. What do you know? Did it come from Ukraine? Moldova? Belarus? At least you know that much, no?"

Barbara watched this dialogue. Altmayer was trying to avoid answering, Beth was determined that he would answer. When he tried to wriggle from a question, Beth pushed him in a slightly different direction. He might reveal something if he answered that new question. If not, then Beth was determined to return to the first question. It was an excellent education in interrogation. Barbara wondered if this was a technique used in high-level diplomacy or something that Beth learned at Stearns and Mandeville. What she noticed was Richard was moving closer to the conference table. Beth nodded to Richard. Barbara waited to see what would happen.

Richard leaned close to Altmayer and slammed the flat of both of his hands on the table. Altmayer's coffee cup tipped and spilled the last dregs of his coffee on the table. Richard immediately picked up a napkin and wiped up the spill. As he wiped up the spill, he spoke quietly to Altmayer. "*Entschuldigen.*"

Beth smiled again and said, "Herr Altmayer, apologies for my colleague's outburst, but if we are going to help you and prevent difficulties with the *Bundeskriminalamt* and, perhaps, EUROPOL, we need you to be honest with us. It is in all our interests. I'm sure you see that now."

Barbara watched carefully as Altmayer's face shifted from anger to fear and, eventually to compliance. At that point, Beth looked at Barbara. Clearly it was time for her to play a role. She assumed her job was to offer herself as Altmayer's confidant and collaborator. She started by saying, "Herr Altmayer, we all know how business is accomplished. Sometimes, the best way to do business is to ask as few questions as possible. Sometimes, it means you have to provide some," Barbara paused as she took a sip from her coffee cup, "compensation to ensure the deal serves everyone's needs. We are simply asking for that small bit of compensation so that we can avoid complications for both your establishment and for our clients. It isn't much to ask for you to tell us where you acquired the paintings. It is a small thing. Please help us."

Altmayer listened to Barbara and then looked at Richard and finally returned his gaze to Beth Parsons. He said, "I believe the paintings came from a client in Odessa. There is an antiques dealer in Odessa who is liquidating his stock so that he can move to Moscow. The reasons are unclear. But, his stock included many pieces and my firm acquired most of them. They included sculpture, porcelain, paintings and even some Faberge items. Very valuable and very rare."

Beth nodded and said, "Herr Altmayer, that was most helpful. This is precisely why we wanted to work with you in the first place. We have mutual interests here that will mean we can all profit when we cooperate. Now, the only other thing that we need you to do for us is to give us access to the paintings so that we can determine if the paintings you have are the paintings that belonged to our client. It will take no time at all. An hour at most. Is that possible?"

During her time in service, Barbara had participated in recruitments of terrorists who went through the various stages of hostility, denial, false compliance, and eventually full compliance. It was a puzzle to her why a human might fight against a requirement at first and, eventually, become fully compliant. Of course, the challenge was always to determine what compliance really meant. Still, once the target's defenses eroded — and assuming the officer involved made the target feel that he had made the right choice for his own reasons — the transition could be quick. Stunningly quick. This was precisely what happened as Altmayer sat across the table from Beth.

"Of course, Madame Ambassador. It is only complicated by the fact that the entire shipment from Vienna is currently in a storage facility in Aachen. We often place valuables in Aachen so that they can be delivered to anywhere in Western Europe. Next week I can move the paintings back to my own warehouse in Frankfurt for your convenience."

Beth smiled. The last defenses were collapsing, but Altmayer was still playing with them. She said, "No need, Herr Altmayer. We will be happy to drive to Aachen. We can be there tomorrow by 1400hrs. Will that be acceptable?"

Altmayer realized his last ploy had failed. He nodded and said, "Absolutely. I will meet you in Aachen tomorrow. Here is the address of the warehouse I use. It is in Germany but very close to the Dutch border." He passed a business card to Beth. Beth immediately handed the card to Richard. She smiled and stood up. She offered her hand to Altmayer and said, "Herr Altmayer, I want to thank you for your time and your willingness to help. I am certain that it will be to all of our advantage."

Altmayer stood up. Barbara could see he was some the worse for wear after an interlude with Beth Parsons. He reached over, took her hand and bowed slightly. "It has been a pleasure, Madame Ambassador."

Richard opened the door and Altmayer took no time at all to leave the room. Beth reached under the table and picked up the small jammer. Before she shut it off, she said to both Barbara and Richard, "That went about the way I expected. Thanks to you both for your roles in this little passion play."

Richard nodded and Barbara had to laugh. Beth shut off the jammer as they packed up their things and headed to the suite. Richard remained for a moment to double check the conference room for any items left behind and caught up to them as they walked down the hallway. He said, "I think it might be useful for me to pre- cede you into the suite. Just in case."

Beth nodded. Richard walked quickly down the hall to the stairs. Beth said to Barbara, "Normally, I don't like it when a bodyguard takes his role too seriously. I think this is one of those times when I will accept his advice."

"Good choice," was all Barbara had to say.

A WAREHOUSE OF CURIOSITIES

A fter heading north for over an hour, they turned onto an east-west highway toward the German border with Holland and Belgium. The rolling hills of the Rhine receded and the gothic cathedral in Cologne, known to medieval scholars in Europe as "God's battleship," disappeared in the rear window. Beth related a tale of her first visit to Aachen as a young graduate student researching medieval Europe. She pointed out that Aachen was the location of Charlemagne's throne after he was crowned Holy Roman Emperor in 800AD. Despite the "Holy Roman" title, Charlemagne rarely demonstrated Christian values as he conquered large portions of Europe through what Beth described as blood and thunder. From the front of the Mercedes, Richard nodded and said, "At that point in time, there was only going to be one type of emperor: a man willing to fight for the job. He led the Franks and their allies all over Western Europe and into Italy. A large man with a very long reach."

Beth said, "I am always fascinated with the stuff that you know."

"I read a lot."

Barbara laughed and said, "And remember a fair bit as well."

"If it is about warrior kings, warrior monks, and condottieri, you are absolutely right."

"You would have been a good companion for my friend Max Creeter."

Richard whistled and said, "Now there was a man to admire. Warrior, PhD, professor and a man who died in battle. I didn't know you knew him."

Barbara paused for a moment. Her comment on Max had been frivolous and now she was trapped in memories of a short love affair and a very brutal final battle. She said, "He was all of those things and a loyal friend. He died in a gunfight that we had with some Russians."

"In Syria?"

"In Northern Virginia."

"Barbara, we definitely need to talk."

Beth interceded. "Ask her sometime about her gunfight when a creep threw a grenade at her. She dropped him with her 2-inch Smith and Wesson."

Barbara laughed and said, "Well, did you tell Richard about our high-speed car chase in Greece facing Russian assassins? And, by the way, when did you fit graduate school into your CV that includes law school as well?"

"I was a pretty boring woman in my 20s. Focused on lots of schooling."

"And then became a diplomat."

"And ended up traveling in war zones because of all that education."

Barbara laughed again. "I got all the war zones I wanted and only had a BA."

Richard said nothing. He shook his head and looked back in the rearview mirror. Clearly, both women had stories he needed to hear. Unfortunately, this was not the time since he was on the German autobahn driving the heavy BMW at 200kph.

Altmayer was good to his word. He met them at the storage facility at 1400hrs. The building was an old brick structure south and west of the old city of Aachen. It looked to be one of the few survivors from World War II. Most of its neighbors were concrete slabs with metal roofs. Instead, it was a two-story red brick building with a flat roof. As they walked into the building, Altmayer commented, "I'm sure you noticed the age of the building. It was saved from Allied attack only because it was a field hospital for the German defenders of Aachen. My family bought a share of the building after the war. It had many purposes, but now it serves as the primary storehouse for art treasures that we are going to place at auction. Far enough away from big German, Dutch and Belgian cities that we have little risk of crime. But, close enough that we can deliver items by truck to every country in Western Europe." Altmayer was clearly proud of his building, his storeroom of treasures. He took Beth on a guided tour leaving Barbara and Richard behind.

When they entered the interior of the warehouse, Barbara could see why. Inside what appeared to be little more than industrial warehouse space was a second brick structure. That structure had a separate heating and air conditioning system as well as a high-security steel door with both a cipher lock and a combination lock. Barbara wasn't an expert on how to enter secure spaces, but it looked to her as if you would need a welding torch and a couple of hours before you would get through the door.

As Barbara completed her visual assessment, Richard walked up and whispered, "Smile, you are on camera. Surveillance cameras everywhere and, if I am correct, the cameras are on at least two different systems for redundancy. I would have to get a closer look, but they also look like they have infrared cameras for night vision and maybe even audio surveillance. This guy is serious about his security. He is hiding in plain sight. Did you see the sign on the door? It says *Waldhaus Maschinenteile GMBH*. Machine parts, indeed."

Barbara whispered back, "I wonder if Beth understands that this guy's company is not exactly what he claims it to be. Perhaps I am just a suspicious type, but this place looks more like it is associated with transnational crime than simply shipment of art treasures."

Richard nodded. "It smells like trouble. I don't know what Stearns and Mandeville have been doing with this guy, but I would recommend dropping him like a hot rock as soon as we get this Nazi loot sorted." Barbara nodded.

Beth returned from her tour of the warehouse. She said, "Herr Altmayer showed me around and set up a small room for us to review the paintings. Let's go see what we can determine." Beth turned on her heel and walked along an aisle between two ten-foot-high metal racks filled with carefully wrapped items. Each one had a paper label identifying what it was — painting, sculpture, jewelry — and an alpha-numeric serial number which most probably matched some digital listing. As they walked down the aisle, Richard pointed out that each parcel also had an electronic tag that Barbara suspected held a GPS tracker. This was her first trip to an auction warehouse, but the more she saw, the more she suspected this was not merely an auction warehouse.

They walked into a small room with a conference table with four wrapped parcels. Altmayer said, "Would you like some coffee or tea? I don't know how long your work is going to take. My staff can deliver whatever you wish."

Beth spoke first. "Herr Altmayer, I think we would prefer to keep focused on the paintings and avoid anything that might spill. If you don't mind, we would like to be on our own while we conduct our review."

Almayer did a small bow and said, "Absolutely, Madame Ambassador." He turned on his heel in what could only be described as a military-style about face and left the room, closing the door.

While Beth and Barbara pulled out laptops, cameras, and infrared lights, Richard walked around the room. When he had completed the circuit, he reached into his pocket, pulled out a 3X5 card and a pen and began to write. As he did so, he asked in a conversational tone, "What can I do to help?" As Beth looked up, he handed the card to her. In small printing, Richard had written: We are under video and audio surveillance. Beth nodded and pushed the card over to Barbara who was assembling a pair of small tripods for the camera and the IR lights. Barbara was not surprised. She palmed the card and put it back in the camera bag.

It took longer than expected to confirm the provenance of the paintings. They matched the images of the ones owned originally by the Mayerhaus family. Identifying whether they were the originals was far more complicated. Barbara was surprised to see that Beth

Parsons had some degree of expertise in both the Bauhaus painters and the late Impressionists. Not exactly consistent with either her law degree or her years as a foreign service officer, but Barbara assumed that Beth was always a quick study. It was when they started to use the IR light that Barbara realized that she trained a bit before their departure.

Beth said, "The IR light will energize the paint. Then we take a reading from this spectrometer of the frequency." Beth pointed to a small electronic device sitting in front of the painting. "Now, this reading won't tell us who painted the painting, but it will tell us if the paint is similar to that used before World War II." Beth turned to Barbara and said, "Go ahead and illuminate the first painting with the IR light."

Over the next two hours, they reviewed the five paintings. The two from the Hungarian Bauhaus painter, Lazlo Moholy-Nagy and the one by a Russian impressionist named Valentin Serov matched the images from the Mayerhaus collection and were painted with materials common before World War II. The painting identified as one by the Russian Vladimir Baranov-Rossine did not pass the spectrographic review. According to this basic check, the Baranov-Rossine painting was done with modern paints used only after 1950. Beth concluded, "OK, that's as much as we can do for now. We will have to let Herr Altmayer know that these three paintings need further adjudication before they can be either returned to the Mayerhaus family or released for auction."

As they were replacing the paintings in their secure boxes, a memory stick fell out of the dust jacket paper on the back of the Serov painting. It had been placed behind a small slice in the paper wrap. Richard caught the stick before it fell to the floor. He looked at Beth. She nodded and he put the stick in his trouser pocket. Based on the way the paintings and their cameras and equipment were set up, Barbara knew the entire action had been invisible to the camera in the room. What she didn't know was how Beth intended to use this new information.

When they were finished, Beth opened the door and walked to Altmayer's office which was a few yards away. "Herr Altmayer, we have concluded our investigation. The Moholy-Nagy paintings and the Serov painting are of the right era and will need to be reviewed by an independent art expert before you can either sell them or return them to their rightful owners. I'm sorry to tell you that the Baranov-Rossine painting is likely a forgery. It is an exceptionally good forgery, but the paints used are simply not consistent with the time frame when the painter lived. We have no interest in that painting and will defer to you on what you do next with that painting."

Beth noticed Altmayer seemed relieved at their determination. That was surprising since she also knew an original Baranov-Rossine painting would be the most valuable of the four. Further, if his firm paid for an original painting and now, he had to sell it as a copy, the value was even less. Beth continued, "With your permission, we will take our leave and return to Bad Soden. Please withdraw the three paintings from the upcoming auction. In the end, you may still be able to sell the paintings once we determine if the paintings belong to my client, but until we have a formal authentication, we can only request that you do not sell what may be Nazi-looted art."

Altmayer stood up and offered his hand. The handshake reinforced Beth's view that Altmayer was relieved with their findings. He said, "Madame Ambassador, you can be certain that I will comply with your wishes. I look forward to a follow-up from the specialists that you will be sending to me. In the meantime, I hope you have a safe drive to Bad Soden and a safe return to the US."

As they drove east toward Cologne, they reviewed the results of the day. Beth opened the discussion by stating, "I think we made real progress today. I was a bit surprised that Altmayer accepted our findings without any grumbling. He almost seemed relieved."

Barbara nodded and said, "I suspect Altmayer has more than one business arrangement in the warehouse and he probably was relieved just to get us out of there before we found something that we might have to report."

"Such as?"

"Well, call me suspicious, but I think the fact that the warehouse is listed as having machine parts along with the level of surveillance and security in the warehouse argues that Altmayer might be using his art dealership to move other items around Europe. Do you know Altmayer's background?"

Beth shook her head. "His firm started in the early '90s. First in Vienna and then in Frankfurt. When the USSR collapsed, the communist elite shipped anything they could to the West for hard currency. Our firm was involved in some of the litigation based on ties to a Dusseldorf firm that Altmayer used. This was before I retired, so I don't know much about those cases. What I do know is Altmayer is an *Ossi*."

Richard had finally pulled the rental car onto the autobahn so he was less focused on driving as he accelerated the BMW to an easy cruising speed of 120kph. He looked at them through the rearview mirror of the BMW and said, "A what?"

Barbara took over. "He was an East German. *Ossi* is slang for an East German. When Germany unified, there were plenty of former East German citizens who profited when the German government offered a one-for-one exchange between Deutschmarks and Ostmarks. There wasn't much to buy in East Germany and no one in the east trusted the communist banking structure, so they just stored their currency in their houses ... "

Beth interrupted, "Or other hideaways ... "

Barbara continued, "So, suddenly some of the East German citizens were pretty wealthy. And, if they had connections ... "

Beth again interrupted, "As Altmayer apparently did ... "

"Then they had a chance to profit from unification. It irritated many in West Germany but it probably was the only way to make unification work." Barbara looked over at Beth and said, "Do you think he was in the Stasi?"

Beth said, "We never found any evidence that he was anything other than a civil servant in the transportation ministry in the German Democratic Republic."

"Transportation in the GDR. Right." Richard's sarcasm was clear.

"Most of the records were destroyed simply to prevent the sorts of checks that we might otherwise have completed. Altmayer's connection with Russia argues that he might have proven valuable to the Soviets before he started his art gallery."

Barbara nodded. "And, perhaps is still valuable to the Russians now since he moves art all over Europe." She continued, "I smell a rat."

Beth laughed and said, "You always smell a rat."

"That's because there almost always is a rat."

Richard interrupted, "Well, let's just see what we find on that memory stick when we get back to the hotel. That should tell us something."

Beth said, "I knew bringing you along might be trouble."

ROOM SERVICE

They returned to Bad Soden after a long day on the road. Beth said, "How about we get room service and review what we saw today and take a look at that thumb drive?" Richard and Barbara nodded as they went into their separate bedrooms to change clothes. Barbara was the first to come out. She was dressed in navy-blue sweats and tai chi slippers. She found Beth on the couch in the sitting room dressed in what appeared to be a silk kimono and matching silk pajama pants. Once again, Beth looked fabulous and Barbara felt underdressed. Luckily, Richard arrived dressed in almost the same outfit as Barbara except his sweats were forest green and he was wearing some sort of workout shoes with toes. Barbara looked at the shoes and said, "What are those?"

Richard smiled and said, "Turns out they are the best workout shoes I've ever had. Forces me to focus on foot placement when I'm doing kick-boxing practice on the heavy bag. You hit with the ball of your foot or you are reminded quickly why you should."

Beth looked at her two companions and said, "Listen, enough commando talk. Let's order dinner and get to work." Barbara was looking forward to the discussion. So far, Beth hadn't offered what might be called "the rest of the story." Barbara hoped Beth would be forced to do so as they talked about the results of the day's work.

A half hour after they assembled, there was a knock on the door and Richard went to answer. Rather than a small peephole common in older hotels, the Schlosshotel had a small camera fitted above the door in the hallway and a video screen inside the room to the left of the doorjamb. He turned back to Beth and Barbara and said, "Hotel staff pushing two carts. It looks like coffee, tea, and three plates under a silver service. Dinner?"

Beth nodded, "Dinner."

As Richard opened the door, there was a crash as the first attendant pushed his cart hard against the door, causing it to fly out of Richard's hands. With the noise, Barbara jumped up and grabbed the nearest object she could use as a weapon. It was one of Beth's laptops. As she ran to the door Barbara said to Beth, "Stay here."

By the time Barbara had crossed the room to the door, Richard was doing his best to handle two men, one brandishing a stiletto and the second carrying a small pistol with a long suppressor barrel. He had a grip on both wrists holding the weapons, but he was losing ground as the two men pushed their way into the room. Barbara swung the laptop against the head of the first assailant she could reach. There was a loud crunch as the edge of the laptop hit the assailant's neck near the base of his skull. Barbara dropped the broken piece of polymer and reached for something more substantial. She found it in a silver coffee pot, filled with steaming hot coffee. As the dazed assailant turned to address this new threat, Barbara swung the coffee pot into his temple and the assailant dropped like a rock. Once he hit the ground, Barbara kicked the knife from his hand, spun around and kicked again, this time catching the assailant under the chin. As his head snapped back, there was a sickening crunch.

Once Richard had only one assailant to handle, he made quick work of him. He took a two-hand grip on the pistol, twisted it out of the man's hand with a simple wrist lock, and tossed the weapon deeper into the room. The man was reaching for a stiletto tucked into his belt when Richard hit him in the throat. The sound of crushed bone echoed across the room as the knife clattered to the floor. Richard gripped the man's head and twisted. There was no noise as the man dropped to the floor.

Richard peered into the hallway. With no other assailants or hotel guests in sight, he closed the door. He turned to Beth and said, "Boss, I will start cleaning up the mess. You might want to think about how we sort out two dead bodies."

Beth had been shaken by the sudden violence. She said, "Two?"

Richard said, "Barbara made quick work out of that guy." He pointed to the first man lying in a puddle of spilled coffee. I have heard bones break before and I think she broke more than a couple."

Barbara was leaning against the wall trying to calm down using her yoga deep-breathing technique. As her vision cleared, she said, "I'll get some towels and blankets from my room. We need to wrap these mopes in something before they mess up the carpet."

Richard nodded. "Good idea." He leaned the individuals against the collapsed tea caddies and started working through their pockets. He found little other than an electronic master key for the hotel. In the inside pocket of the first assailant, he found a small photo of Beth Parsons and a room number. "Well, we can rule out some type of random attack. These guys knew precisely who they were after."

He continued to search the second attacker and found another sheet of paper. "It would appear they weren't here to kill us. Only to kidnap you, Boss."

Beth walked over to Richard and looked at the paper in his hand. It was a typewritten note that read: *Let the sale continue and Parsons will be released.*

Barbara arrived with towels, a couple of pillowcases and the two blankets from the closet in her room. As she started wrapping the bodies, she said, "It would appear the Russians are serious about acquiring all of these paintings. What in the world makes them worth the risk of kidnapping you?"

Beth finally recovered. She walked over to the devastation in the entranceway. "I have no idea. It is clear we need to take a real hard look at that memory stick." She paused and looked at Richard and then Barbara. "I suppose we don't just call the police."

"And tell them what, exactly?" Richard was not trying to be rude, but his tone was less than polite.

Barbara decided to take over before the adrenaline in Richard's body caused him to say something he might regret. "Beth, I think we can clean up as much of this mess as possible without involving the police. I can call in a favor and see what happens. My biggest concern is there may be other bodies here someplace. Somewhere there are two missing hotel staff. Guys like this don't leave any witnesses behind. Our only hope is that they intercepted the real staff outside the building. Otherwise, there will be police for certain. For now, we are lucky that January is a slow season here in the Taunus. We may be able to get these stiffs out of our room without anyone noticing."

Richard smiled and said, "On a positive note, we now have a pistol."

Barbara said, "Up until twenty minutes ago, I would have thought a pistol was not something we were going to need."

Beth shook her head and said, "Me neither."

Barbara went back into her room and recovered her parka and an Iridium satellite telephone. She walked into the living room of the suite, opened the sliding glass door, and walked out on the small patio that overlooked the Schlosshotel grounds including a golf course and a small park. Barbara noticed the large snow drift two floors below. She had several numbers on the speed dial function of the phone. She called one simply titled Martha. The phone rang three times and a voice on the other end said, "7963."

Barbara responded, "Please tell Mary it is Barbara."

Barbara looked at the luminous dial on her watch as the seconds slipped by. In less than a minute, a familiar voice came on the phone. "This can't be good."

Barbara smiled. "It's good to hear your voice as well, Mary."

"When we gave you the number, there was an agreement that it was to be used *in extremis*. Knowing you as I do, I suspect it is not a social call."

"Do you have a set of cleaners in Europe? I have a mess that needs work."

There was a pause on the end of the line. "Cleaners. I don't know. I will have to call an old friend of yours named Patty Dentmann. She is the boss there."

Barbara knew the layout of the Headquarters building. Mary Sanderson was one of the seniors in the Counterintelligence Center. Her office was not far from the front office of the Europe Division. "Can't you just walk down the hall?"

"I could but Patty is in Europe. Where are you right now?"

"Bad Soden."

"Check. Patty is in Germany right now. I don't know where exactly. I will have her give you a call soonest. I'm assuming it is urgent."

"About as urgent as you can imagine."

"How many?"

"Two."

"Who are you with right now?"

"Beth Parsons and her bodyguard."

"Richard?"

Mary's comment surprised Barbara. She hadn't expected her Agency colleague to know anything about Beth except her status as a former ambassador. She said, "Yup."

"OK, so you are safe right now. I will send an immediate to Patty and she should be in touch soonest."

"Thanks."

"You realize this makes up for the fact that we caused your house to be firebombed."

Barbara smiled. The last time she worked with Mary, the result had been less than perfect from the Agency standpoint and even less so from Barbara's standpoint since the double agent ended up trying to burn down Barbara's house. "Deal."

"By the way, is this going to interest me?"

"Absolutely. I think you are going to want to see what we have. At the very least, it was something folks were willing to do us harm to recover."

"It wasn't what you expected?"

"Not at all."

"OK, I will do my best to get to Frankfurt by tomorrow. Meantime, expect a call from Patty."

"Thanks, sister."

"You have always been trouble, Barbara."

"As if you weren't?" Barbara thought about their long-term relationship including a period when Mary was working as a double agent against the Russian GRU and under the direction of her father-in-law.

"OK, I'll get to work. Out here." The connection ended. Barbara looked out at the snow-covered golf course below. She had an idea how to pass the time while she waited for her call from Patty. She opened the sliding glass door and walked back into the hotel suite.

Richard said, "Is the cavalry on its way?"

"I hope so."

Beth looked up and said, "The sisterhood?"

"Exactly."

Richard asked, "What do we do in the meantime?"

"I have an idea. Take a look outside and see what you think."

Richard was outside for a minute and returned. "I think it will work. At least for a little bit."

Beth looked worried. "What are you planning to do?"

"We can't keep these guys in the room and we really can't get them out of the room without drawing some attention in the hallway. My recommendation is we carry them out onto the balcony and dump them over the side. They will fall into what looks to be about a ten-foot-deep drift of snow. It isn't a great plan, but it's the only plan I can think of until the cleaners arrive."

Richard looked up. "THE cleaners? Really?"

Beth said, "Who are THE cleaners."

"Agency folks who help make messy stuff disappear."

"Like aliens in Area 51?"

"That's a myth."

"Or Jimmy Hoffa."

"That definitely wasn't the Agency."

"Sure."

Barbara smiled. She walked over to the first body wrapped in a blanket. "Richard, are you going to help me or not?"

Richard walked over and grabbed the other end of the blanket. Beth stood up and opened the glass doors. They leveraged the body so it balanced on the patio railing and then unrolled the blanket, launching the first body into space. It disappeared with a thump into the snow drift. They moved quickly and the second body went over the side. Another thump.

"If we are lucky, it will snow some tonight."

"And if not, we have to just deny any part we might have played in all of this. Let's get back to cleaning up the spilled coffee."

Beth shook her head and said, "Should I ask for more room service?"

Richard shook his head. "I think one delivery is enough."

Richard said nothing more as they cleaned up the spilled coffee and the pieces of broken plastic from the laptop used as a weapon. It was as if he had done it all before and Barbara wondered if he had done so for Beth. Beth had taken it in stride, so perhaps her time in Stearns and Mandeville had been more adventurous than Barbara knew. Either way, during Richard's time with SOF he had experienced far worse.

Barbara's own experience working against terrorists had given her time with special operations professionals. They were often unassuming men who did not look the part of killers. Some were well-muscled men that an outsider might identify as a rugby, soccer, or hockey player, but certainly not the heavily muscled men who played commandos in the movies. Others were smaller, lean-muscled men who could carry heavy rucksacks for days or move lightning-quick on a karate or judo mat. Barbara's longtime friend and former lover, Max Creeter, had been the former. Jake Longstreet, retired Green Beret and now security specialist working with Stearns and Mandeville, the latter. No matter what shape or size, they all shared one trait. They were all taciturn. Richard was certainly that.

THE DREAM

Barbara O'Connell was walking the streets of the city, trying to determine the location of no-man's-land in the midst of an urban civil war. The provisional US embassy was two blocks away from the main square where the two sides fought gun battles virtually every night. During the daytime, the rebels and the Tajik government forces retreated to their safe havens in opposite sides of the city. Those breaks in the fighting allowed residents to go to the marketplace for what little food was left in the city. Rural villages in this newly independent state of the former Soviet Union didn't seem to care which faction would win. They only wanted the fighting to end so they could transport their goods to market in the two main cities of Tajikistan, Dushanbe and Khojand.

Barbara needed to determine the no-man's-land for an entirely different reason. She was responsible for creating an embassy escape and evasion plan in case the conflict reached a point where it risked US lives. There were five Americans assigned to the embassy in Dushanbe and Barbara was the only Agency officer as well as the de facto security officer. Along with the primary job of keeping people safe, she was expected to provide daily reporting on the battle. Knowing where the two sides drew their battle lines was critical to both jobs. As a woman on the streets, dressed in drab European garb, wearing a locally purchased head scarf and carrying a worn fabric shopping bag, Barbara passed through the residential areas with little notice. Today, she intended to define the edge of the war zone, then go to the market to buy whatever she could find and return to the house that served as the embassy and the residence for her colleagues.

As she walked along the buildings south of the main street, her boots kicked up brass cartridge cases from the firefight the previous evening. The government forces — a mix of paramilitary police and former members of the Soviet Army stationed in this country bordering Afghanistan — were the most disciplined, but also the least willing to fight. The resistance forces — Islamic extremists, former Soviet dissidents, and ethnic Tajik nationalists — were nothing more than a well-armed rabble, but they were the most violent. Barbara knew she could probably talk her way out of a confrontation with the government forces. It wasn't clear if she would even get a chance to talk if she was confronted by the resistance.

Evidence of the recent firefight seemed to show that the next cross street served as the temporary boundary between the two sides. She looked up at the stucco walls of the apartment buildings, pockmarked with hundreds of bullet holes from small arms fire. It was definitely time to return to the market and then to the embassy. She would take out the map she kept in the only safe in the building, mark this new boundary, tell the ambassador, and then send the information to Headquarters. Her time in Tajikistan was not at all like conventional espionage. It was more like something out of 19th century military intelligence of "go spy the land." Luckily the assignment was temporary. No more than four months, probably less if the fighting got worse. Then she could return to her work for the Counterterrorism Center. Hunting terrorists appeared to be less dangerous.

As she progressed a few blocks along the residential street, she heard the sound of heavy military trucks. She stopped and looked back at the crossroads. Four olive-drab cargo trucks with canvas-covered beds pulled into the four corners of the intersection. The tail gates of the trucks dropped, the canvas drew back, and dozens of men jumped out. Dressed in grey-green military uniforms more commonly seen in NATO forces, these men looked nothing like either side of the civil war and nothing like the Russian soldiers assigned to the Dushanbe airport. Their weapons and load-bearing equipment were well maintained, their boots well worn, and they wore green knit caps. Barbara was not about to walk back for a closer look, but it appeared that the men were professional soldiers who were used to living and working in war zones. There were plenty of Russian veterans from both Afghanistan and Chechnya. Violent, brutal wars with no rules. These men were ready for a fight.

As she watched, an officer jumped down from the front of the first truck carrying a loudspeaker. The officer looked young, but hardened from years in combat. He used the speaker to deliver a message in Russian. "We are the Special Purpose Mobile Unit. Come out now and surrender." Barbara had heard of the Special Purpose Mobile Unit known colloquially as OMON based on the Russian acronym. They were the Russian Ministry of Interior special forces, used to combat terrorists and silence dissidents. Their arrival in Dushanbe was not a surprise, but this was the first time Barbara had seen them.

As the officer spoke, the doors of the apartment buildings opened. Old men and women dressed in long wool coats, mufflers and knit caps walked out to see what was going on. After all, it was only two years ago that the Soviet Union offered peace and security in this border town. Poverty to be sure, but still good order. They knew how to respond to the demands of a security unit from the Ministry of Interior. It was important to obey the state.

When the crowd finally assembled inside the crossroads, the officer deployed search teams into the apartment buildings. In short order, the search teams came out with young teenagers in custody. The teenagers were assembled on the street. The officer raised the loud-speaker again. This time he was speaking to his men. He only said one word. "Fire!" The teenagers were the first to die. The old men and women started to run. The soldiers keyed on the runners. After they dropped, the soldiers started to fire at the pensioners.

Barbara ran. She had been far enough away that she hoped to escape notice. Clearly, this new force in town was one that intended to control the population by any means. They would take no prisoners. What wasn't clear to Barbara was which side was it on. Supporting the Tajik government led by members of the old Soviet oligarchy, some element of the Tajik resistance, or perhaps some third force that had yet to emerge in this civil war? Barbara disappeared down another side street and headed to the center of the city. She could hear the sound of military boots chasing after her. They were gaining, while she seemed to be losing momentum. Had they seen her? Did they want to eliminate witnesses? As she turned another corner, she could see OMON troops in front of her.

Barbara woke up with a start. She forced herself to remember she had been dozing on a couch in the Schlosshotel. The Dushanbe images slowly receded from her memory. It wasn't the first time she had suffered from the nightmares that she simply called "the Dream." It usually followed some confrontation in the real world and she assumed her dream world simply processed the events in some other way, bringing up events from her past, mixing them with the present and terrifying her in her sleep. She hadn't thought about Dushanbe in years and she wondered precisely why her brain would dredge up this old story. Barbara knew that self-analysis was rarely useful. So, she got up from the couch, stretched and headed to the bathroom. A hot shower might help. Hot tea would be even better.

A REUNION

The Cleaners arrived early on 16 January. They reached out via the satellite phone at 0600hrs and said Beth, Richard, and Barbara should check out of the hotel at 1000hrs and drive toward Frankfurt. They promised to resolve what they called "the situation" at the hotel before the three checked out. They also promised to give further guidance once the BMW was safely on the road.

As they drove out of the Taunus, Beth received a call on her mobile. The voice on the other end said, "We are coming up behind you in a Volkswagen transporter. Please follow us." Beth relayed the message to Richard. He slowed the BMW down to 120kph.

Richard said, "Are you sure?" Barbara nodded.

"I'm sure about their bosses. I've worked with them for over two decades."

Richard nodded. "One way or the other, here they come." A grey Volkswagen Transporter van passed them and pulled into their lane. Richard matched the speed with the van and they drove into Frankfurt. After twenty minutes, they exited the autobahn and stair-stepped through Frankfurt streets near the *Bundesbank*, formerly the head of the German currency and now one of the centers for the Euro currency, and the *Europaturm*, the giant telecommunications tower that watched over the city. They slowed as they drove past the *Palmengarten* and into a neighborhood that seemed untouched by either World War II or the modern development caused by the booming German economy. They pulled into a gated driveway and parked next to a small brick two-story house. In front of the VW van was a BMW 750i that looked remarkably like the one Richard was driving.

The van door opened and four men got out carrying black duffle bags. Richard, Beth and Barbara exited their car and walked to the side door of the house next to the parked BMW. As they walked in, they were greeted by what could only be described as a harsh woman's voice saying, "Barbara O'Connell. If you had to cause trouble, why in the world did it have to be in my division?"

Barbara edged past Beth and Richard and said, "Patty, you know I didn't cause the trouble. It just found me."

"You can keep saying that just like you daughter says stuff isn't her fault, but I don't believe it."

"Neither do I!" Mary Sanderson's voice echoed from the sitting room of the house.

Patty Dentmann's voice adopted a more formal tone. "Welcome to your new, temporary residence while we sort out what is going on. Ambassador Parsons, thanks for agreeing to see us. And Richard, thanks for keeping these two ladies safe."

Richard said, "Actually, Barbara was the one who kept me safe this time."

Patty laughed loud and long until she stopped with a snort. She caught herself as she saw her men looking a little bewildered by the introductions. She said to them, "It's a bit of a reunion. Barbara was a senior when I was a peanut in the Agency. Richard and I worked together on something that is probably best described as ... irregular."

Richard smiled and said, "Irregular definitely describes it, Patty."

Barbara saw again that Richard was more than just a bodyguard for Beth. She wondered how much more she would find out during this reunion and decided quickly that the answer was very little.

Patty welcomed them into a tiny living room furnished in wood and leather and surrounded on all four walls with large lawyers' bookcases in oak. As Barbara walked by the bookcase nearest the door, she noticed the books were leather-bound European classics. She was tempted to stop for a moment and check out one to determine its provenance when Patty said, "Barbara, please don't pull out one of those books. Knowing you, I suspect it would result in you finding some place to settle in and read. Plus, the books serve a purpose: they cover a Cold War relic Faraday cage that traps radio and digital transmission. We could go downstairs to the basement where we have a SCIF, but I thought this would be more ... amenable."

Beth smiled and said, "Given what we went through last night, amenable would be very nice."

"Excellent. Well, the guys here have made us some coffee and," Patty paused for a moment and laughed. "Homemade kuchen, no less! You never know what your security detachment is going to be like when you become a division chief. In my case, I have some serious shooters who also just happen to like baking!" Patty was interrupted as one of her men rolled in a cart with a silver coffee and tea service and a tray of cakes. Patty nodded to the officer and said, "Thank you, Peter. Please close the door. We will be fine for at least an hour."

Barbara noticed the security officer had a Glock in a waistband concealed-carry holster on his right hip and a small radio on his left. As he walked to the door, he pulled a leather panel out from the door frame, attached it to the door and then gently closed the door with a thud.

"Please help yourselves. Barbara, I had them make Earl Grey tea for you and an Italian roast coffee for both Beth and Richard. I hope that is satisfactory."

Barbara remained puzzled as Patty served up the coffee and tea and offered slices of the cinnamon coffee cake. Why in the world was an Agency division chief in Frankfurt and why in the world was she playing the domestic host to them? She didn't have to wait long to find out.

After they had all settled in around the coffee table, Mary started the conversation. "I heard from the Cleaners that you had more than a bit of trouble last night. Honestly, I wasn't surprised when I heard about your contact with Altmayer. You are nibbling around the edge of a particularly confusing operation that we have been tracking for almost two years. I think your role in this started a few years ago when you and Beth rounded up an Irish assassin who, if I'm not mistaken, was an O'Connell." Mary finished the last sentence as a statement of fact rather than a question, so Barbara just nodded.

This time Patty took the lead. "Then Barbara served as bait for a counterintelligence operation that resulted in a narrow escape by some unknown assailants." Patty paused to sip from the china cup. "We worked with the Canadians to track the perpetrators who barely made their escape in a light plane that I heard had at least two rounds from your revolver." Patty looked at Barbara and this time, Barbara decided to comment.

"Well, they did firebomb my house and destroyed my old Range Rover."

"So I was told. Sadly, we found the aircraft in Southern Ontario, but lost track of the perpetrators in Toronto." Another sip of coffee and then Patty turned to Beth. "It was just this past winter when we realized that your firm was involved in the recovery of the Mayerhaus paintings that I sent Richard to keep you safe." Barbara looked over at Richard. He simply shrugged and continued to eat his cake.

Beth said, "And it would seem that was a good idea given the events of last night."

Mary nodded. "Indeed. At the time, we didn't know for sure that our counterintelligence operation was going to involve Altmayer or the Mayerhaus paintings. In fact, most of the CI analysts in my office thought there was little chance of a connection. I just had a feeling that the linkage between Altmayer and Russian oligarchs was just too dangerous to ignore. Clearly, they were wrong, and at least for once, I seem to have been right."

"How much can you tell us about your side of this?" Barbara asked. She pulled the memory stick out of her pocket and said, "Other than last night's attack, this is the only thing that I know of that might have something to do with Russians."

Patty said, "Richard, would you take the stick to the cyber gurus in the other room. I think you know the tale I'm about to tell."

Richard stood up and said, "Check, Boss." He took the stick from Barbara and left the room.

Patty returned briefly to her hostess role. "How about some more coffee or tea? And, for that matter, some of this delicious cake. Who knew that my security detachment were also bakers?"

ONCE UPON A TIME

When everyone had refilled their cups, and after Patty Dentmann ate another slice of the coffee cake, Mary began the tale: "Like all good stories, it starts with once upon a time. So, once upon a time, after the collapse of the Soviet Union, there were still members of the KGB and the GRU operating under commercial cover in Vienna. They had small businesses trading in electronics, pharmaceuticals, and German cars. Each of the businesses was designed to disguise a Soviet espionage network, but once there was no Soviet Union and before the reforms took place creating the new Russian services of the SVR and the FSB, these individuals were on their own. As we all know, a close look at a good espionage network reveals similarities to transnational criminal enterprises. After all, you are holding clandestine meetings, you are paying for access to confidential information and you are transporting, more accurately described as smuggling, information, people and sometimes technology from one country to another." Mary stopped to refill her cup with the strong, black coffee available on the tray.

Barbara turned to Patty. "Patty, I suspect Mary has already relayed it was the GRU that murdered Peter and then murdered his father."

Patty nodded. "It was a dangerous time, and sadly, Peter paid the price." She paused just long enough to look Barbara in the eyes. She looked at Mary and when they were both certain that Barbara was ready to listen to the rest of the story, Mary continued.

"The Agency, the FBI and Treasury worked together to identify these networks. By the late 1990s, the GRU and the SVR worked to recover their initial investments and the people involved. Return them to the fold, so to speak. Many did return, but some chose another route. These individuals joined with some of the oligarchs who were pillaging Russian resources. Now, the press often refers to these new networks as "Russian Mafia," but unlike some of the other transnational criminal organizations, these networks were more para-statal rather than independent. They are only partially independent of the Kremlin. And hardly any of them have an ethnic or familial connection like Italian organized crime. The Russian government is willing to work with these networks, even fund some of them. In exchange, these new organizations accept tasking from the Kremlin. It has allowed some Russian intelligence operations to be completely deniable."

Patty took over the briefing. "In the post 9/11 world, one of these networks, named SWORDFISH, began to offer what they called advanced security services in Europe. It claims to be a private con-tractor that offers expertise in several areas of security and intelli-gence, military training, cyber defense. SWORDFISH employees that we have identified are all former members of the GRU and Russian SPETSNAZ. At least we think they are *former* members. What has been surprising over the past two years is SWORDFISH expanding their client base. They appear to be supporting front-com-pany operations for both the GRU and the European operations of Chinese People's Liberation Army General Staff Department Second Department or 2PLA."

"The Chinese version of the GRU."

"Exactly, Barbara. So, now we are facing an adversary who is accepted by multiple European countries as simply an international security company that is also linked to the two military intelligence organizations from our major adversaries."

Beth said, "Why in the world would the GRU tolerate their sup-port to 2PLA?"

Mary answered, "They wouldn't, but this outfit seems pretty good at compartmentation, so why would the GRU know?"

Barbara shook her head. "I still don't quite understand what this has to do with our work with Altmayer or the creeps who tried to do us harm in Bad Soden."

Patty took another sip of her coffee and said, "Perhaps because SWORDFISH uses Altmayer to move items and money around Europe. Small things, of course, since an art and antiques dealer would be subject to inspection, but since SWORDFISH is an official part of the Russian Federation, they can't move items around Europe using a diplomatic courier."

As Patty finished, there was a knock on the door. Richard stuck his head into the room and looked at Patty. "Boss, you have to see this." Patty stood up and left the room.

Once she was gone, Barbara turned to Beth and said, "Exactly when were you going to tell me that Richard was working for the Agency and not working for you?"

Beth shook her head. "It isn't that straightforward. After our interlude in Croatia, the Agency sent a representative to Stearns and Mandeville. They offered Richard to serve as my bodyguard in exchange for some information that we had on Russian organized crime. They made a strong case that I was in danger, and they did not want a former US ambassador to end up in some sort of hostage situation. At first, I thought they were overreacting but the partners in the firm thought it was a fair trade of information in exchange for someone to help me work in some of the less savory parts of Eastern Europe and the Balkans. I honestly had no idea that he was involved in what Patty just identified. By the way, do you have history with Patty?"

Barbara smiled at Beth's effort to change the subject. Instead, Barbara turned to Mary. "And, what exactly did you know about this?"

Mary was about to answer when Patty returned.

She shook her head and said, "OK. So, we have an entirely different operation than any of us expected. I'm not entirely sure what is going on. Mary, I think you need to get back to the asylum on the Potomac. We are going to need the big brains to assist."

Barbara was annoyed at this exchange. "Compartmentation prevents you from telling us?"

"Nope. Translation prevents me from telling you. The memory stick data is a mix of Chinese, Arabic and Russian all of which is encrypted. I've got the Russian hands working on one of the files in the basement. We don't have any Chinese or Arabic speakers at the safe house. We also don't have the capability here to decipher the encryption. We are going to need some help from DC."

"Nothing?" Beth was intrigued and about to offer her help when Patty answered.

"The Russian files that weren't encrypted are pretty much what you might expect. Business discussions and financial transfers between Moscow and SWORDFISH on acquiring technology and infrastructure. The technology is one part that you already suspect, since I'm assuming you sent Longstreet and his gang to *Sternbild GMBH* to check on their security protocols."

Beth nodded, "The US end of that company is a client. They have several different software designs that are very promising in satellite security. We figured industrial espionage was very likely."

"Beth, industrial espionage is the least important threat. The GRU and 2PLA are both interested in their intellectual property for anti-satellite weapons, and we also think transnational terrorist organizations are after a prototype that they are building."

Barbara shook her head. "So, SWORDFISH wanted us to stop the art sale because there was a memory stick in the paintings with requirements for their folks in Germany?"

Mary said, "And because one of their clients is a senior Russian oligarch and he wanted the paintings."

"Now what?"

"Well, until we know for sure that you aren't going to be snatched off the street, we are going to keep you here. At least until we get the memory stick translated."

Mary said, "And that is my side of the bargain." She looked over at Barbara. "Always a pleasure, dear. I hate to say this but I have to leave before you get involved in some other nefarious activity. Please give me a call when you return. I'm sure there will be time for tea."

Beth interjected, "Or wine!"

Barbara smiled and turned to Patty, "And Altmayer?"

Patty smiled, "I have Altmayer covered."

Barbara said, "Covered as in under surveillance or covered as in you have him in some other safe house or perhaps under six feet of dirt?"

Patty paused for a moment. "That would be telling."

A COLD NIGHT ON THE DANUBE

16 January 2012 — Vienna

After a 10-hour train ride from Frankfurt to Vienna, Sue was in ill humor. They left Frankfurt at 2200hrs and arrived in Vienna that morning. The first-class coach on the high-speed intercity train was about as comfortable as first-class seating on an aircraft with far more amenities. But it did mean 10 hours instead of a flight of less than 2 hours. And, 10 hours in relatively comfortable seats still meant 10 hours with her prosthetic rubbing against the remnants of her left leg. She spent a good portion of the trip walking in the aisles and between rail cars just to ease the pain.

On arrival at the main Vienna train station, they took a taxi to the Bristol Hotel a few blocks from the Vienna Opera House and St. Stephen's Cathedral. After they checked in and cleaned up, Sue met Jamie in the lobby. He said, "OK, so if you are up for a little sightseeing, we can take a walk around the Opera House and St. Stephen's Cathedral and end up with a lovely evening at the Café Central. What do you say?"

Sue started to grumble. The thought of walking in the freezing January weather in Vienna didn't seem very attractive at all. As she prepared a sarcastic remark, she remembered what Massoni said about partnerships. She simply said, "Sure. But why did we travel by train instead of aircraft, and now, why are we staying in a five-star hotel instead of something less ... ostentatious?"

"It's all part of the master plan, Sue. We needed to be sure we were clean. Our contact, FIVEKNOT, is a long-term asset. We need to keep him alive since he has been with us for nearly forty years. So, just roll with it. Ready for a bit of tourism?"

Sue nodded. "Lead on, Jamie."

As they walked out of the hotel, Sue found that the wind off the Danube made the already cold day bitter cold. She had on as many layers as she could wear and still move, and they didn't seem enough. All of the layers were manufactured material designed to whisk away sweat and keep the owner warm in any level of activity. She topped those layers with a sky-blue waterproof windbreaker and a sky-blue ski cap.

Jamie said, "One of our cover stops is going to be a shop where we will buy you a serious winter coat. Not to worry, it's all part of my master plan." Jamie was wearing a heavy wool coat in navy blue. Calf length, it looked like it was from another era when men walked to work in whatever weather. He had a matching navy wool scarf and a fur hat that made him look nearly six inches taller. He had a leather brief case over his shoulder.

He looked at Sue and said, "In the meantime, take my scarf. I have another in my pocket." He handed her his wool scarf and pulled a second one, this time in a red wool, out of his pocket and wrapped it tight around his neck. Sue was surprised how much warmer she felt with the plush wool around her neck, but it still didn't help with the wind.

Jamie pulled Sue close and linked their arms. He said, "We are just two tourists enjoying a brisk stroll."

"Brisk indeed!"

"Hey, can I help it that you didn't come prepared for all contingencies?"

"Right, so what's this all about, Mr. Boy Scout?"

"We started our surveillance detection route last night by taking the train. You probably noticed I had the tickets at the train station waiting for me rather than purchasing them online or in-person. I still believe there is some creep out there tracking Sue O'Connell and I didn't want to make it easy on the creep by putting us on Lufthansa and giving up our names for a flight manifest. Now, the Bristol Hotel may be five stars and it may be a classic hotel focusing on what the Austrians call *gemutlich* style — meaning cozy and congenial in case your German isn't up to speed. But the best thing is it has an old-style reservation management system that isn't easy to access even when you are looking for a room. I'm not saying we are invisible, but we are close. That reminds me, you did put your phone in the Faraday bag like I asked, right?"

Sue nodded. She didn't tell Jamie that she had used the phone on the train to text Jasper Derry what she hoped was a cute note saying she missed him and would be in touch as soon as her work was completed. After that, she put the phone in the bag well before they arrived in Vienna. Sue's view was that Derry was inside her "circle of trust" and she wasn't giving anything away because she didn't say where she was or when they might be back in touch. She just needed him to know that she was not some creep leaving him hanging out in USAEUR headquarters.

Jamie continued, "OK, our first stop is a classic European department store. I want you to go to the women's section, find a heavy wool coat, a scarf, leather gloves and a real hat — preferably fur — and pay for the items using this card." Jamie handed her a pay-as-you-go credit card. "It has a thousand Euros loaded. I suspect you can get by with that."

Jamie bared his white teeth under his exceptionally large mustache. Sue wasn't sure if that was a smile or a sneer or just a grimace because of the cold. Either way, she took the card and nodded. "I will be loitering in the men's section looking for anyone who might follow us into the store. Buy the items, go to the changing room, put them on and put your current kit into the shopping bags. Then we will start our real walk. I just don't need a partner who is a popsicle when we get to our meeting. OK?"

Sue nodded. She noticed they were at the front entrance of the department store as Jamie reached across her and opened the large glass door. A rush of hot air greeted them as they entered the store. It had been years since Sue was in a department store; probably since she was in college. Her mother would take her to stores in Northern

Virginia prior to each class year. Her current shopping habits included online shopping at camping equipment stores and whatever was available at the PX at Camp Ederle. That experience had eroded her shopping skills as she tried to balance her needs — both personal and professional — with her limited time. She knew her closet in the BOQ in Italy had a series of uniforms for both garrison and field and then a rack of clothes that looked like an advertisement for an expedition outfitter. Suddenly, she was awash in high European fashion. She hoped she could cope.

When she came out from the women's department, she was dressed in a very fashionable, maroon, ankle-length coat with a matching scarf and wool beret. She found Jamie standing just outside the men's department dressed in forest green loden coat with navy blue collar and a wool hunter's cap complete with a leather hat band and pheasant feather. The only item that remained the same was the briefcase. Sue looked at Jamie and said, "I preferred the other outfit."

"Me too, but the goal is to look different when we leave from the side door."

"Well, you look different."

"*Danke.*"

"I'm afraid I'm not going to be much help with my long-forgotten college German."

"Don't fret, Sue. I will answer any questions we might face, though I hope we don't face any. FIVEKNOT is fluent in at least five languages including English, so we are good on that front."

"So, you think we are under surveillance?"

"No evidence so far, but you never know. I figure it doesn't hurt to make it as hard as possible in case someone either might be following us now or might use street cameras to track us after the fact."

"Are we worried about the Austrians?"

"Of course. They are good at the trade and they are friendlies — well, sorta-kinda friendlies. But, any country outside the Five

Eyes who have surveillance cameras probably bought them on the open market. More likely than not, from a Chinese vendor. If so, that means they can be hacked, and if they can be hacked, we must assume they will be hacked. Now, enough chit-chat, it's time to get to work. Follow me."

"*Genau, mein Freunde.*"

Jamie's smirk under his mustache was just barely visible.

Sue had to admit the heavy wool coat was far warmer than her previous layers. She was slightly burdened by the bags she was carrying marked *Peek and Cloppenburg.* As they left the store, she noticed Jamie wasn't carrying his bags. She said, "Did you just abandon your kit?"

"Hardly, I had them send my stuff to the hotel."

"And, exactly why didn't you have them send my stuff as well?"

"Nothing better for blending into a shopping district than having a woman carrying shopping bags."

"And men?"

"Men don't shop."

"Remind me later to kick you someplace you might regret."

"Promise?"

Sue smiled and said, "Shut up."

They walked along as the sun disappeared to the west. January in central Europe rarely offered excellent weather and the early evening was no exception. As they walked up Kartnerstrasse to St. Stephen's Cathedral, the sky darkened and a light snow began to fall. An already grey day began fading into black. The lights on the cathedral captured the snow as it slowly settled on the steep Gothic roofline. Jamie smiled and said, "It certainly looks like we are clean. Even a good team would have to close in on us in this weather. I think we can move relatively quickly to Café Central. Some *café mélange* would be welcome, don't you think?"

"Along with a bit of Sacher torte?"

A real smile came out from under Jamie's mustache. "I prefer the

Imperial torte recipe, but we shall see what they have available. If not, we will just have to stop at the Sacher or the Imperial on our way home for dinner *und torte mit schlagsahne.*"

Sue knew enough German to recognize the word for whipped cream.

They stair-stepped along several streets heading generally west and north. Jamie said, "If we have time, we should visit at least one of the museums here. It has been years since I enjoyed some high culture and I can't think of anyone I would rather share it with than you."

Sue shook her head, "Really?"

"No, I just said that to build rapport." Jamie tried his most sincere smile which Sue thought looked very insincere. "You have been acting unhappy for the last two days, so I thought I should be nice to see if that might make a difference."

"Did it?"

"Nope." Jamie switched to a relatively amusing faux German accent. "Perhaps some hot cocoa for madame?" Sue chose not to answer.

The weather switched from attractive light flakes to wet, heavy snow and the wind picked up. Both were covered with snow as they reached Café Central. They stopped under the awning of the ancient coffee shop to shake off the snow and then entered a room of polished wood and brass and the smell of coffee, pastries, and various liqueurs. They hung their coats on a nearby coatrack and found a table in an isolated corner. Jamie ordered for them and the waiter arrived with a tray of coffee, small pastries and two glasses of a clear liqueur.

Sue said, "Slivovitz?"

Jamie said, "*Genau.*"

Sue leaned across the table and said, "I grew fond of this stuff in the Balkans."

Jamie nodded. "Me too! *Prost!*"

Sue looked at the luminous hands of her watch. It was approaching 2000hrs.

Jamie said, "You know, we should have purchased an appropriate watch for you as well. A steel men's watch is not consistent with your image of the young European sophisticate."

"And your steel dive watch with tritium hands and markers is?"

"I'm the one who must keep us on track. Plus, let's face it, I would look sophisticated no matter what watch I wear." Sue was thinking about a retort when Jamie said, "No time for small talk, it's show-time."

Sue looked over her shoulder to see FIVEKNOT walk into the restaurant. He was wearing a grey wool coat and grey hat and gloves. They matched his grey complexion and the grey moustache and goatee. He took off his black tortoise shell glasses as they fogged from the change of temperature and humidity. Sue noticed even his eyes were grey. Sue's best guess would have been that FIVEKNOT was in his mid-sixties. Jamie whispered, "I'm going to introduce you as my colleague from the US. Who do you want to be?"

"How about Anna?"

"Deal. I'm Bruno."

The grey man came to the table. He wheezed as he sat down. He spoke in a flat, unaccented English that he probably learned listening to Voice of America. "Bruno, you know I don't like to come out in bad weather."

"Stephan, I wouldn't have called if it wasn't an emergency. And, I suspect you already know that you have been well compensated for the inconvenience."

The grey man said, "If you hadn't paid in advance, we wouldn't be meeting." He tried to smooth over the remark by a small laugh which ended into a rasping cough. "I hate the fact that we can't smoke in restaurants anymore."

Sue was very pleased that they couldn't smoke in restaurants simply because she suspected the grey man was a chain smoker. Her biggest complaint in working the Middle East target was her sources were almost always chain smokers, filling her car with blue smoke from cheap cigarettes.

Jamie said, "Stephan, this is my colleague from the US, Anna."

Stephan looked at Sue across the table in a manner that was both disinterested and rude. It was as if Jamie had been introducing the grey man to a piece of furniture. Stephan turned back to Jamie and said, "Are you going to buy me a drink?"

Jamie nodded and waved to the waiter. Stephan said, "*Cafe und schnapps.*"

Sue wasn't entirely up on European courtesy, but she would have expected the grey man's request to sound less like a demand. The waiter looked at Jamie, who nodded, and then disappeared back to the bar.

"Stephan, I don't wish to keep you long. Do you have the information?"

"Yes."

Jamie smirked. "Are you going to give it to me?"

"Yes."

"Anytime soon?"

"After my schnapps arrives. Then you will get the information and you can leave me in peace."

The waiter arrived with a tray including a black coffee, a tray of coffee biscuits, and a glass of clear liquid. Jamie said, "*Danke.*" He handed the waiter a fifty Euro note and said, "*Stimmt so.*" The waiter nodded and left.

The grey man said, "You paid too much."

"It is to keep his silence."

"Perhaps."

"My information?"

The grey man took a tissue out of his pocket, blew his nose and left the tissue on the table. Jamie picked it up and put it in his pocket. "*Danke, Stephan.*" Jamie nodded to Sue. They stood up. Sue picked up her parcels and they left the restaurant together. As they left, Sue

looked back at the grey man who had pulled out a dog-eared leather-bound book and started to read while he drank his coffee.

When they got outside, Sue said, "I will never complain about any of
my contacts again. That man is about as nasty as they come."

"Sue, he is an ugly old man, but he has been a source for years.
In his youth he used to be a legal traveler for us into Yugoslavia and
into Romania. If he was caught in those days, the best he could hope
for was a bullet in the back of the head. I have heard stories that
make him sound like a hero. Today, FIVEKNOT is just a reliable,
but cranky source."

"So, why did I need to come with you?"

"Because I like your company?"

"Nope."

"Because I needed some muscle, just in case."

"Maybe."

"Because a man and a woman together are less likely to draw surveillance than a single man?

"Now you are coming close to the truth."

Jamie smiled and said, "Maybe I just wanted you to watch my
operational brilliance."

Sue tried hard not to laugh. She just said, "Sure, that's it."

As promised, Jamie led them back to the Sacher on another stair
step through the city. Once they were in the Sacher he said, "Sacher
torte?"

Sue was chilled and said, "With plenty of whipped cream and a
pot of coffee."

Jamie nodded and put in their order. They enjoyed their sweets
and coffee surrounded by nineteenth century elegance. After an hour,
they headed back to their hotel. As she picked up her bag, she noticed
that sometime during their walk Jamie had dropped the tissue into
her bag. She was both impressed and disgusted at the same time.

They had a late dinner in Jamie's room at the Bristol. Sue noticed that while her room was a dormer garret on the top floor, Jamie's was a more substantial suite. She said, "What's up with the suite?"

"I thought you would like the dormer. It overlooks the city, you get to see the cathedral and it is very romantic, no?"

"How do you know that?"

"This isn't the first time I have stayed here."

"Fine. Now how come you get a suite?"

"Because we needed a suite for work. We are going to work, right?"

Sue nodded toward the cart in the corner of the room with two silver covered trays and a coffee service. "After dinner."

"Excellent. Did you bring the tissue?"

Sue used two fingers to pull it out of her pocket. She dropped it in Jamie's lap and said, "Yuck."

"Yup. Stephan does his best to disgust me every time we meet. This was particularly disgusting."

"I assume somewhere in there is a memory stick or a flash drive?"

"I certainly hope so. Otherwise, you have been carrying his snot around for a couple of hours."

"YUCK!"

Jamie took the tissue into the bathroom. Sue heard the sink run and then Jamie returned. "If you want to wash your hands, feel free. It is going to take me a minute to open this up on my laptop." Sue took his advice.

As soon as she went into the bathroom, Jamie put the memory stick into his laptop, pulled up the files and pushed three images into a photo library. He then opened the remaining files. When Sue came out of the bathroom, he showed her the files. "Just what we were after."

Sue looked at a string of numbered accounts with listings of deposits and withdrawals. She said, "And what does this tell us?"

Jamie said, "Well, the first listing is of bank account numbers we already know are managed by SWORDFISH."

"Not exactly earth-shattering news."

"Well, the next listing shows financial transfers from those accounts to other accounts throughout Europe, the Persian Gulf and even the USA. Remember, the goal here is to capture as much of the SWORDFISH network as possible so the gurus tracking the money can turn that into what SOF likes to call actionable intelligence. Our job is simply to feed Seymour good data."

"As if you Klingons don't action targets."

"Well, sometimes we resolve targets ... kinetically."

"So, I've heard."

Jamie said, "Are you going to talk and watch me starve to death or are we going to have dinner."

"Dinner."

"Excellent!"

After they finished dinner and rolled the cart into the hallway for the staff to recover, Jamie finished his coffee and said, "I think we have done well on this. Of course, if FIVEKNOT was just a little younger, we could have completed this task through some electronic comms, but he is old school. I can't blame him. He's stayed alive all these years because he follows old-school rules."

"You said nearly forty years?"

"Yup. He learned the trade back in the days when it was all dead drops, brush passes and very brief encounters. He beat the KGB, the Yugo service, and even the Romanians on the streets and he is still collecting long after they are gone."

"His access?"

"Again, very old school. You might call him an intelligence entrepreneur. He built up his own network in Central Europe. He started doing so during the Iron Curtain days when we couldn't get across, but he could. He was in old-school parlance a legal traveler. He knew what sort of information we needed and found the right sources.

Today, we could meet his sub-sources, but he won't give them up. It drives the CI gurus crazy. Personally, as long as we can vet the information and he successfully finishes operational testing that we throw at him, I'm fine with paying him to collect for us. And, I really don't think the Agency has the manpower or the skills to reach into the networks that he built over years. If we fired FIVEKNOT, we would have to start all over. And, let's face it, where would we get this sort of banking data? I doubt any Agency case officer would convince a banker in Europe to break his trust for … what? A bit of dough? FIVEKNOT probably went to school with the guy or has some leverage over the guy that I don't want to know about and all he had to do was ask. Politely, of course."

"I have a hard time imagining FIVEKNOT doing anything politely."

"Perhaps not. He may be a creep, but he is our creep and that's why we took the measures we did to get the data. Seymour will be pleased. Dierdre? I'm not so sure."

"Why?"

"Because Dierdre comes from a law enforcement background. She was London Met Special Branch before moving over to BSS. She is very good at what she does, but so far, she hasn't shown quite the tolerance for ambiguity that is consistent with … "

"Jamie's world."

"Exactly. She is going to focus on the chain of acquisition and whether it meets British court requirements. Ah, the trials I suffer … "

Sue said, "Yes, it must be so hard to be you."

"Exactly. So many men jealous of my good looks and so many women … " Jamie didn't get to complete his sentence as he dodged a napkin she threw at his face. "OK, enough about me. Back to work. The real question now is how soon can we get back to the PANOP-TICON? I will check my book on trains."

"Book?"

"Remember what I said about minimizing our electronic footprint. I could use the computer, but then I would be leaving tiny tracks that might make a difference. While we were in Frankfurt train station, I purchased a Europe train schedule. Old school. Sometime tomorrow, we will show up at the Vienna Main Train Station, buy our tickets and our holiday will be complete. I will let you know tomorrow morning. OK?"

"OK. But what about the museums?"

Jamie smiled. "Sweet dreams."

"In my dormer room."

"Well, I hope you brought something to read. I always carry a long book so that I never run out of reading material."

"What are you carrying now?"

"*The Portable Tolstoy.* All his short stories. I will never finish it."

"I didn't bring a book."

"You want to borrow Tolstoy?"

"Then what will you read?"

"I also pack *The Meditations* of Marcus Aurelius."

"Sheesh!"

"You thought I was just a pretty face, right?" Jamie tossed her his dog-eared paperback.

"Something like that."

As soon as Sue left, Jamie returned to his laptop. He opened his photo library and then opened the last three photos saved in the library. The first one was a surveillance picture of two men meeting at a coffee shop somewhere in Europe. Jamie recognized both men from the briefing in Stuttgart: the two SWORDFISH targets that were now the subject of the PANOPTICON surveillance operation. Shemkovich and Chesnik. The time stamp on the photo was from 13 October 2010. There was a GPS coordinate on the lower right-hand corner of the photo. FIVEKNOT might be a cranky old man but he was thorough. Jamie closed the screen and pulled up some commercial map software. He loaded the GPS coordinate to find the location. It was a coffee house near the Goethe University Boathouse in Sachsenhausen on the Rhine. That meant that the data provided by HICU was either incomplete or incorrect. Both SWORDFISH targets had not just arrived. Rather, they had been in Germany for at least all of 2011. Interesting, but whether it was helpful, Jamie was not sure.

The second photo had Chesnik in front of an antique shop. The glass storefront showed a mix of paintings and jewelry. Painted in classic gothic script was the name *Altmayer Kunst*. The date on the photo was 10 January 2012; the GPS coordinates looked to be only a few kilometers from the first photo. The photo offered no further information.

The last image was another one of two men entering the same Sachsenhausen coffee shop. This time it was Chesnik and another individual Jamie recognized. Out loud, Jamie said to himself, "This is not good."

Jamie walked on the sidewalk around the Vienna Opera House. It was still snowing and the wind off the Danube was biting. He had his laptop case over his shoulder. The weight of the laptop, all his peripherals, and his mobile phone all packed in a Faraday bag bit into the shoulder of his wool coat, forcing gaps in the button holes that allowed the wind to reach into his sweater layer. But he knew the reason for the inconvenience. It was just one of his personal rules. On TDY, never, ever leave anything electronic unattended. If you want to keep your kit safe, you carry your kit with you. Too bad if it is heavy and you are walking on slippery sidewalks in the snow. Embrace the suck.

It was late enough that he had no expectation of interruption as he pulled out a satellite phone. Normally, he would have waited until he returned to the PANOPTICON to pass information, but he knew that Patty Dentmann would want the information and want it NOW.

Dentmann answered her phone with more than a little annoyance. "Is this something that is so important that it can't wait until I wake up tomorrow?"

Before Jamie started working for Dentmann, several seniors he knew in the outfit had warned him that she was not strong on rapport. The adjectives they used were in the following order: brilliant, grumpy, imaginative, cranky, and brilliant. Jamie assumed this was the grumpy Dentmann on the phone. He said, "Boss, given what you are doing and what I am doing, I thought it was something you needed to know now."

"And?"

"Both of your assumptions were correct. Both the useful one and the ugly one."

"You have evidence?"

"Surveillance photos."

"No chance of manipulation or misinterpretation?"

"None."

"OK. You were right. I needed to know that now. When are you coming back?"

"Tomorrow early on the ICE. We should be back late afternoon."

"Call when you return to your building."

"Wilco." Jamie heard the connection end. No goodbye, no thanks, just dead air. Well, he figured working directly for one of the barons of the Agency would be a challenge. He figured right. Now, all he had to do was get back to Frankfurt RFN. He used the satellite phone to make two first class reservations on the morning ICE heading back to Frankfurt. It departed at 0630hrs. He looked at his watch. 2330hrs. Time to annoy O'Connell by letting her know she had to get up at 0500hrs to get to the main train station on time. After that, he would arrange an early checkout, write up the report, drink tea and pack. Plenty of time to sleep on the train.

IN THE MIDDLE OF THE MESS

Barbara looked across the dining room table at her former colleague. It was just past six in the morning and at that latitude, it was still pitch dark outside. She had expected to have her first cup of tea alone and in the kitchen. After working for Beth for a few years, she knew that Beth was a night owl, often reading well past midnight. That meant Beth would not be up before eight. Barbara found Patty Dentmann already in the dining room with a pot of coffee in front of her, an uneaten German pastry on a plate to her left and an e-tablet to her right. Barbara assumed the electronic device was something that allowed Patty to carry classified on her trips untethered from the Agency network. There was a teapot on the table. Barbara poured milk into a mug, added tea, and waited for Patty to engage.

The two had first met when Patty Dentmann was a junior officer working in Dubai and Barbara was on the TDY circuit hunting various terrorists. Over the years, she had kept track of Patty's progression through the ranks. Dentmann was good at the trade and ambitious enough to know how to balance time in the field with time in headquarters. Her expertise mirrored Barbara's own. She had focused on counterterrorism operations. Barbara lost track of Patty after she saw her in Nicosia when she was the COS and Barbara was unwittingly part of a counterintelligence operation that resulted in the arrest of one of Sue's classmates from the Farm.

Now, Patty was a very senior woman in the Agency, a division chief, a "baron" in Agency parlance, and the weight of the two different responsibilities showed. Anyone who would serve as a senior would have to accept long hours, hard choices and none of the excitement and adrenaline rush that went with espionage. Add to that, Patty was carrying the weight of serving as an example for younger women in the Agency. She had to show them that serving as a senior did not mean mimicking the less-than-ideal leadership techniques that the workforce knew were common among the men who ran the outfit. It was all part of serving the sisterhood.

Barbara had been retired for several years and in that time, she had focused on lifestyle changes that were simply not possible when she was a serving officer. She had a very reliable sleep pattern. She focused on a healthy diet and exercise. And, she had less stress. With that thought, Barbara had to laugh. Less stress? She had been in more gunfights and life-and-death struggles since she retired than her entire time in the Agency. What was that all about? Perhaps her son was right. She needed to rethink her personal choices. Still, as she looked at Patty, Barbara was convinced that Patty looked older even though she was ten years younger. The weight of the sisterhood. Barbara noticed it in her serving friends like Mary. They carried that weight every day.

After Barbara poured herself some tea, she sat quietly waiting for Patty to engage. When she did, it was as if Barbara was entering the middle of a conversation rather than at the beginning. "When did the Altmayer connection start?"

"You mean when did I know about Altmayer or when did Beth know?"

"Either works."

"I found out about Altmayer on the plane when we went through our briefing papers. I think Beth knew about Altmayer when her research assistant identified the art sale."

"So, you really don't know anything about Altmayer?"

Barbara looked up at Patty and said, "Richard has been your guy from the start, right?"

"And?"

"Then you know everything I know and more. I don't know that

Beth's firm did much more than a basic background check on Alt-mayer and his antiques shop. Why?"

"Because Altmayer is a member of SWORDFISH."

"I thought he was German."

"And that makes a difference?"

"I suppose not. If he was STASI before 1989, he would have had plenty of connections with the KGB and possibly the GRU. You said SWORDFISH is a GRU creation, so sure why not?"

"Well, take my word for it. He is part of SWORDFISH. Son of a German woman and a Soviet military intelligence officer stationed in East Germany in the 1950s. That means there is more to this story than stolen paintings."

"We already knew that when we recovered the memory stick."

"Right. Well, until we hear from HQ, there is no telling what's on it. Did you notice anything while you were in Aachen?"

"As Richard probably told you, the warehouse looks less like something for an art dealer and something more like a warehouse used for nefarious purposes."

Patty laughed. She had been drinking her coffee, so the laugh turned into a choking cough. "Nefarious! You've been hanging out with Beth too long. According to Richard, it looks like a safe house designed to move men and material around Europe."

"I didn't want to jump to conclusions."

"Fair."

Barbara took a sip of her tea. "So, now what?"

"Now we go back to Aachen."

"A covert entry?"

"We call it close target recce or CTR nowadays." Patty smirked. "But we both know it's a simple case of breaking and entering." Patty took a sip of coffee and said, "You know, Longstreet and his gang are some of the best in the business. And they are right here in Germany. I could whistle up some folks, but it would take some time. It would also take more permission than I could get anytime soon. Good folks with those skills are in high demand these days as we go after terrorist cells all over the world. Do you think Beth would release them to our loving care?"

From the door leading into the living room, a voice said, "Release whom?"

Barbara turned to see Beth walk through the door. As always, Beth looked like she was preparing for an interview with an international newspaper. Perfect makeup, hair properly brushed, and wearing a workout top and bottom that was in some sort of high-tech material in a deep burgundy. She was wearing rope-soled tai chi shoes. Barbara said, "We didn't expect you up so soon."

"You were hardly quiet when you got up this morning and I won't even talk about the kitchen crew at 5 a.m."

Patty smiled and said, "That would be me."

"Figured. So, who do you want released and why?"

"I need Longstreet and his gang. We need to get back into the Aachen facility."

"Can I come?"

"Absolutely not."

"Then the answer is no."

"If you come, will you follow orders?"

"Have you ever known an ambassador to follow orders?"

"Sorry, foolish question. OK. If you come, will you work with Richard?"

"Of course, silly."

"Then after breakfast let's get Longstreet into the game."

"Dandy. Now, who's up for bacon and eggs?"

Barbara looked at Beth and said, "Are you doing the cooking?"

Beth did her best impression of a Lucretia Borgia smile. "Of course, silly."

NOT FUN AND GAMES

Jamie walked from the safe house quarters to the **PANOP-TICON**. It was 2200hrs and the cold air from the junction of the Rhine and the Main created what the meteorologists called freezing fog. Whatever it was called, it was a cold walk made even colder by what Jamie would have to do next. When he entered the secure spaces, he kept his winter coat on for a few minutes to ward off the chill that seemed to reach into his bones.

The night shift was working and the interior lights had switched over to red to ensure those going in and out of the building kept their night vision. He walked around the workspaces, greeting folks as they tracked various terrorism and counterintelligence leads throughout Europe. Jamie had to remind himself that **PANOPTICON** was not focused on a single target. **GINGERHAWK** was his operation and, based on the most recent information from **FIVEKNOT**, was about to get very messy. But it was not the only target set in play. There were dangerous terrorism leads that needed to be tracked in Europe. With luck, those leads would result in capture operations based on the hard work the analysts did this night and every night. After making the rounds, he walked up to the box in a box and let himself in using the cipher-lock combination.

Jamie was surprised to see Massoni and Flash looking at one of the computer screens in the room. Assuming they worked the morning shift which started at 0600hrs, they were definitely working late. He said, "Something I should know?"

Massoni shook his head and said, "We are just trying to wrap our heads around the video footage from the surveillance teams."

Flash looked particularly distressed. Jamie replied, "Given the way you look, it must be really bad."

Flash nodded. Jamie was concerned since it was not like Flash to remain silent when asked an open question. He turned back to Massoni. "Jim, what is so bad that even Flash can't cope."

Massoni asked his own question. "Where's Sue?"

"In her quarters. Our train from Vienna was supposed to be high speed. Apparently ice on the tracks made it more like a slow freight train. Our ten-hour trip took fifteen and, unlike yours truly, Sue doesn't sleep on a train. Once we got back and made the transition from the train station to Wiesbaden and then had one of the guys pick us up, she looked beat. I told her to put her head down. I reckon she will be down for the count until morning."

"Then we have some time to talk through what we just saw."

Jamie nodded. He said, "I suspect I have my own version of this. I didn't bring it into the box. It is sitting outside with one of my tech gurus shifting the data from a memory stick we picked up from FIVEKNOT. He had to wash it through the various security measures before pushing over to my personal logon in here."

Finally, Flash spoke. "What did FIVEKNOT say?"

"You will hear soon enough from Sue that FIVEKNOT doesn't say anything. He passes information from his own network to us through a memory stick. We pass funds to his Swiss bank account. He has been in the business longer than anyone currently working for the outfit. He doesn't waste time and he is a grumpy guy."

Massoni said, "Even with charmers like you and Sue?"

This time it was Flash who didn't want to hear the normal barracks banter. She looked at Jamie and said, "You are wasting our time. What gives?"

"OK, so show me what you have on your screen and then I will tell you what FIVEKNOT gave me."

Flash hit the keys on her keyboard in the proper sequence and a series of files appeared on the screen. The files were videos labeled with date-time groups and the collection source. Some were labeled MIKE surveillance serial, some LAMBDA serial and some DORSET serial. Jamie knew the labels identified the three surveillance teams and their shift work. Flash clicked on the LAMBDA file dated: 15 Jan 12 0600–1400hrs.

Jamie watched as the surveillance video started. At first, it was clearly taken from a video camera mounted in one of the MIKE vehicles. There was basic narration identifying the start point in Sachsenhausen named ALPHA1, a description of the vehicle which had been described as Charlie4 and the individual in the vehicle identified as Bravo2. Jamie already knew that Bravo2 was the SWORDFISH employee they had identified as Chesnik. He asked Flash to stop the video for a moment and said, "FIVEKNOT has identified an alias for Chesnik. He runs an antique dealership in Frankfurt under the name Altmayer."

Flash nodded and said, "That helps in the context of the rest of the video. Both MIKE and DORSET teams identified the Sachsenhausen location as his bed-down location and named it ALPHA1. I'm going to jump ahead since Chesnik conducted an hour run to detect surveillance. Your guys are good at what they do. He didn't catch them." She restarted the video as Chesnik pulled up to the Schlosshotel in Bad Soden. "They didn't penetrate the hotel. They expected a hotel meeting and simply didn't have the manpower to manage it." Flash used the mousepad on her screen to the end of the video. "Basically, after the hotel, LAMBDA switched off to the MIKEs. Chesnik returned to his bed-down location in Sachsenhausen: a shop with a gothic script on the glass front: *Altmayer Kunst.*" Flash moved the mouse to the next video: the DORSET file dated 15 Jan 12 2200hrs—16 Jan 12 0600hrs.

The video once again was narrated by one of the surveillants. The narrator described what he called the NSOP or night standing observation point in the neighborhood around ALPHA1. The SBS team set up on the street using two different vehicles as well as regular foot surveillance. The SBS team were using night-vision cameras so the images were grainy and had a faded green color. Flash said, "It is pretty slow for the first two hours." She moved her mouse and the images raced across the screen until she reached 2355hrs. As the minutes passed on the screen, Jamie was afraid of what he was going to see even if he knew what to expect. At exactly midnight, the lights came on in the shop and a man in a long winter coat and hat walked down the street and entered the building. Flash said, "If the SBS guys hadn't covered both angles of the street, we would have never captured the face of the visitor. But, with a little bit of editing, we have the face." She clicked her mouse and an enhanced image of a man's face filled the screen. Jamie nodded.

Massoni said, "You knew?"

"Let's just say I expected. Is there more?"

Flash nodded. She clicked on the next LAMBDA file labeled 16 January 0600–1400hrs. She said, "Chesnik leaves the shop at 0700hrs and heads north on the highway. Your team followed him all the way to Aachen and to a warehouse. The signage said *Waldhaus Maschinenteile GMBH*.

"I have to hand it to your Black Sheep," Flash continued. "I don't know how they got the next bit of video. A map search of the area shows nothing but warehouses and junkyards. They labeled this new location ALPHA2." Flash paused and said, "Anyhow, here is the important part."

She clicked on the video as a BMW sedan pulled up. Three people got out and met with Chesnik. Two of the faces were obscured, but the third was instantly recognizable. Flash said, "That's Sue's mom!"

Jamie said, "Yup. And the guy is one of ours."

"YOU KNEW THIS WAS GOING DOWN?" Flash's shout echoed against the polymer walls of the box.

"Not exactly. I knew that my guy was working with Sue's mom and a former ambassador. I didn't know it was linked to SWORDFISH until I got the data from FIVEKNOT."

"Well, we aren't through with this yet." Flash clicked on the MIKE video set for 16 Jan 1400–2200hrs. The screen showed a scene in a park. The narrator identified the park in Bad Soden. The video showed a meeting with four individuals. Chesnik was one of them. The narrator said the other three were unidentified Bravos. Jameson put them on the target registry as Bravos 3, 4, and 5. All four targets were dressed in heavy winter gear and turned away from the camera. When the meeting ended, they turned toward the camera and walked away. The narrator reported that given their instructions, the MIKEs stayed with their Bravo and watched him return to ALPHA1.

Flash concluded, "As you already know, we have identified one of the guys."

Jamie said, "I suspect we will be able to identify the other two. I will need to check with the Cleaners."

Flash looked puzzled. "Cleaners?"

Massoni said, "When the Klingons make a mess, they don't want the authorities to know. So, they have folks who clean up their mess."

Flash still looked puzzled. "Mess?"

Jamie said, "Bodies."

"Bodies?"

Massoni said, "Well, let's face it. This isn't a war zone where we can just bury them anywhere."

Jamie smiled and said, "We could try. Lots of forests in Germany."

Flash was still trying to process this new situation: "Who called these Cleaners?"

"None other than Barbara O'Connell."

"So, the two guys tried to do harm to Barbara?"

"And my guy Richard and a former ambassador named Beth Parsons. It was not a wise move on their part."

Massoni smiled and said, "Not our pal Richard Smith?"

"One and the same."

"Then they really were foolish."

Flash said, "So, what do we do about our other problem?"

"We wait for tomorrow and then talk through what happens next with Sue. In the meantime, Dentmann is working on sorting out Bravo2 and ALPHA2. Our job is going to be focused on our other SWORDFISH target, Shemkovich or Bravo1, and our new target, Bravo3. I have already informed the surveillance teams that they don't need to look for Bravo 4 and 5. They are permanently out of the picture." Jamie concluded with another of his scary smiles.

He walked over to his workstation and logged on. There was a new email from his cybersecurity officer. He clicked on the email and then opened the file. He said, "FIVEKNOT gave me a series of banking reports on financial transfers from what he identified as the SWORD-FISH front company in Vienna to several banks in Switzerland and in Germany. For now, the most important financial transfers are to *Altmayer Kunst* and to *Waldhaus Maschinenteile GMBH.* I have already told Sue about that set of transfers." Jamie paused and said, "Any chance you two have any coffee in here?"

Flash said, "Coffee? I thought you drank tea."

"I do, but right now I need caffeine and I need it right now."

Massoni handed him his mug of steaming brew just poured from a stainless-steel thermos. He said, "Just what the doctor ordered."

Jamie took a sip and said, "Yup. If ordered by Dr. Mengele."

Flash said, "Who?"

Massoni and Jamie shook their heads and said in unison, "Never mind."

Flash nodded. "Again, what's the next file?"

As he opened the file, he said, "I didn't show Sue these pictures." The file included a dozen surveillance photographs with both Chesnik, Shemkovich and two men — one Asian and one Arab. Eventually, another man enters the picture. They were in a series of coffee shops in Salzburg and in Munich. There were other photos of the new man walking into a small warehouse. The sign on the outer door was written in Gothic script: *Sternbild GMBH.* This individual, previously identified in the surveillance videos as Bravo 3 was Chief Warrant Officer Jasper Derry.

Jamie said, "FIVEKNOT says that Derry has been meeting with these guys at least once a month for nearly two years. His sources identified Derry as an American and he told me that in our brief phone conversation setting up the meeting. The Agency and Army CI have had Derry on their watch list for the better part of a year. His travel patterns were inconsistent with his stated work or leave trips.

We didn't have any evidence to open a full investigation. Two months ago, we received a report from the BfV that Derry was traveling to Southern Germany and Austria on a regular basis. Some of those reports were linked to ski trips he made with Sue. When they parted, he often went on another excursion outside of Germany."

"The Germans had the GPS on his phone tracked. Eventually, they built a network analysis of several phone numbers associated with SWORDFISH and, of course, Sue's personal number in Italy. Once they realized that Derry was a senior CI investigator, they reached out to Berlin Station. Berlin contacted Headquarters, Dentmann contacted me. We engaged Army CI headquarters at Ft. Belvoir. And that's why I needed to get to Vienna and that's why I took Sue with me. I didn't want her to have a chance to meet with Derry until she knew."

Flash said in what could only be called a moan, "Was the entire GINGERHAWK gig a ruse?"

Jamie shook his head. "Nope. GINGERHAWK is real and the SWORDFISH interest is real. We think SWORDFISH is working for the GRU and for the Chinese and maybe for themselves. Sadly, we now know they are using Derry to gain access to the *Sternbild* team. A modified false flag operation. Up until now, that was all supposition. The FIVEKNOT photos and the surveillance work from our surveillance teams were the first time we had any hard evidence."

Flash said, "Can we pick up this creep right now and show him some wall-to-wall counseling?"

Massoni nodded. "I'm with Flash."

"I know of some alternative techniques that don't involve walls," Jamie said. He took another sip of the coffee and made a face. "But my orders are we need to play this out a little while longer. At least until my boss, Richard, and Sue's mom sort out what is going on in ALPHA2. Since the SWORDFISH guys are not on the diplomatic list, if we can build a good case against them, the Germans can arrest them, detain them, and put them on trial. It might not stop SWORDFISH, but it will certainly disrupt them. For the near term, we need to keep Derry in play and that means getting Sue to work with us."

Massoni shook his head. "Tomorrow isn't going to be fun and games."

Jamie said, "This isn't the first time I've had to work on a counter-intelligence case for Dentmann. It is always ugly when you start digging around in peoples' lives. The best you can do is try not to make too much of a mess with the innocents' lives. That way, when those innocents associated with the target get back to work, their world isn't completely destroyed."

"Good luck," was all Flash could add.

OLD-FASHIONED BREAKING AND ENTERING

18 January 2012 — Waldhaus Maschinenteile GMBH

Jake Longstreet looked at the bright tritium dial on his watch. 0230hrs. He was sitting in the windowless back of a Ford Transit van. The only light in the van other than his watch was from his laptop computer. He spoke into a headset. "How long is this going to take?"

Barbara and Beth were sitting behind Jake in a pair of captain's chairs that were designed for space efficiency rather than comfort. Both Barbara and Beth were wearing headsets but without the boom microphone. Patty Dentmann offered to let them listen but not participate. In the front seats of the van were Richard and another of Jake's team who Barbara knew only as Mutt. Mutt was behind the wheel. Two miles away in a grey Volkswagen camper van, Patty Dentmann was sitting with Longstreet's tech guru Mark. One of her security detachment was in the front of that van.

Mark's high-pitched squeak responded to Longstreet's question: "Do you want to do this right or do you want to do this fast? I can't do both."

Longstreet turned to Barbara and Beth and said, "He is such a perfectionist." He turned back to the computer and keyed his microphone. "I would like to accomplish this sometime before dawn."

"If you stop interrupting me, we might make some progress. This isn't just old-fashioned breaking and entering. These guys have a sophisticated system with multiple redundancies and … "

"I get it, Mark. Just let me know when you have bypassed the cameras and the alarms. Then Richard and I can get to work."

"Patience, grasshopper."

They waited in the dark. With the van parked and shut down, the January cold quickly seeped into the back. Barbara noticed she could now see her breath. She was glad Patty gave them blankets before they left the safe house. Both she and Beth had them wrapped around their legs. Beth was wearing a fur hat which Barbara had thought looked ridiculous when they left Frankfurt. Now she was jealous.

Mark's voice came through their headsets. "OK. I am about to bypass the alarm system, and the cameras are playing a video loop that will last thirty minutes. On my mark, now. It is 0240hrs. You have 30 minutes. I will keep track of the time and the system."

Jake looked at his watch. He set the timing bezel with the luminous pip to 0305. That would give him a visual warning when they needed to get out of the facility. He said to Mark, "Thanks, brother."

He turned to Barbara and Beth and said, "Please use the onboard exterior cameras to watch outside and, please, stay here. We should be back by 3. Let us know if there is anything happening out there." He pointed toward the van wall. He rapped on the bulkhead door and spoke into his headset. "Richard, time to go." He pulled on a grey watch cap that matched his grey ski jacket and pants, opened the sliding door, and disappeared into the night.

Barbara moved to Jake's seat, where she chould observe the incoming images and access his microphone. He had set up the large laptop screen so there were four images. Two showed images from the two cameras mounted on the front and rear of the van and two were linked to small cameras that Jake and Richard were wearing. Barbara noticed Beth was standing behind her. She didn't want to miss the show.

Back in the original safe house rehearsal, Mutt expressed his disappointment that he wasn't going to be on the ground with Jake. Mark was dismissive of the complaint. At the end of the briefing, Jake made it clear, while Mutt could listen in, he needed to be ready if a quick departure was in order. At that point, Barbara thought the face of Mutt looked like it was pouting. She decided at the time not to laugh out loud.

Jake and Richard walked along the fence on the side street that led to the warehouse gate. They stopped at the gate and Jake rammed a small wedge between the hasp and the lock and the lock popped open. He worked slowly on the chain around the gate, opened it just enough so they could slip through and then tightened the chain so that from the street it would look secure.

They moved across the parking lot to the warehouse door. Richard shined his red-filtered penlight on the cipher lock on the door. Jake pulled a small metal box from his shoulder bag and placed it over the cipher lock. He threw a switch and the box began to work through all of the possible combinations of the four buttons on the lock. While the machine was working its magic, Jake reached into his bag again and pulled out a locksmith's lock gun, which he inserted into the deadbolt lock just above the cipher lock. The lock gun worked the pins inside the lock with the simple squeeze of the handle. Just as he felt the deadbolt come free, the small green LED lit up on the metal box.

Richard said, "Pretty slick."

"We used to have to pick these locks and then get one of the employees to give up the cipher. Now, it's all technology, all the time. I got us in, now you need to earn your keep. After all, you're the one who has been inside."

"Let's see what is waiting for us in Aladdin's cave."

ALADDIN'S CAVE

Richard led Jake through the warren of crates with various customs and destination markings. As they walked the aisles, Jake shook his head. "You realize that just about all of this might be associated with SWORDFISH and some sort of criminal enterprise."

"Yup. But, for tonight, we are interested in fine art."

"As if you aren't always interested in fine art."

Richard smiled and said, "That's me."

They made it to the art vault in less than a minute. They faced another cipher lock and waited another minute as Jake's black box opened the door. Richard said, "The memory stick was in the most recent shipment from Vienna. Why don't we see what else we can find behind these paintings?"

Altmayer might be a criminal, but Jake realized quickly that he was an organized criminal. They had no trouble finding all the paintings and works of art that had been recently shipped from Vienna. They turned on the light in the vault and placed each of the paintings on the large worktable in the center of the room. One by one, they carefully inspected the dustcover paper on the back of the paintings. They didn't waste their time with the rest of the Mayerhaus paintings since they had already been inspected. There were a half dozen early- to mid-20th century paintings in the shipment from lesser-known artists in the art deco, abstract and Dada styles. After the first three, Jake said, "Are they forgeries?"

"Beats me. I'm guessing some are, some are not. What we really are interested in is whether Altmayer and his cronies are using these paintings as mules for other deliveries." As he felt the back of a Soviet-era painting, Richard noticed the label on the dustpaper simply listed the name of the artist — Kazimir Malevich — and two red stars. As he ran his hands along the base of the frame, Richard found a small bulge that was invisible to the eye but revealed by touch. He said, "Jake, it looks like I found something."

Longstreet walked over to Richard's side of the table and said, "Let's just make a small tear and see what happens." He pulled an X-Acto blade from his bag and made a half-inch slice in the side of the dustpaper. Richard turned the painting on its side and out slid a clear plastic bag. The bag was filled with diamonds.

"Now that makes this painting far more valuable, eh?"

Longstreet handled the bag and said, "My guess is each are about a carat. Not exactly a fortune."

"But a nice little prize in your Cracker Jack box, no?"

"Did Altmayer say how often he takes deliveries?"

"Nope, but the paintings are in chronological order and it looks like there is a delivery from Vienna about once a month."

"Not a bad payday. Do we keep them or put them back?"

"I think we photograph them and then put them back."

Jake frowned. "Rats."

Richard photographed the bag, the dustpaper, and then the front of the painting using a small digital camera he had pulled from the left cargo pocket of his winter pants. "Hey, we are the good guys, remember?"

Jake smiled. "At least you are. I'm a civilian now, remember?"

He carefully slid the bag back into its concealment and closed the slice with some invisible tape recovered from his bag. While Richard pulled down another painting from the same shipment, Jake pulled one from the shelf dated December 2011. Again, simply the name of the painting and two red stars. He said, "Here's another one." They repeated their careful effort of opening the dustpaper. Richard turned the painting on its side and more diamonds slid out.

Jake said, "I suppose these go back as well."

Richard said, "Yup. But what about this memory stick I just pulled from my sample. Do we take it?"

Jake shook his head. "We don't have to." Once again, he reached into his shoulder bag and pulled out a small black box with two USB ports. Longstreet pulled out a memory stick from the bag and pushed it into the left port. He took the newly discovered stick and pushed it into the right port. He thumbed a toggle switch on the side and a red LED came on. The light slowly changed color from red to amber and then to green. When it showed emerald green he said, "That's all it takes to get a copy. Let's put this one back in place."

"Just curious, but what other little toys do you have in the bag?"

Before Longstreet could think of an amusing reply, Mark's voice came through their earpieces. "You need to get out of there, now!"

Jake looked at his watch. It was only 0250hrs. "Hey, I thought we had until 0310?"

This time it was Barbara's voice in their earbuds. "Except Mark's magic tracker has identified Altmayer's phone heading your way. He is six to seven minutes out based on the map on the computer."

"Shit," was all Jake had to say. The two intruders carefully placed the paintings back in the rack, checking the placement based on the digital photo they took before they started pulling the paintings off the rack. Once they were satisfied the rack looked correct, they shut off the light, left the room, closed the door. They checked to confirm that the cipher engaged properly and ran for the main door.

As they closed the main door, Jake said, "We need to relock the deadbolt and then get out of here."

Richard looked confused.

As he used the lock gun, Jake said, "If you open a lock using a lock gun or a lock pick you have to manually reset the pins in the lock." As he worked, they could see headlights coming toward the compound. At least two, possibly three trucks.

Mark's squeaky voice said, "It would be best if you left pretty soon."

Jake said to Richard, "Go out to the fence, pull the chain tight and close the lock. They need to see that all is well. We are going to have to do some fence jumping as soon as I get this door lock finished."

Richard ran to the fence and pulled the chain tight, rotated the chain and lock to the outside, and closed the hasp. The lock snapped shut. Richard could imagine the sound was also a warning for them to get hidden and hidden soon.

Jake appeared next to him. "Move to the right along the fence line. When they pull in, that part of the fence will be in the deepest shadow."

"A guess?"

As they ran along the fence line Jake said, "Please! This is what I do for a living. A map recce showed the dead zones along the way. We usually do this for the client instead of against a target, but it's all the same to me."

Mark's voice said, "I'm going to have to turn the cameras and alarms back on. You need to hunker down for a bit until the targets themselves shut off the alarms. Pulling the plug in twenty seconds."

They found an area that was tight against the wall along one edge of the building. Jake pushed Richard down. They were lying prone against the chain-link fence. All he said was "Blind spot."

Mark's voice said, "Cameras and alarms back on."

The bright blue-white headlights of a Mercedes SUV flashed across the yard as the vehicle pulled in front of the gate. Now it was Barbara's turn to speak. "We have a Mercedes GLV and a Volvo cargo truck pulling up to the gate. Looks like four in the GLV and two more in the Volvo."

Now it was Patty's voice. "Does it look like Altmayer? Are any of the goons armed?"

"Can't say yet. Wait, out." Barbara stared at the computer screen. She recognized two different individuals coming from the Mercedes. One looked like Almayer. The other looked very familiar. She just wasn't ready to say anything ... yet.

Inside the Volkswagen van, Patty shook her head. It had been years since someone told her to wait. She smiled and thought to herself, "That's what I get for working with civilians."

Barbara could feel Beth's breath against her neck. She was staring over Barbara's shoulder at the screens. Barbara thought this might be the first time Beth had watched an intelligence operation using a live feed. She also knew that Beth had a soft spot for all the guys in Condottieri Malatesta and most especially for Jake Longstreet. Barbara also knew from experience it was harder to watch than to do the mission. The laptop split screen now only had two images. The other two, those worn by Jake and Richard had gone black. Beth asked, "Where are they?"

Barbara shrugged. "My guess is they are lying flat on the ground against the wall. No image because the camera is face down. It will be all right." She hoped she sounded more confident than she was.

They watched as the two vehicles pulled into the yard and parked in front of the warehouse. As expected, a total of six men got out of the vehicles and walked toward the warehouse door. There was no sign that they were in the least bit concerned about their own security or the security of the warehouse. One of the men stood in front of the door and after a few seconds opened it and turned on the warehouse lights. The bright lights blurred the night vision cameras in the van. Blurry or not, Barbara could count six men headed into the warehouse. When they closed the door, she said, "Six men in the warehouse. Warehouse door closed."

Mark's voice came on the net. "I can delay the feed from the outside cameras for 30 seconds. Shut down in fifteen seconds. Ten. Five. Go!"

Jake and Richard sprinted for the gate. They made it and were headed down the street at a dead run when Barbara said, "Door opening. Two men coming out and headed to the cargo truck. There is a garage door opening on the side of the warehouse. The truck is headed into the building."

As she finished, she heard a light tap on the sliding door of the van. She turned to Beth and said, "I think someone is knocking."

"Someone?"

"OK, don't fret. It must be our pals. Otherwise, Mutt would have been making noise."

She opened the door and the two men jumped in. Beth closed the door behind them.

Richard pulled on a headset and said, "Boss, what's the next step?"

From the other van, Patty's voice said, "We go home. I don't suppose you captured the van plates?"

Longstreet shook his head. "As if we would forget?"

There was a cackle in their headsets. Mark's voice squeaked, "We never forget."

SHOCK AND DENIAL

Sue woke early. She hadn't realized she was so tired until she looked at her watch. It was 0540hrs. She had been asleep for eight hours. A record. And, sleep uninterrupted by a nightmare. Amazing!

She climbed out of bed, took a moment to stretch before she stood up and hopped over to the chair where her prosthetic had spent the night. She paused for a moment. Shower or just get dressed? She had showered before she went to bed. Thankfully, she had a dreamless night, so no night sweats. She thought to herself, "I think a simple cleanup will do." Next to her prosthetic was her black nylon track suit, a pair of shorts and a black t-shirt, socks and a single running shoe. The other shoe was already laced on the prosthetic. She hopped over to the bathroom and in ten minutes was back out and ready for the day.

As she dressed, Sue pondered her current life. While it wasn't easy, she finally had come to terms with the amputation. Most of the time, her new prosthetic didn't rub her leg raw. While she still couldn't run normally, she was able to keep up what the Army called an "airborne shuffle" for two miles without any pain. She had a good job and good colleagues. And, for the first time in years, she had a man in her life. All in all, she realized it was a pretty good deal.

She shook her head over her recent bout of depression and grumpiness. She definitely had to make another set of apologies before she left Germany. Sue smiled and thought, "Who needs a psychiatrist? All I needed was a full night's sleep!"

Fully dressed, she pulled her new wool coat over her track suit and headed over to the SCIF. Even if no one was up, she might be able to log on to the military system and see what else was happening with HICU. She smiled again as she thought, "My team."

Just before she left her room, she looked at her watch again. 0604hrs. She grabbed her phone. She could have a short call to Jasper before she headed into the SCIF. Just enough to tell her she was thinking of him. When she got outside, she waded into the freezing fog from the river. She had plenty of experience with cold in Afghanistan, but there was something about this damp cold in Central Europe that cut like a knife. She realized her call would have to be short if she was going to keep from shivering. She dialed Jasper's mobile number. There was no ring tone.

A computer-generated voice on the phone spoke in German: *Keine verbindung. Keine verbindung.* Sue looked at her phone. She had five bars of connectivity, so she knew she had a connection. If the German Telekom said there was no connection, then it had to be at Jasper's end. Perhaps he was on the road? Or in an aircraft? He hadn't said anything about travel when she talked to him just yesterday before she left Vienna. But he might not be able to tell her anything on an open telecom circuit any more than she could tell him what she was doing. Sue shrugged and headed into the SCIF.

As she entered the first set of doors, she shut off her phone and placed it in one of the bins. She noticed that Flash's electronics were already in the bins. Flash was not necessarily an early riser. Did she pull an all-nighter? If so, was there some problem at HICU? Sue worked the cipher lock and rushed into the PANOPTICON.

Inside, the night shift was packing up and the day shift was filling in the desks. There was no greater sense of urgency than the last time she was there. And, there was no sign of Flash at the military workstation in the SCIF. Sue hung her coat on a coatrack next to that workstation and headed to the central "box inside a box." Perhaps the answer to this puzzle was inside there.

She worked the cipher lock combination. It didn't work. She tried again. Still didn't work. It hadn't been that long since she was here. Just two days. She tried a third time. Just as she was about to kick the door, Jamie opened it.

"You want to come in?"

"Is the gang in there?"

"Yes."

"Any reason why I can't come in?"

"Nope. But you have to promise you will keep your temper."

Sue smiled. She hadn't been the best guest in the world. She thought Jamie was simply pulling her chain. "I promise."

Jamie nodded. "Come on in."

The first thing Sue noticed was the room was full. She expected to see Massoni and Flash. She wasn't really surprised to see Dierdre. But she was surprised to see both Patty Dentmann and Jed Smith. And, she noticed that all of the workstations in the SCIF were blank. What sort of work can you do at this time of the morning and not have a single bit of electronics up and running? Sue wasn't entirely certain what was going on, but it wasn't a good sign.

Once the door was closed and locked, Jamie offered her the last remaining chair in the room. He said, "Sleep well?"

Sue nodded. This wasn't going well. It reminded Sue of her final board during selection for Surveillance and Reconnaissance. She decided to be careful, even if it was among her friends and colleagues. She said in her most professional voice, "What's up?"

Smith took the lead. "Sue, when was the last time you were in contact with Jasper Derry?"

Sue thought for a minute. The last few days ran together. She said, "Yesterday morning. Just before we got on the train in Vienna." She could feel her blood pressure rise and her skin flush. Was this how someone told you about the death of a loved one? She said, "Why? Has something happened to Jasper?"

Flash said, "You tried to call him this morning, right?"

Sue noticed there was an edge to Flash's question. Not her normal, smart-assed edge but a formal tone that she hadn't heard before. "Yes, just before I came into the SCIF. There was no connection."

Jamie looked over at Smith and Dentmann. "He's in the wind." He turned and left the room.

Smith said, "Sue, you must pay attention. What I'm about to say is not something that you want to hear."

Sue thought. This is it. Jasper's dead.

Smith continued. "We have been working on multiple cases inside the GINGERHAWK project. One of these you know. It is collection on SWORDFISH and their links to the *Sternbild GMBH* project. We were all focused on the risk of losing their technology to either the Russians, the Chinese, or some terrorists." Smith paused and Sue nodded.

"The other case in GINGERHAWK was a counterintelligence operation focusing on the leaks related to the SOF communications channel."

"I know. We shut our leaks down nearly two years ago. One in California and one in Dushanbe. You were involved in hunting the leak in the Gulf when you were ... "

"Yes, when I was wounded. As you know from your job as acting chief in HICU, the leaks continued, though not as dramatically as they did before you shut down the SWORDFISH data farm in Dushanbe."

Sue looked at Smith and said, "At least we weren't losing assets anymore."

Dentmann spoke for the first time. "But *we* were losing our counterterrorism sources in the Gulf and here in Europe. It would appear they shifted their targeting from SOF to the CIA."

Smith added, "Well, not entirely. We lost a SOF support asset in the Balkans in November and a liaison partner from GSG9 was killed in an ambush in the UAE in December."

Sue hadn't heard of any of these losses. Losing assets was always a risk in espionage. Bad tradecraft on the part of the handler and/or the asset caused most losses. Bad luck explained almost all the rest. She knew a small number were losses related to an active penetration of a service or its communications systems. She was especially puzzled by the loss of a member of the German national police *Grenzschutzgruppe 9*. They were one of the premier counterterrorism forces in the world and a close ally of SOF. And why was he in the UAE? An assassination of a German counterterrorism officer? Unthinkable. No matter what, she should have heard about these cases through the normal reporting feed from SOF. She said, "Why didn't we hear about those losses?"

Smith said, "Because we didn't send the reports to HICU."

Sue lost all her concern about Jasper Derry in the blink of an eye. Her temper got the best of her. She spoke without thinking. "Exactly how were we supposed to maintain our security if we didn't hear about these threats?"

Dentmann said quietly, "Because Sue, for the past six months you were part of the investigation."

"HICU?"

Massoni reached out and touched Sue's hand that was resting on her left leg. "Not HICU, Sue. You."

"Me?" Sue's temper flare was replaced by complete confusion. "Why me?"

Smith said, "Because for the past six months, we have had an open counterintelligence investigation that included Chief Warrant Officer Jasper Derry."

"Jasper, no way!"

"You silly cow! He was using you as cover for his operation." Dierdre's voice was cutting. It forced everyone to stop.

Sue looked across the table at Dierdre. She looked around for something to use to beat the Brit senseless. She decided her chair would have to do. Sue stood up, grabbed the top of the chair and was about to swing it across the room when Massoni grabbed her around the shoulders in a bear hug. He squeezed and Sue couldn't move.

Patty Dentmann turned to Dierdre and said, "Ms. Macomb, that was uncalled for. Also, it didn't help one little bit." Dentmann's voice turned cold. "*IF* you intend to stay in this room, much less on this investigation, I think you'd best apologize to Chief O'Connell. *NOW*, please."

Dierdre Macomb thought for a minute. She only recently met Dentmann. The woman was barely five feet tall. She spoke with authority and had been introduced as a CIA senior. Still, she had seen plenty of CIA seniors in the past. Tall, old white men. Dentmann was a short, middle-aged woman. Macomb suspected Dentmann was no one who would matter to her bosses. She turned to Dentmann and said, "I don't think that is going to happen."

Dentmann smiled and said, "Fair enough." She turned to Massoni and said, "I think Sue could use some air. How about we take a moment to get some coffee and tea."

They stood up and walked one at a time out of the room. The last ones out of the room were Massoni, Flash and Sue. Massoni said, "Sue, this isn't going to be pretty, but you must listen. You really must listen. Not talk, listen! I'm not giving advice, I'm giving you instruction. Please, listen."

Flash shook her head and said, "Listen, sister. The only way out of this jam is by listening to what happened and what is happening. And pay no attention to the Brit bitch. It's one thing to be rude to us kids, it's another thing to be rude to someone like Dentmann. I don't think Ms. Dierdre Macomb will be coming back."

PAIN AND ACCEPTANCE

Massoni and Flash sat next to Sue in the cafeteria. They did their best to calm her down, offering milky tea and little in the way of conversation. Massoni had a long Army career and he had seen more than a few cases of bad news delivered badly. He thought about how Smith and Dentmann might have done better. He was certain that the BSS officer should not have been quite as blunt. He suspected Jamie would have taken care of that. However, Jamie was not in the mix and Massoni knew why.

If there was going to be a manhunt, it needed to start immediately, and Jamie had the resources both in the PANOPTICON and with surveillance teams to get the job done. He didn't expect to see Jamie again until Derry was in custody. While they were finishing their cups, the SBS team came into the cafeteria for breakfast. They had just finished their serial and their turnovers to the MIKEs. They were in a jovial mood. Another bit of night work behind them. They were ready for a meal and some sleep. Everyone on the team recognized Sue and greeted her. She couldn't meet their eyes and didn't respond to their greetings.

Smith came over to the table and said quietly, "I think it's time we reconvene."

They walked back together. Flash could see that Sue was just one step away from emotional and physical collapse. She walked next to her friend and made sure that she got through the cipher to the main SCIF and again into the interior SCIF. When they arrived, Smith and Dentmann were already sitting in their chairs. Macomb was noticeably absent as were all of her notes, her laptop and any sign that she had ever been in the room.

When the HICU team sat down, Dentmann opened the conversation. "Sue, I apologize for Macomb's comments. She will not be returning to this meeting. She will be returning to the UK on the next available flight out of Frankfurt. One of Jamie's security team has escorted her out of the facility. She will be allowed to pack her kit and then Jamie's guy will drive her to the airport. She will be met at the airport by a BSS security team and will be taken to a safe house to be debriefed and signed out of the GINGERHAWK compartment."

Smith said, "That was fast."

Dentmann said, "I happen to be quite close with both the head of BSS and several seniors in SIS. It only took a call. Let's not worry about Ms. Macomb. I'm sure she will be encouraged to reconsider her future when she returns to the UK."

Flash said, "I still think we should have let Sue beat the snot out of her."

Dentmann smiled for the first time that morning. "She would have had to wait in line. But, sometimes, it is better to let bureaucracy do the wall-to-wall counseling." Flash wasn't sure if Dentmann was smiling or sneering when she finished.

Smith said, "So, now we need to proceed. Sue, I'm sorry that this comes as such a shock. In part, it is because only yesterday we were able to confirm our suspicions. Up until then, we had to allow Derry to live a normal life, though we watched him carefully."

"We were under surveillance?"

"Not you and Derry, just Derry. He was always under technical cover but that is normal since we all are subject to periodic technical cover. It is part of the job."

"Even the Flash?" Flash spoke out of turn and Smith gave her a stink-eye stare that said "NOT NOW!"

Smith continued, "The story goes back to your first contact with Derry in Monterey. Once the FBI and NCIS took over that investigation, there were several loose ends that just didn't make sense. The individual they arrested was clueless on what was going on and there wasn't any good reason why he should have been allowed to manipulate the computer system if the counterintelligence team at Ft. Ord had been doing their job. We noticed shortly after the network compromise was resolved, Derry applied for reassignment to USAEUR."

"He said he wanted to be closer to me. It was all about working through our relationship." As Sue said this, she realized the argument sounded empty — even to her.

"At that point, we had no idea that Derry was anything but a well-respected Army counterintelligence officer. A wounded Green Beret who decided to stay in the fight. We were still losing assets until the Dushanbe operation and until I was hurt in Bahrain." Sue noticed Smith took a moment after he described his near-death wounding during the ambush in Bahrain.

Smith continued, "Once I returned to SOF headquarters, I could see a bigger picture of SOF and Agency counterterrorism operations. It didn't look good. It did have a pattern, however. It looked as if the counterterrorism operations that were stand-alone operations, our penetrations of terrorist organizations, were untouched. Only those operations that were associated with terrorist transnational supply networks were compromised. I thought about what we learned from the Beroslav case about the links between Russian organized crime and terrorist supply chains."

Sue nodded. Along with a generational vendetta against the O'Connell family, the Beroslavs worked as intermediaries between Russian organized crime and terrorist networks. They supplied the terrorists with sophisticated weapons and equipment. In one case, they even offered up nuclear waste which would have been used in a dirty bomb. The HICU team had put an end to the Beroslav network, but Sue realized it was probably one of many.

"So, the SOF commander allowed me to pull on that thread with the Agency," Smith continued.

Dentmann took over. "Jed first took it to the counterintelligence folks in our building. They were interested and invited me into the discussion because of my experience with the Beroslav family," Dentmann looked at Sue, "and the O'Connell family. By that time, I was the Europe chief and didn't have the personal time to spare to work with Jed."

She took a sip from a coffee cup. "There was a little luck in the timing. It turned out that Jamie was rotating out of Afghanistan. He worked with you guys on SWORDFISH. Jed knew him from the HICU reporting and from the Jameson rescue operation. I pulled him into my division and set him up with several other..." Dentmann paused as if she was searching for the right word, "...specialists and gave him the job of sorting out whether Jed's intuition was right. And, we all know he was right."

Smith returned to the discussion. "We knew SWORDFISH operators traveled through Europe on a regular basis on legitimate commercial business. We suspected those business trips served as cover for their efforts to engage terrorists. After all, Europe remains a crossroads and an international banking hub — especially for terrorists. We sent Jamie to the PANOPTICON with the job of using these resources to focus on the SWORDFISH network. I worked with Jamie to use the resources of the PANOPTICON to track SWORDFISH travel and build a network analysis of who they met, where and when. Once those resources were turned on, it was only a matter of time before we created a network analysis of their connections. And then we brought Patty's colleague Seymour into the game to focus on the terrorist and SWORDFISH financial network. Sadly, that was when we uncovered a series of coincidences connecting Derry with SWORDFISH."

Smith pressed on, knowing that any delay in the conversation would only make Sue's dilemma even worse. "Over the last three months, we have been working with the Germans to cover all his mobile phone conversations working off German Telekom. Between what we were doing here and what we got from the Germans, we know Derry regularly traveled out of Germany, sometimes with you and sometimes alone. He made multiple trips to Vienna over the past two years. He wasn't a formal target until December when we noticed he was also engaging members of *Sternbild GMBH*. He had no good reason to do so."

Smith nodded. "In the past few days, surveillance coverage of the

SWORDFISH visitors and the intelligence you and Jamie collected from FIVEKNOT confirmed our suspicions and moved Jasper Derry from being a curious anomaly on the edge of a counterintelligence operation to one of the targets of the operation."

Flash said, "Sue, we have two separate surveillance reports of his meetings with the SWORDFISH team, a bunch of other foreigners and the *Sternbild* employees. FIVEKNOT provided banking details that show funds transferred to a German bank account in Derry's name."

Sue shook her head. Her voice was quiet and sad. "So, his interest in me was all cover? I was just a prop to keep you off his tail?"

Dentmann offered, "Honestly, we don't know. We won't know until we start to interrogate him."

This time Sue's voice reflected nothing but blazing hot anger. "Where is he?"

Smith said, "We don't know. That's why we asked when you last talked to him." He paused and said, "When you did talk to him, did you give him any information that might have warned him of our interest?"

Sue felt like her head might explode. There was too much to understand. And now, she had to wonder: Did she help him escape? She said, "I don't think so. Anyway, I didn't know anything."

Flash said, "He did know of our interest in the SWORDFISH guys based on when we reached out to him about Shemkovich and Chesnik. We thought he might offer some of his assets to track them."

Dentmann shook her head and said, "That might have been enough." She looked over at the HICU team. "There was no way you could have known."

"I should have known. I thought we had a future and now I know he was playing me." Sue's comment was more of a cry than a simple statement. Her head was bowed and her voice was barely audible.

Massoni said, "Sue, take it from me. You can't know everything about a person. You can never know everything about a person."

Smith agreed. His voice changed to a more parental version of

Smith. "That is the nature of treachery. If we could read people easily, treason wouldn't be possible. And, we don't know why Derry did what he did."

Dentmann paused for thought. She wavered for a moment before deciding Sue should hear the rest of the story. "Sue, you need to know that Derry also was involved with a team in Bad Soden that attacked your mom and Beth Parsons."

Sue's head snapped up like she had been hit with an electric shock. "Mom? What the hell is she doing in Germany?"

Dentmann said, "Your mother and Beth were not hurt, but it was a near-run thing. They are in Germany on a legal case that ran headlong into SWORDFISH. They were involved in the recovery of art looted by Nazis during World War II. They didn't know they were in trouble until they were attacked. We have them in a safe house in Frankfurt. It turns out they were exceptionally helpful in uncovering another part of GINGERHAWK."

Smith said, "Patty, I don't know if you have heard the latest on that since your return from Aachen. The first memory stick they took from the warehouse in Aachen had some encrypted files, but nothing DC experts couldn't crack." Dentmann nodded and Smith continued. "It seems that one of the files has an outline of GRU undercover operations in Syria and Ukraine and a request for SWORDFISH paramilitary assistance in the next two months. The DIA analysts are going nuts."

Massoni, Flash and Sue said in unison, "Ukraine?"

Dentmann said, "The Russians never liked the fact that several of its Warsaw Pact partners have become members of NATO. Ukraine is an important part of what the Kremlin thinks of as Greater Russia. They are determined to make sure Ukraine remains part of their orbit and never ever becomes part of the West. As to Syria, we know that Russia and Syria have been allies for decades. How that fits into the Syrian partnership with Iran remains an open intelligence question. But there is no reason to believe that the Russians won't support Assad in his civil war."

She paused to take a drink from the coffee mug in front of her. "Before I left for Aachen, the translators in headquarters sent me their work on the Chinese files on that stick. It's an outline of a complex sale of *Sternbild's* intellectual property through SWORDFISH and the Chinese to a private entity based in Pakistan. Given the strange brew of Islamic extremists, the Pakistan Intelligence service and the Chinese partnership with their advanced weapons systems, there is no reason to imagine that this is good news. And, by the way, SWORDFISH earns a neat two million Euro for simply brokering the sale."

Massoni shook his head. "Lots of moving parts."

Dentmann said, "Especially since one of the line items in that transaction was payment to a subcontractor. The Chinese pictograph used was for the word dairy."

Flash shook her head and said, "Oh my."

Dentmann said, "Sue, we just did a CTR of the SWORDFISH warehouse in Aachen. As we left, we captured photos of SWORD-FISH personnel entering the building. One of those entering the building last night was Jasper Derry." Dentmann paused to let this last bit of information sink in. She said in a calm, almost motherly voice, "Sue, that's all we know. I want you to think about your travels with Derry. Did you travel someplace that might be where he is hiding while he sorts out how to get out of Germany? I know it's hard right now, but we need you to concentrate on how we can find Derry."

Sue nodded. She realized that she had to earn her place once again. She needed to deliver on this question and do so quickly. "Give me a couple of hours and I will have a full description of all our meetings since we got together. A lot of them are going to be locations maintained by the military, but a couple were civilian locations. I think I have some of the records on my phone." Sue wondered if anyone in the room would believe her. She certainly hoped so because she needed to stall them so she could sort this out on her own. She remembered being told more than once in the Army and nearly every month in SOF: your mess, you clean it up.

A QUICK MEAL

After the debriefing at the PANOPTICON, Dentmann returned to the Frankfurt safe house to shower, change clothes, and start on the next phase of GINGERHAWK. That meant a conversation with her German counterparts focused on the two known members of SWORDFISH in Germany and the hunt for Jasper Derry. Her driver made the standard circuitous return to Frankfurt to ensure they weren't under surveillance from friend or foe. After an hour's drive, Patty Dentmann walked into the Frankfurt safe house.

The first thing she saw was Barbara, Beth, and the two members of Condottieri Malatesta sitting around the dining room table finishing what was left of a large pizza and working on a large carafe of red wine. The sight and the smell reminded her that she hadn't eaten in at least twelve hours. She looked at the large face of the steel Rolex watch on her left wrist. She had lost track of time. It was well past three in the afternoon which meant she only had coffee and a German pastry in the last eighteen hours. Her stomach grumbled as further reminder.

"Boss, I'm afraid they finished my pizza, but I made you a calzone with the remainder of the dough and opened some red wine. I figured you deserved it."

"Richard, I didn't know you could cook."

Richard smiled. "Boss, there are lots of things you don't know about me." He paused for a second and said, "But, please don't ask Jamie. He will only exaggerate."

Dentmann turned to the kitchen and said, "Where's that calzone?" Once she had finished the lunch made by what she now knew was her even-more-mysterious employee, Patty joined the folks at the dining room table. The question in her mind was whether she should reveal to Barbara O'Connell that her daughter was at the center of their work against SWORDFISH. Many times in her life, she had to make the decision on need to know. Did Barbara O'Connell need to know? By the time she entered the dining room, she decided the answer was no.

A RACE ACROSS GERMANY

Sue returned to the cafeteria hoping she would find one of her SBS colleagues still there. Her luck held. George was sitting at a lunch table nursing a cup of tea. He looked tired. It had been a long night and likely a series of long nights as his team conducted surveillance serials across Central and Northwestern Germany. Sue had no idea where they had been, but she knew from experience that night surveillance was twice as hard as day surveillance. Get too close to the target and you reveal your interest. Keep a loose trail on the target and risk losing him entirely. The SBS team was only four guys which meant they had four vehicles in play. Sue hoped at least one of them would work for what she had in mind.

In an effort to make her initial interest appear casual, Sue walked over to the stainless-steel boilers and made herself a cup of tea. She sat down across from George and said, "Long night?"

"Too right, Sue. We have been running across Germany trying to keep up with the Bravo. We covered him in Sachsenhausen, in Frankfurt proper and then did a long stretch to cover him in Aachen, then a return to Frankfurt. Seems clear he didn't see us, but it was serious work."

"Night work is always hard."

George nodded. "OK, Sue. What do you want?"

"Me?"

"Hey, it's not as if we have spent a good portion of the last few days just chatting over our mugs of tea. What do you want to know from the serials?" He wasn't sure what she might ask and given what

Massoni had told him, he wasn't sure that he knew what his answers would be.

"George, I got the debriefing next door. No need to give me the ugly details. I just want to borrow one of your cars."

"Borrow one of Her Majesty's vehicles? You must be joking." George smiled as he said it, but Sue realized he wasn't happy about her ask.

"I just need it for a day or so. You could just tell the powers that be that it was in the shop for servicing after all the road miles."

"Ah, so you want me to give you a piece of UK Ministry of Defence property *and* you want me to lie about it."

Sue could see this wasn't going precisely how she planned. If she had been talking to Jameson and the MIKEs it might have been slightly easier, but even then she knew Jameson would have wanted a detailed explanation. Unfortunately, the MIKEs were already out on their serial, most likely following either Shemkovich or Chesnik. She decided to tell the truth. It might not work, but she figured it was her only choice. She and George had been through more than their share of adventures together and he might, just might, see this as reason enough.

"Here's the deal. You know you found Bravo2 meeting with a US person. That US person is an Army CI Warrant Officer named Jasper Derry."

"That much I know."

"How?"

The voice behind her spoke up. "Because I told him."

Sue spun around to see Flash and Massoni standing behind her. "How did you sneak up on me?"

Massoni said, "Motto of the sergeant major guild: Always know everything all the time."

Flash said, "We figured you were going to try something stupid and we are here to help."

Sue smiled. "Help do something stupid?"

Massoni said, "Help you so that you didn't do something *really stupid.*"

"Like?"

"Like steal a car from the Brits."

"I just told him I wanted to borrow the car."

George nodded. "That's what she said."

Massoni shook his head. "She trained at the Klingon school and is the daughter and granddaughter of spies. Along with her secret decoder ring and her cloak of invisibility, they taught her to lie, cheat and steal."

George said, "As if they didn't teach you the same at Ft. Bragg."

"Different."

Sue looked at Massoni. "How?"

"By working through the chain of command ... informally."

"Eh?"

"I convinced Smith that the only way we were going to get anything out of you is by indulging you in your pursuit of Derry. Remember, I served with you in S&R. It's not like you don't go off on your own sometimes." Massoni was careful not to look down at Sue's left leg as a reminder that her wound in Jalalabad was a result of her aggressive nature.

Sue didn't need that reminder. She said, "So, what did Smith say?"

Flash was tired of being what she might have called "wallpaper" in the back-and-forth between Sue and Massoni. "He said, do whatever it is you intend to do. Just don't get killed."

George said, "So, I'm no longer going to risk jail time at Her Majesty's pleasure?"

Massoni smiled. "Well, that all depends on how much you want to help."

George said, "If you are on a command-instructed job, then it's all good. How many of the team and what vehicles do you need? I need to know soonest because I need to know how many of the mates need to wake up."

"As if they were in bed yet. I'm guessing all three of them are in the weight room."

"Too right, Sergeant Major. Now, please answer the question."

Before Sue could answer, Flash said, "We need your two fastest vehicles and, just to be fair, you and one of your guys."

George shook his head. "It's all of the team or none."

Massoni smiled. "Well said, George. Here's the deal, I don't know where Sue is going to take us. So, I figure we take your team but only three vehicles. Your teammates can ride in the back and put their heads down as we get started. Sue, Flash and I will do the initial turn at the wheel. Fair?"

"Excellent, Jim. Give me a half hour to assemble the team and another half hour to get the vehicles ready." He looked down at his SBS issued black dive watch. "So, half nine?"

Sue nodded and said, "Thanks, George."

He said, "Always fun when you are around Sue. Oh, by the way, do we pull our weapons out of the arms locker?"

Flash smiled. "Guns? Did someone say guns? We don't have any guns. Yes, please!"

Massoni nodded. "Good plan, but don't share them with us Americans."

George was already headed to the cafeteria door. He looked over his shoulder and said, "As if."

At 0930hrs, they loaded into three SBS surveillance vehicles. Sue and George were in the lead vehicle, a silver Audi A4. Flash and her favorite SBS team member, Dozer, followed in a navy-blue Opel Vectra. Massoni and the two remaining members of the SBS team were in their communications vehicle, a Ford Transit. Massoni insisted that all the SBS weapons were stowed in the locked metal gun safe in the back of the van. That was precisely how the SBS team brought them to Germany from Akrotiri and, as far as he was concerned, that was where they would stay until and unless they were needed. Massoni had two concerns: first, he did not want to create some international incident and, second, he did not want Sue O'Connell near firearms when she met Jasper Derry.

Flash's voice sounded through the comms on all three vehicles. "So, where are we going?"

Sue keyed the microphone in her vehicle. "North."

"I get that, Doctor Obvious. We are northbound. Where are we going?"

"On one of our trips together, Derry told me about his grandfather fighting in the Hurtgen forest outside of Aachen. He mentioned that he knew a guy who had a forest cabin there. At the time, I thought he was planning on taking me there. When you told me about the surveillance operation that took the guys to Aachen, I figured it was the only place where he might go. Call it a hunch."

Suddenly there was a new voice on the network. Jamie said, "And a dandy hunch for sure."

Sue looked in the Audi rearview mirror. All she could see was the SBS vehicles. "Where in the world are you?"

"I'm about ten miles in front of you. The comm network among all the surveillance teams are linked and, well, they are all linked to me as the … *Master of the PANOPTICON*."

Flash said, "OK, Mr. Master, how do you know where we are going?"

"I don't know where you are going, but I do know where Derry is headed. I had the LAMBDAs surveil him. He ditched his phone, but we have a tag on his car. When he took it to Frankfurt airport and rented a vehicle, they put a quick plant tag on that one."

Flash jumped in. "So, that means we have a parade of your surveillance team and probably a group of German security service folks as well as our little caravan of crime?"

"Nope. The BfV wants to keep the US side of this in the hands of the US. They are currently focusing on the SWORDFISH guys. Once we showed them the reporting on SWORDFISH smuggling operations and their effort to steal German technology, that was all they needed to do a full-court press on the Russians. The Black Sheep have returned to Frankfurt to work for Patty. It's just us kids. Do you want me to pull over at the next layby so you can enjoy my company? I'm in a silver BMW X5."

Massoni said, "How about we just keep on the move and head to Aachen?"

Jamie said, "Fine by me. I was just trying to be a team player."

Flash said, "Did you really mean that?" Even through the digital encryption, her sarcasm was evident.

"Nope." Jamie's transmission ended.

In good times, the drive from Wiesbaden to Aachen is lovely. The Autobahn A3 is smooth and weaves in and out through vistas of the Rhine River valley to forested areas, north to Cologne. In January, it was far less lovely: a mix of black ice and freezing fog, heavy equipment haulers appearing out of the fog as they lumbered up the hills, and insane German drivers blazing past at 250kph in giant Mercedes and BMW sedans and SUVs. Once they approached Cologne, they exited and joined a similar convoy of madness on the German Autobahn A4 heading west toward Aachen.

Normally, Sue would have been one of those reckless drivers, but she knew that she needed to lead this convoy if she wanted her own revenge against Jasper Derry. She looked over at George dozing in the passenger seat. He had been a good sport to allow the use of the SBS surveillance vehicles, especially after his team had pulled an eight-hour surveillance serial. As she headed north toward Cologne, Sue was alone with her thoughts. What would she do when she got to Aachen? If she could get Jasper Derry alone long enough, she thought she might use a choke hold and save the US money on housing a traitor in a super max-prison. Given the fact that both Massoni and Jamie now were involved in this pursuit, she expected she wouldn't get any time alone with their target and her former lover.

This wasn't the first time she had helped to uncover a traitor. While on her first tour, she worked with a classmate from the Farm, Stan Cyzneski, an Agency counterintelligence officer. He turned out to be a sleeper agent for the Russian government, running disruption operations inside the Agency while monitoring and ensuring Russian organized-crime activities were consistent with the goals of the Kremlin. He had tried to kill both Sue and her mother to cover up his treachery. Sue eventually realized he wasn't exactly a traitor. He had been a Russian agent his entire life. An enemy to be sure, but not a traitor. Her thoughts switched to Nicolai Beroslav who first tried to kill her as part of a vendetta that started in the forests of Southern France in World War II. Beroslav died in her arms as he protected her colleague Jameson. Beroslav had intended to defect, but a Russian sniper round ended that plan.

It was his defection and the intelligence he passed before he died that led them to targeting SWORDFISH. Now, she had another man in her life who proved to be nothing like the man he claimed to be. Separate from his treachery and his betrayal of Sue's trust, it turned out Derry was involved in a plot to harm her mother. Had he intended to kill her? That was another question that Sue intended to ask him — ideally after punching him several times in the face. Sue's hands gripped and released the Audi's leather steering wheel. Sue's chest tightened with the grief of personal loss. The feeling reminded her of when she heard her father had died. Now, she had lost the only man she thought might have been willing to share the rest of her life. Her chest was tight and her head throbbed. But right now, with adrenaline coursing through her veins, her brain told her to fight and her training gave her the emotional tools to do just that. Still, the questions kept coming and she had no answers at all.

As they approached the junction with the A4 to head west toward Aachen, Jamie's voice crackled through the onboard radio network. "The tag on Derry's vehicle has stopped in a very remote part of the Hurtgen forest south of Aachen. We need to exit the A4 at highway 1238 to Stolberg. It looks to be about 45 minutes on the A4."

Sue answered first. "Roger, exit at 1238."

Flash's voice came on next. "Check."

Massoni last. "Roger."

Sue wondered about this new twist. She knew little about the German-Belgian border. In fact, the only thing she knew about the area was what Jasper told her about his grandfather in World War II. How much of that was true and how much fiction? She had no idea as she drove west on the A4. She only knew one thing for sure: the confrontation was probably less than two hours away.

DIVIDING TO CONQUER

After a half hour on the A4 autobahn, a new voice came on the radio. Sue had trouble recognizing it at first through the static and the encryption. Eventually, she realized it was Mac. Apparently both he and Brian were awake now and working in the SBS van. "I'm doing a map recce and it looks like Stolberg is a lovely tourist spot. So lovely that it has a small airfield. Small commercial service, but it has both private aircraft and gliders flying there during the summer."

George was fully awake now and said, "OK, Jamie. How do you want to deploy?"

Jamie's voice came through the speakers. "Here's my idea. Sue and George stick with me. We track down the rental car and try to sort out where Derry is located. Flash and Jim head toward the airfield. If there is going to be any need for the long-range optics that you have onboard, it is probably going to be at the airfield. Plus, the van has the weapons. I don't expect any trouble with Derry, but we still don't know who else is in play. Make sense?"

George nodded. Sue keyed the microphone. "Sounds good to us."

Flash responded next. "Yup, sounds about right. Can the van vector us toward the airfield?"

Mac responded. "Roger. We need to exit on highway 264 rather than taking the Stolberg exit. After you exit, wait for us and we'll take the lead."

Dozer nodded to Flash. She said, "Got it."

Jamie said, "And Flash, please give us reporting on what you see."

Flash tried to think of something smart to say. She couldn't decide between smart and rude so she opted for silence.

Sue followed Jamie's lead as they exited the A4 and headed south on a two-lane road that passed through a narrow valley. Now that they were close to their confrontation with Jasper Derry, Sue had trouble staying behind Jamie as he wound through the valley. Both hillsides were snow-covered while the valley floor was filled with fog so Sue would periodically lose sight of Jamie's taillights, then regain visibility and then lose them again. Finally, she keyed the microphone and said, "Are we going to Stolberg or not?"

Jamie responded. "Hey, I'm alone in this BMW trying to stay on the highway while watching the display on my laptop as it tracks the tag, so give me a break!" He continued, "To answer your question, it looks like we aren't going to enjoy a Stolberg pub meal. I'm trying to find the road that turns off this one and heads east southeast. I'm slowing down. Wait, out."

Sue almost collided with the BMW as it appeared out of the fog. George said quietly, "Do you want me to take over?"

Sue faced him. She was about to say something rude when she caught herself. George was only trying to be helpful and she was driving too aggressively. She said, "Nope. He caught me by surprise, that's all." She looked up to see the BMW's brake lights closing fast. She hit her brakes just a little too hard, forcing George toward the dash.

George reached out and touched her shoulder. "Sue, I know what you are going through. Shortly after we lost Paddy to a car bomb in Basra, we identified the bomb maker who created the IED. We were the only team nearby and set up a hasty raid on his house. Everyone on the team, myself included, wanted to fill the guy and anyone else in his house full of lead. For once, the Rupert involved said something useful. He said: 'We need him alive so we can destroy the network.' He was right. It took discipline, and it created some pain on the team, but we did take him alive. That was a good thing because there were a dozen other residents, all innocents: a couple of geezers, three women and four kids. And, we did destroy his network. Sue, I'm here to play the Rupert for you. We have been working on this target for weeks. We need this guy alive so we can destroy his entire network."

Sue considered George's story. His "Rupert," the name the British operators gave their officers who were assigned to a special operations unit but didn't go through selection, had said the right thing. George had said the right thing. It just didn't feel like the right thing. As Sue was pondering the advice, the BMW made a sharp left turn on a side road that headed up a hill. Sue noticed the trees on both sides of the road were perfectly trimmed and there was no undergrowth. It looked more like a garden than a forest.

George noticed her looking to the left and right. He said, "When I was a young Royal Marine, we regularly trained in Germany. We noticed the forests were immaculate. German forest rangers keep the forest floor clear. I'm not sure if it is because of fire risk or just because of a German sense of order. Either way, it's beautiful. However, it also means we need to watch our distance to the target. Our lights will carry a long way." George reached for the microphone and said, "Jamie, you need to kill your lights and slow down if we intend to have anything resembling surprise."

The BMW lights went out just as the paved road ended and a well-groomed dirt road began. Jamie said, "We are close now. I'm going to pull off the road here."

George said, "Mate, don't forget to combat park."

Even through the encrypted channel, Jamie's sarcasm came through. "Oh, what a great idea." He pulled across the road, did a K-turn and pointed the BMW back toward the main highway. Sue pulled past the BMW, did the same and pulled the Audi just off the road.

George said, "Not to worry. This is an Audi Quattro. We won't get stuck." Sue nodded as she watched Jamie exit the BMW and walk toward their car.

Sue and George got out of the car when Jamie said, "The tag is about 200 meters away." He smiled. "I hope it is still attached to the car and Derry is still here."

Sue started off down the road at a quick pace. So quick that it took both Jamie and George a brief jog for them to catch up. Jamie continued, "When we get there, I think it makes sense for you to call out to him. I don't know if he is armed, but we aren't."

George said, "Speak for yourself, mate. You didn't think I was going along with this adventure and not have something to protect myself. We both know how traveling with Sue can be dangerous."

Jamie said, "Fair point. So, at least one of us won't have to throw rocks at our target."

Sue said, "Let me get him to come to us."

George said, "Remember what I said, Sue. Give him a chance to surrender."

Jamie nodded. "We still don't know enough about his participation in this entire mess. Please do not punch him in the throat."

They located the rental car in front of what was clearly a hunter's blind in the forest. As they approached, Sue turned to Jamie and said, "No promises."

She pulled ahead of her two colleagues and walked toward the blind. She shouted, "Jasper! You need to come out now. We need to know what is going on."

Behind Sue, George had pulled up next to a three-foot-thick pine. He wasn't entirely sure it would stop a bullet, but it was the only cover he could find. He pulled out a Sig Sauer P226 from a holster in the middle of his back. He looked over at Jamie who was behind another of the pines. Jamie had a Glock19 in his hand. George whispered, "I thought you said you weren't armed."

"I lied."

Sue was now about five yards from the door of the hunter's blind. She called again. "Jasper, you need to come out and tell me what is going on. You owe me that much."

The door slowly swung open, revealing a small portion of the darkened interior of the blind. Derry's voice came from within. "Come on in if you want to talk."

Jamie whispered to himself, "NO, NO, NO," as he watched Sue walk into the blind. Jamie looked at George.

"This is not what we recommend in SBS."

"No fooling." They left their cover behind the pines and moved to opposite sides of the doorframe of the blind. They wouldn't be able to prevent Derry from harming Sue, but they might prevent him from killing her.

A PLAYGROUND FOR AMBITION

18 January 2012 – Hurtgen forest

The late afternoon light barely illuminated the interior of the blind. Derry sat in a green nylon folding chair with a hunting rifle across his lap. When Sue entered the blind, he used the barrel of the rifle to point toward another nylon folding chair on the other side of the blind. Sue obeyed. She assumed that if he intended to kill her, he would have done so already. This was a man who wanted to talk. She intended to keep him talking, at least for now.

"Sue, you should have let this one go. This entire case, the whole operation had nothing to do with you or your unit."

"That's not how we saw it."

"I realize that now."

"Jasper, what's going on? I thought we were..." Sue paused searching for the right word. "I thought we were lovers. I thought there was something between us."

Jasper shook his head. "Me too."

"When did this start?"

"When did what start?"

Sue worked hard to keep her temper. If she didn't have a prosthetic, she would probably already have jumped across the room, taken the rifle and beaten him senseless. Over the years, Sue realized that while she might appear to be 100 percent physically able, that was not the reality. Sitting in a nylon chair, she wouldn't get enough leverage from her good leg to make the leap across the room. She wondered if Derry had realized that when he invited her in.

Derry broke the silence. "When I got back from Afghanistan and spent the months recovering in San Antonio in the burn center, I came to realize that all of this was a sham."

"This? What this?"

"All of the Global War on Terror."

"Did you forget about 9/11?"

"Oh, I don't mean finding, fixing and finishing al-Qaida and destroying the Taliban. That was righteous. I mean afterwards when SF and the rest of SOF started on the carousel of rotations. Twelve months downrange followed by six months home and then twelve months downrange again, but in a different place. Hell, sometimes in a different country. What's up with that?"

Sue didn't really know what to say. She had been on that same rotation cycle for years. She didn't mind. The work was good, the targets were bad guys, and she was with her teammates who were her family. Sue didn't try to sort out the politics. It was her job and from her perspective, all the missions were righteous. To reply to Derry, she just shook her head. She remembered her interrogation training in military intelligence school, reinforced at the Farm: once the target starts talking, keep them talking.

"I realized foot soldiers — Americans and all of our allies — were simply mowing the lawn. We kill them and then we leave and when we come back, we have to kill them again. No one wins. Everyone loses. Well, not everyone."

"Jasper, we did good work in Afghanistan and Iraq. We protected the homeland from seriously scary psychopaths."

"Sure. But mostly when a Special Forces team was out in some godforsaken base, we weren't hunting terrorists. You guys in SOF were doing the righteous stuff. We were just mowing the lawn."

Sue wasn't sure at this point how to get him off this topic. Finally, she said, "You were at the Ft. Sam Houston burn center."

"I was finishing off my rehab, staying in a BOQ, and walking to therapy every day. I was trying to decide what I wanted to do with my life. The doctors had said I could get eighty percent disability. Remember, I was in a National Guard SF Group. I was about halfway through law school when 9/11 happened and the Regiment mobilized the entire group. I thought about going back to school. I had been away for three years. I wasn't sure I could get back into civilian life. I wasn't sure about anything."

Again, Sue could hear the pain in his voice. She wanted to respond, but couldn't think what to say. She had made the transition from recovering wounded warrior with the help of her family and a dozen of her closest friends. If Derry didn't have that, he probably felt so abandoned. All she could say was, "And?"

"Well, one day I'm coming home from PT and a guy comes up to me. I remembered him from Afghanistan. He was a Special Forces team sergeant there named Joe Dieb. He ran another team from an active-duty group. They had lost their team leader and warrant in a car bomb. He survived. You could see the burns on his face and hands. I figured he was in rehab. We had a coffee and talked."

"What did he have to say?"

"He said that war zones were playgrounds for ambition. Anyone downrange had to decide for themselves if they were going to survive or thrive. He said he decided to thrive. First, he said he accepted what his teammates called 'big-boy rules.' When he was out in some remote base, he and the boys did whatever they needed to do to accomplish the mission but also to keep themselves healthy with an eye toward their future back home. He said if that meant killing folks, you killed folks. If it meant keeping fit through steroids or using amphetamines to keep sharp on patrol, then so be it. If you had a chance to bring home something valuable from the war zone, you did. And, at no point did you ever report the entire story to higher. So long as the team lived by big-boy rules, that really didn't matter. He said the senior chain of command, officers and senior NCOs were all focused on how their operations looked to higher in Kabul or in Baghdad. They were looking for the next promotion and the next assignment. That was what he called the playground for ambition. Grunts did the killing and the dying; command got the awards and the promotions."

Sue knew from experience that there were plenty in the chain of command who were not interested in awards and decorations. She also knew there were plenty who died downrange. She thought about Smith who nearly died in an ambush that Derry might have facilitated. She kept her temper. She had to keep him talking, so she asked, "What did you say?"

Derry shook his head as if he was trying to clear his mind. "I said I knew exactly what he meant. I was back in CONUS, I was broken, and I had no idea what I was going to do next. For sure, my injuries would keep me from staying a Green Beret. That was who I was."

Derry emphasized his point by putting the thumb of his left hand in the middle of his chest. The burn scars on his hands and his neck seemed to turn red in the reduced light. Sue assumed it was just a trick of the setting sun. She said, "What happened next?"

"He introduced me to some other SF guys, a couple of Rangers and a couple of SEALs who were still in rehab. They called themselves the Boys of the Trojan Horse. For the first time in months, I felt like I was back in a family. We talked about how we were going to thrive back in CONUS. Dieb said the Boys needed to work together. He had some contacts with a private military contractor. They were getting contracts with US forces, UN forces and even Arab countries. Real money for not much work. We all agreed that it was the right way to go. The six of us met with a recruiter for the company. It was just like Joe said. Real money for very little work."

"And?"

"Well, I took some leave and did a thirty-day with the company. I figured I deserved a little fun before I decided what I was going to do next. They flew us down on a private plane to Mexico. We did some training for an armed paramilitary force there. Basic tactics like you would use in special operations or in a police SWAT outfit. It was easy and they paid $2,000 a day. We had to live in a police barracks in the middle of frigging nowhere but it was clean and they fed us, so the dough went entirely in our pockets. It was sweet." Derry paused at this point and said, "You want a beer?"

Sue was completely taken aback. She noticed for the first time there were empty beer cans on the floor next to him. She couldn't imagine a worse idea than drinking a beer with Derry, but she also knew one of the rules of a debriefing: if the target offers you food or drink, take it. "Sure."

Derry threw her a can of Belgian beer. He opened another beer and watched as she opened her beer and it foamed out of the top of the can. He smiled and said, "Sorry."

Sue took a sip of the lukewarm beer and said, "No problem." At any other time, it would have been a relief to drink a beer after a full day of driving. Instead, it tasted sour.

"Joe told me that there was no reason to leave service. I could still work for the PMC and stay in if I wanted to do so. They would pay me a retainer of $2,000 a month and I could work one weekend a month on some project nearby. I asked him if this meant leaving the Boys. Joe said no. We would still work together. He would be my point of contact. And, that's how it started."

Sue nodded. "When did you realize that the PMC was Russian?"

"Oh, that was right away. They made no secret about it. They said they were registered in the US, Mexico and Germany. They are a multinational enterprise."

"When did you realize they were targeting us?"

"They weren't ever targeting us."

At this point, Sue lost her temper. She said, "What about our communications? What about the fink in Monterey?"

"Nothing to do with me, Sue."

Sue knew that wasn't the case. She also knew that in an interrogation you worked slowly, forcing the target to give up information in pieces. The worst thing to do early in an interrogation was to contradict the target. You had to keep them talking. She said, "So, what were you doing for them in Germany?"

"Didn't work in Germany until the last couple of months. Mostly, I worked with Joe and the PMC in Serbia and Belarus. Same as the stuff we did in Mexico. Small arms, tactics, and some intelligence work."

"How did you get there?"

Derry smiled. "Remember when we went skiing in Austria last winter and then last summer when we took the Glacier Express? Well, afterwards you went home and I just headed east for the rest of my leave."

"OK, so what about Germany?"

"OK, so I did set up a meeting between the PMC, some foreign dudes and a German satellite firm. What's the harm? Everyone was happy when they signed the contracts. They just needed an American face to close the deal. The local German from the PMC, a guy named Altmayer, said the German firm would be more comfortable with me. He was right and the pay was exceptional. No harm to anyone."

"Until they tried to kill my mom."

"What?"

Sue lost her temper. She stood up and threw the can of beer across the room. "Don't bullshit me, Jasper. You met with the guys who attacked my mom in Bad Soden."

Sue watched as Derry's face paled. "They were supposed to grab something from a hotel room."

"Yeah, they were going to do more than grab something."

"Your mom?"

"Beats me. They never got the chance."

"Police?"

"Nope. Mom and another guy finished them."

"As in *finished finished*?"

"Yes, Jasper. As in dead on arrival. So, you didn't think this was all that dangerous a game?"

Derry appeared to lose his composure. "I did have a couple of jobs that involved trips to Baja California. We did put a couple of guys in the ground. Drug smugglers. Same in Serbia: foreign internal defense. It was nothing important."

"Or so you were told."

"Joe wouldn't lie about that. It's part of big-boy rules. We don't lie to each other."

"But you would lie to me."

Before Derry could answer, Jamie and George came around opposite sides of the doorframe, pistols aimed at Derry. Jamie said, "Jasper,
we can do this the easy way, or you can leave feet first. Your call."

Derry looked at the two men in the door. The light in the doorway
made it hard to see their faces. The four beers made his limbs heavy.
He thought he might be able to take one out with the rifle, but not
both. Plus, he would have to handle Sue as well. Derry decided to
raise his hands. He let the rifle slide down his legs to the floor. Sue
walked over and picked up the rifle. She worked the bolt. There
was no round in the chamber. She thought about slamming the rifle
stock against Derry's head. Then she thought about his comment on
big-boy rules. She was not about to go down that path. She said, "It
would seem that big-boy rules don't apply in this part of Germany."

Derry nodded and said nothing as he stood up. Jamie holstered his
pistol, pulled a set of nylon flexcuffs from his waistband and put them
on Derry. Jamie was kind and put the cuffs on with Derry's hands to
the front instead of the standard of hands behind the back. As he did
so, he whispered to Derry, "You are one lucky shithead. I think she
was about to kill you." He paused and said to everyone, "It's time to
go."

George stepped down from the door, holstered his pistol and
helped Jamie control Derry as they walked into the late winter sun.
For the first time that day, the fog receded and a sunbeam stretched
across the small clearing next to the hunter's blind. Sue had trouble
adjusting to the sunlight after the dark interior and nearly tripped as
she walked out.

PHITT. There was no sound other than the impact of the bullet
on clothing.

Derry started to fall backward and Sue grabbed him from behind.

PHITT. This time the round went through Derry's neck. It hit
the watch on Sue's wrist and ended up in Sue's shoulder. The impact
spun Sue around as she fell back with Derry to her side.

NOW ISN'T THAT ODD?

After Jamie and Sue separated from the other two vehicles, Mac guided the Ford Transit van and the Opel toward the small airfield east of Stolberg. Flash observed the same problems as Sue as she followed the van. The freezing fog made the grey van disappear and reappear at the most unexpected times. After the third time that Dozer shouted "Watch out," Flash said to him, "Hey, I got this and I'm trying to stay close enough that we don't lose them in this fog. Unless you have a map onboard, we need to keep track of the van so we can get to this airfield. OK?"

Dozer felt well and truly chastised. He had a soft spot for this American intelligence officer. He had wondered for several years if she might go out on a date. Every time he had considered asking, they had been involved in a gunfight or she had flown to some other war zone. He apologized and decided to ask. "Hey, when we are done with this op, you think there might be time for a meal?"

Flash smiled as she braked hard to avoid the van for the fourth time in the last twenty minutes. "And so much more, Dozer. So much more. But first, we need to get through this bit of trouble."

"You think Sue is going to cap that bastard?"

"Maybe if she gets a chance, but I'm thinking Jamie and George will keep her from doing any real harm. We need to know the link between SWORDFISH and Derry. Derry is the only one who can tell us." She was about to give a more detailed explanation when the van braked and stopped in the middle of the road. Flash looked in the rearview mirror. She was afraid some madman might speed right into them. Mac got out of the van and walked back toward the car.

"We are about one K from the airfield. We think the best plan is to pull off the road and walk in to the target."

Dozer nodded and Flash said, "Any suggestions on where we ditch the vehicles?"

"The satellite map shows a layby just ahead. Room enough for both of us. Just follow us." He turned and walked back to the van. As soon as he was inside and before sliding the door shut, the van inched forward about twenty yards, pulled across the road and into a dirt shoulder that was just wide enough for the van to get all four tires off the road. Flash followed and tucked the Opel behind the van. The lights of the Opel cut through the fog enough that she could see the left taillight of the van was on.

Dozer said, "When you shut down, turn the left blinker on. It will serve as a parking light so we don't return to find the back end of the car crushed and the front end rammed into the van."

Flash complied and got out of the car. It was late afternoon and the fog was settling into the valley. She opened the left rear door, took out a down parka and pulled it over her black fleece. From the jacket pockets, she pulled on gloves and a black watch cap. She noticed Massoni and Dozer already had on winter kit. When Mac and Brian opened the rear doors of the van, the first things they pulled out were heavy fleece and British camouflaged field jackets. They donned gloves and caps before they opened the metal case that served as their arms locker.

Flash rubbed her hands and said, "So, what toys do I get?"

Dozer shook his head and said, "Binoculars? Long range camera, night vision scope, directional microphone?"

"How about a sniper rifle?"

Massoni joined into the conversation. "She is SOF qualified on both the Remington .308 and the Barrett .50, but if it was me, I would give her a sidearm and the surveillance kit."

Flash said, "Sergeant Major, you are such a spoilsport."

Mac handed Massoni and Flash a pair of SIG SAUER P226 pistols and two spare magazines. "That's what we have to spare."

Flash and Massoni did a quick function check on their weapons. After she slipped the pistol into her parka pocket, Flash said, "Where's the optics?"

Brian pulled a nylon bag out of the side of the van. He handed it to Flash. She didn't miss a step as she shouldered the thirty pounds of equipment. She stared at Brian and Dozer, challenging them to say something about who should carry the kit.

Dozer pulled out his long-gun case. Mac took two MP5 machine pistols and handed one over to Brian. Mac raised the MP5 sling over his head and settled it at rest on his chest. The last thing he took from the arms locker was a green nylon duffle bag containing four sets of night-vision goggles. Flash said, "Green eyes! Which one is mine?"

Brian pointed to the bag over her shoulder and said, "Flash, yours is in the bag. On a tripod."

Flash shook her head. "Rats."

With the kit distributed, Mac closed and locked the back doors of the van and Brian did the same on the side door. Mac looked at the GPS on his wrist and said, "We should reach the airfield fence in about a kilometer."

They walked for half an hour, taking care not to create too much noise or too much damage to the forest floor. When they approached the airfield fence, they noticed multiple points of entry where weather or vandals had damaged it. They agreed that they didn't need to enter the airfield at this point, so they stayed on the forest edge and set up their observation point. Flash opened the duffle and found a tripod with two separate mounts: one for a spotting scope and one for a night-vision scope. She pulled out an electronic tablet with a set of peripheral cables linking the two scopes. She was assembling the surveillance equipment when her phone vibrated, announcing an incoming call.

She spoke quietly into her headset microphone. "Yes?"

Jamie said, "Trouble at this end. Let the mates know that we have come under fire."

Flash tried to sound as unemotional as Jamie. "All well?"

"Not exactly, but we are all good. At least one shooter and one spotter, though for all we know, it could be more. That was all we identified. They are in winter camouflage and definitely pros."

"Check. Anything else?"

"Let me know what you see once you are set up. And, be careful. Out."

The connection ended. Flash reached out to touch her closest colleague to her right, the SBS operator Dozer. He was prone behind an L118A1 sniper rifle on a bipod, scanning the airfield through his telescopic sight. He looked over at Flash. She said, "The other team came under fire. Bad guys in winter camo. That's all I know."

Dozer nodded. He touched Brian who was to his right and said, "Looks like we may have company. Winter camo."

Brian nodded and said, "Numbers?"

"We don't know. George took fire."

"Check."

He got up from his prone position and tapped Mac. He pointed behind them. In a crouch, he walked back ten meters. Mac followed.

Flash tapped Massoni on his shoulder. He was in a prone position to her left behind the loaned SBS MP5. Flash said, "The other team came under fire. Bad guys in winter camo."

"How many?"

"At least two. Winter camo."

"The team ok?"

"Jamie said they were ok."

Massoni nodded. He had wondered why Brian and Mac had moved behind them. Now he knew. They needed a secure perimeter if they had an enemy out there. He said, "Anything on the scope?"

Flash looked down at the tablet. "Two planes on the tarmac. One is a twin-prop engines with a T-tail. One is a nice and shiny small jet. Both have doors open. Pilot or co-pilot walking around the aircraft doing preflight checks." She pulled off one of her gloves and using two fingers expanded the image. "Prop aircraft has a YU tail number."

Dozer looked up from the sniper scope. He whispered, "Piper Cherokee from Serbia."

Massoni looked up. "How in the world do you know that?"

"Part of the training, mate."

"Really?"

Dozer chuckled. "No. I've been an airplane geek since I was a kid. T-tail Cherokee is a long range turbo-prop. A favorite of Chuck Yeager."

Flash said, "Who?"

Both Massoni and Dozer said, "Never mind."

Flash nodded. She adjusted the screen. "Jet has an A6 tail number."

Dozer looked at the screen. "UAE. And it is a Dassault Falcon. It is a very long-range bird."

Massoni looked up. "Long range as in fly from here to the UAE."

"Not likely. But certainly out of NATO airspace in one leg."

Flash keyed her microphone. "Jamie."

"Go."

"We have two aircraft here. One has a Serbian tail number. One has a UAE tail number."

"Now isn't that interesting? A private aircraft with a UAE tail number visiting Western Germany." He paused. Finally, his voice returned to Flash's headset. "OK, no matter what, let the UAE bird go. As to the Serbian plane, if you can disable it and not get into a firefight, do what you can. I will let the Germans know we have Serbians, most likely armed Serbians, in their AOR. Remember, they are still hot over the death of a GSG9 guy."

"Roger." Flash passed the information to both Massoni and Dozer. They both nodded.

The silence on the forest floor was broken when, through their internal communications earbuds, they heard Mac whisper. "Two vehicles on their way."

At 50N latitude in January, the transition from day to night is like a curtain going down. Flash looked at her G-shock. The light-yellow LED glow from the watch illuminated the dial: 1545hrs. She switched from the spotting scope to the night-vision scope. It wouldn't have the clarity of the spotting scope but soon the spotting scope wouldn't be of any use at all. She turned on the directional microphone and plugged the sound jack into an access port on the tablet. She whispered to Massoni, "What do we do now?"

"If Derry tries to board the Serbian aircraft, we stop him or the aircraft. If he boards the UAE aircraft, we just capture the image and let it go. We aren't going to start a war over a creep."

"Why not?"

Massoni and Dozer both said, "Never mind."

They watched as a Mercedes transporter van pulled up next to the Cherokee. A Mercedes S-class limousine pulled up next to the jet. Massoni said, "Flash, make sure you capture an image of all passengers."

Flash shook her head. "Thank you, Dr. Obvious."

Three armed men came out of the transporter and set up a perimeter around both aircraft. They were dressed in winter camouflage smocks and carried AK74 rifles with folding stocks. Two more exited the van. One carried a long-gun case and one a Pelican briefcase. The man with the gun case walked toward the Piper and boarded the aircraft. The second man with the Pelican briefcase walked toward the limousine. Flash was certain it was their primary target, Shemkovich. She aimed the directional microphone at him.

All four doors opened in the Mercedes limousine. First, two men in the front exited the car and took up security positions on either side of the vehicle. Both were European men dressed in suits and long wool coats. Flash couldn't be certain, but one of the Europeans looked like their other target, Chesnik. They stood guard as the two passengers in heavy parkas got out of the car and walked toward the man with the Pelican case.

Flash realized almost immediately that they were at the maximum range of the microphone. It might be possible for a tech crew back at the PANOPTICON to recover the full conversations, but she wasn't going to hear anything useful. All she could make out was Shemkovich speaking in English and saying something about the plans and the transfer of the funds. As she focused on the two men from the Mercedes, she realized that one might be an Arab and the other South Asian. Pakistanis? Indians? It was impossible to tell. They nodded as they took the Pelican case. As she watched, two men came out of the airplane. They were dressed in suits rather than winter gear. She could see one was an Arab and the second was Chinese or Korean. The Chinese or Korean individual spoke to Shemkovich in Russian. All Flash could make out was "Good work." The Arab spoke to the others in English. He said, "We must go." After that, the four boarded the jet and Shemkovich walked toward the Piper.

As soon as the men boarded the jet, the crew door closed and the engines started up. The armed men cleared the area in front of the Dassault and walked over to the Piper. The jet immediately cleared the area and headed on the taxiway to the active runway. In the dark, the white jet was invisible against the grey background of the forest. Flash watched as marker lights on the wingtips and the top and bottom of the fuselage moved to the end of the runway. In less than five minutes, it was in flight and heading east.

As soon as the aircraft had disappeared into the dark, the driver and the front passenger of the Mercedes limousine went back to the Mercedes and pulled away. The Mercedes transporter followed. The large lights from both Mercedes bathed the forest surveillants in light as they drove away. They heard the engines slowly disappear as the two vehicles headed back toward Stolberg.

Flash said, "That wasn't a good thing."

Massoni said, "When headlights hit you in an ambush position, you figure you are a goner. In fact, the light passed over us for less than a second and no one in the car or on the airfield were looking. No problem."

Dozer said, "Listen to the sergeant major. He knows this from experience."

Flash said, "I captured the images of the players and the license plate of the Mercedes. I didn't see Derry. I can confirm Shemkovich is here and I think Chesnik just left in the Mercedes."

Massoni said, "Well, why don't we ask Jamie?"

Flash said, "Sorry. That was obvious, no?"

Massoni and Dozer said, "Yes."

Flash called Jamie. "Hey, we saw Shemkovich get on the Piper. I think Chesnik just left in a Mercedes. We didn't see Derry."

"Nope. He is still here."

"We got the intel on the players at the airfield."

"Excellent. Now that you have seen the players, do you think you can delay those armed goons. The Germans are on the way and they would really like to talk to them."

"Don't know. Let me ask."

Flash turned to Dozer. "You think you can do something to the plane so that it can't take off?"

Massoni added, "And so we don't get in a firefight with those creeps?"

Dozer smiled. He rolled over on his right side and pulled a foot-long tube from the cargo pocket on his left pants leg. He slid his rifle back so that the weapon was up against his chest. He screwed the tube on the rifle barrel and then moved the rifle back into position. He said, "I can do the needful. We just need to be patient."

They watched as the armed men boarded the aircraft. The crew door on the Piper closed and the turbo-prop engines fired up. The propellers started to turn on the left engine, then the right. The pilot ran through an engine check, taking the rpms up and down. He then released the brakes on the wheels and started to pull away. It was completely dark. The aircraft was lighted only by its left- and right-wing lights and the lights on the top and bottom of the fuselage.

Flash watched as Dozer moved his rifle barrel slightly following the movement of the aircraft. In a calm voice muffled by his cheek against the stock of the rifle, he said, "When I make this happen, we need to get out of here PDQ. Flash, I recommend you start taking down the electronics. OK?"

Flash nodded and carefully began to disassemble the electronics. Massoni helped her fit the equipment back into the duffle bag. Dozer keyed their internal communications and said, "OK, we are going to need to pull out of here shortly."

Mac's voice said, "Check. We are ready to roll."

Massoni said to Flash, "We can pull back now."

"I want to watch."

"Me too, but we aren't gonna." He grabbed the duffle bag with one hand and Flash's parka with the other and pulled. They slipped away deeper into the woods.

Dozer smiled as he watched the aircraft move along the tarmac toward the active runway. On the one hand, a closer shot was easier. On the other, the longer range shot when the aircraft was starting to roll toward takeoff would be safer. Having watched the level of professionalism of the men on the aircraft, he opted for safety. He knew the plane would offer a profile shot when it reached the active runway. It would be a 600-yard shot.

Dozer watched as the aircraft headed down the tarmac toward the active. He took a series of deep breaths to wash the adrenaline out of his system. He took one more breath and held it for a two-second count just as the Piper started to turn toward the active runway. He pulled the trigger and watched as the nosewheel collapsed from the shock of a 7.62 armor-piercing round hitting the wheel strut. The long aircraft nose slowly dropped, scraping the tarmac as the force of the engines pushed the aircraft forward along the collapsed nose-wheel. Dozer didn't see that happen. He was already running deeper into the forest and toward his friends. He wanted them all to be well clear of the airfield before the SWORDFISH team exited the aircraft and examined the damage.

By the time they reached their vehicles and stowed the weapons and kit into the lock box, four helicopters flew overhead. Two Chinook CH47s and two Alouette scout helicopters. As Dozer got into the passenger seat of the Opel, he said to Flash, "I think the Germans really mean business."

Flash nodded. "Good."

THE FOG OF PAIN

George drove the Audi. Jamie followed in the BMW. Sue sat in the passenger seat of the Audi. She wasn't entirely certain whether she should weep or just fume over the situation. The wound on her left arm was starting to stiffen. She wasn't sure if that was a function of swelling or whether Jamie's first aid had pulled the bandage too tight. Either way, it was also starting to hurt. The painkiller he pulled out of the med kit was starting to wear off. One thing the painkiller had accomplished. She had only foggy memories of the past two hours.

Sue remembered her last conversation with Derry. He was a troubled soul who had gotten in too deep and had just kept down the path without knowing how wrong it all was and how wrong it would become. Of course, she knew from her training that was how most intelligence operations started. You take an unwitting individual along a path that he may or may not realize is a path to treachery. Somewhere along the way, the target realizes, or the case officer tells the target, what they are really doing. At the Farm, they teach that the target must know eventually what he is doing if the case is going to be productive. A good case officer makes sure well before the pitch that the target already suspects it is more than friendship that brings them together. In Derry's case, either he understood his path to treachery and didn't admit it to Sue, or perhaps he was deceiving himself from the beginning to the end. Sue would never know.

She remembered the sound of the first round from the sniper rifle as it hit Derry in the left chest. Perhaps the first round missed Derry's heart because of the way he was cuffed. The cuffs had forced him into a slight crouch. She never heard the second round, but she knew he was dead before he hit the ground beside her. All she remembered was lying on the ground, staring at the sky.

She vaguely remembered seeing George and Jamie dropping to prone and firing rounds in what they believed to be the general direction of the sniper. After a pair of rounds from each of their pistols, they paused to see if the sniper would return fire. Instead, what they heard and saw were flashes in the woods from automatic rifle fire. None of the rounds appeared to be aimed at any of them. Instead, the rounds crashed into the wood walls and frame of the blind. The next thing Sue remembered was Jamie's face as he and George pulled her by the jacket collar behind the blind.

After another burst from the woodline, there was nothing but silence. Sue remembered a few sunbeams from the setting sun passing across the meadow. The beams didn't penetrate the forest. She heard George say, "Careful, mate."

Then she heard Jamie's voice from a distance. "They're gone. They did what they wanted to do and nothing more."

Sue remembered seeing the BMW backing up toward her. It seemed as if Jamie was about to drive over Derry's body. Jamie opened the back hatch of the BMW, pulled out a large, ambulance-red medical kit and started working on Sue's wound. She remembered hearing Jamie cut through her coat and shirt. She remembered the sting as he injected some sort of painkiller. After that, she had nothing but foggy memory until she awoke in the Audi on the German autobahn.

George looked over at Sue. "Back to the land of the living?"

"Barely. Where are we?"

"About 25KM from Wiesbaden."

Sue started to sit up. The reclined seat and the tight seat belt prevented her from doing anything quickly. She finally relaxed back into the seat. "I've been out for a while."

"Well, you did get shot."

"Yup. It's not the first time."

"Well, this time it was not real serious. I didn't realize that Jamie had been a medic before he took the dark path."

"Me neither."

"Well, he did some dandy field surgery right there in the meadow. Seems your watch took most of the impact. You ended up with a pretty big hole from the tumbling round. You won't be doing any press-ups anytime soon. Jamie says you will need a visit to the Wiesbaden hospital. He just stopped the bleeding and patched you up as best he could. A few stitches, some antibiotics and a shot for the pain. They will need to dig the bullet out of your shoulder at the hospital."

"Dandy. I don't remember any of that."

"Well, you also were a bit stressed. A bit of shock, eh?"

"Derry?"

"In the back of Jamie's truck."

"What now?"

George smiled. "Beats me. I'm just the driver."

"And I am living in the fog of pain."

"Sorry about that Sue. Nothing else I can say."

"Thanks, George. I'm just glad you were there."

"And, I'm glad you are still with us."

Sue didn't hear George's last comment. She had already dropped off to sleep.

SOMETHING NEW AND DIFFERENT

19 January 2012 — PANOPTICON

Flash sat behind her computer screen inside the box inside the PANOPTICON SCIF. She looked out at the team working into the late afternoon. Smith had let her know that she should take a day or two off, but she couldn't relax. After she visited Sue in the US Air Force Wiesbaden medical facility, she needed time to decompress. For Flash, that meant time spent on the computer looking at the various loose threads left in the recent mission. There were just too many for her to accept as "mission accomplished." She heard the door open and looked up to see Smith, Massoni, and Jamie walk in.

Jamie said, "How's our impatient patient?"

Flash shook her head. "Impatient is right. She has already annoyed three nurses and two orderlies. As I walked to her room, the senior nurse on the ward, an Air Force major, asked me to let Sue know that she needs to stuff a sock in it if she doesn't want to end up with an Article 15 while she is there."

Smith shook his head. "I will take a drive down to Wiesbaden and see if I can do some attitude adjustment therapy on Chief O'Connell. What did they say about her injury?"

Flash noticed Smith wince as he mentioned the bullet wound. She wondered how long it would be before he got over his own trauma. This was not the time for smart-assed remarks, so she gave him the story straight up. "The bullet wound is ugly. Jamie's first aid made it less traumatic than it might have been. It was a rifle round that went through Derry, shattered Sue's watch, and then tumbled a bit. They dug the bullet and pieces of her watch out of her shoulder. Lots of trauma, but no arteries or nerves damaged. It went through Sue's left shoulder sideways rather than what the doctor described in his medical science as pointy end first."

Massoni said, "Flash, he was just trying to make it easy for you to understand."

Flash scratched her nose with the middle finger of her right hand and continued. "He said there was a fair bit of muscle damage but that he expected a full recovery after a few months of PT. No infection. She won't be doing pull-ups for a bit."

Smith said, "Good news."

Jamie said, "Especially since we have a new plan for her."

Flash said, "We?"

Smith said, "Let me explain."

Massoni said, "I already heard some of this. I'm going to try to make some real coffee. Flash, you need some?"

Flash nodded. "Always, Sergeant Major. Always."

Massoni walked out of the box leaving Smith and Jamie sitting next to Flash.

Jamie spoke first. "So, we are pretty happy about how things worked out."

Flash tried not to sound too sarcastic. "Really? Derry's dead. Sue's in the hospital. The creeps got away with the plans to the anti-satellite design. Real success for GINGERHAWK."

Smith looked at Flash. His stare said it all: Cool it!

Jamie continued. "OK, so we wanted to debrief Derry. We couldn't have predicted that SWORDFISH creeps would kill him. As to Sue's wound, again, I tried everything I could to keep her out of harm's way. That, as you know well, is impossible."

Flash nodded. "OK, after trying for years to keep O'Connell out of trouble, I will give you that."

"The Germans stopped the SWORDFISH crew at the airport.

A couple of them tried to be heroes and got into a gunfight with the Germans." Jamie paused and raised the forefinger of his right hand. "Note to self: do not get into a gunfight with GSG9. Especially if they blame you for the death of one of their men."

"Resolved them."

Jamie nodded. "Kinetically."

"All of them? Shemkovich included?"

"They all had guns."

Flash nodded. "No doubt. But the jet jocks got away with the plans."

"They got away with some plans."

"Not *the plans?*"

"Nope."

"When were you going to tell me?"

"I'm telling you now."

"Did you know before this?"

Smith interceded. "When we briefed you in Heidelberg, we didn't know. While you guys were doing what you were doing here in the PANOPTICON, I joined Patty Dentmann for a dinner with the owners of *Sternbild GMBH*. We explained the legal consequences of their negotiations with SWORDFISH and the foreigners. I think they were surprised. These guys are tech geeks who thought they were just getting venture capital money. They were convinced by Derry that it was all good and the others were from Silicon Valley. They offered to help us. They explained that an early prototype of their design had failed both simulation testing and bench testing. They offered to provide that failed design."

Jamie continued, "It's like most technology. We aren't going to stop our adversaries from getting technology. All we can reasonably do is delay them."

"The gurus in the Pentagon say that the plans received from the German firm could delay any adversary's anti-satellite program for up to two years. We are assuming a mix of terrorist groups involved so they might not have the ability to sort out the problems for some time. Their patrons in the UAE, or Pakistan, or China may move more quickly, but by that time we should have already launched a countermeasure."

"So, this was all a massive deception operation."

"Flash, it wasn't deception until we realized that was the only alternative. The SWORDFISH team were already well down the road of acquiring the technology. The best we could do was disrupt and deceive. As you know, sometimes in our CT operations, we must disrupt rather than finish the target."

Flash shook her head. Massoni walked in and handed her a steaming cup of black coffee. "Caffeine," was all he said to Flash. He turned to Smith and asked, "Boss, have you got to the plan yet?"

"Sergeant Major, Flash had to know the end of the story before we gave her a new plan."

"Yes sir." Massoni smiled and looked at Flash. "You are going to love this."

"Really?"

"No. He ordered me to say that."

Smith laughed and said, "As if Sergeant Major Massoni ever followed my orders."

"Sometimes I do, Boss."

Jamie said, "Flash, give them a chance to explain."

Smith said, "I found out last week that there is a new commander coming in for HICU. He's coming from the Navy side of the SOF assault squadrons. He wants to bring with him his Navy master chief as senior NCO. I think it is a good idea and I asked Jim if he would be willing to move. He said he would as long as it wasn't back to Ft. Bragg."

Massoni nodded. "Been there, done that, never again."

Flash said, "And?"

"Well, it turns out that both the Agency and the SOF command wanted to expand the SOF presence here in the PANOPTICON," Smith explained. "I've been tapped to run this place when Jamie returns to his headquarters job."

Jamie nodded. "Pray for me."

"I told the commander I would do so if I could pick a small team to come with me. He tolerates my requests. Jim is coming with me. I would like a shit-hot analyst to come with me as well. Know anyone who might be interested?"

Flash said, "Do I get to play with all these systems?"

"Up to a point."

"Up to a point?"

Massoni said, "Up to a point when you start to break them."

Flash smiled. Her expression changed. "What about Sue? Who in the world is going to take care of Sue?"

Smith said, "Jamie."

Flash looked puzzled. "Jamie?"

"It turns out Patty Dentmann really wants a SOF collector on her private army at headquarters," Jamie said. "So far, it's just me, an old teammate named Richard, and a tech guy. She wants another operator who is willing to color outside the lines."

Massoni laughed. "Is that what you call it?"

Jamie pulled his most serious face. "Yup."

Flash shook her head. "O'Connell and Jamie working together full time. It might be the end of the global world order!"

Massoni lifted his mug. "I'll drink to that."

JUST A LITTLE BIT OF HARM

20 January 2012 — Sachsenhausen

Georg Chesnik was in a hurry. He needed to close the shop and take the night train to Vienna. From Vienna, he would drive to Bratislava, and SWORDFISH would fly him to their headquarters in St. Petersburg. First, he needed to carefully eliminate any link between his alias, Friedrich Altmayer, and SWORDFISH. Altmayer would simply disappear. German authorities would be puzzled at first and eventually wonder what happened to the East German gentleman who ran an art gallery in Vienna and in Frankfurt. The warehouse in Aachen would be a problem, but there were few who knew that it was anything but a trans-shipment point for art purchased in Frankfurt and shipped to the rest of Europe. The SWORDFISH team had already purged all the intelligence material out of the art. The diamonds were packed safely away in his travel case. And the rest of the art? Well, the rest would be considered sunk cost. SWORDFISH seniors knew that operations had a life cycle. Eventually, all clandestine operations either ended or were exposed. In this case, it was both.

Chesnik was sad to leave this job. It had been rather nice to play a wealthy art dealer with seemingly unlimited funds, good taste in art, clothes, wine, and cars. It wasn't the first time he had served undercover, but it was absolutely the first time that he had enjoyed the cover-persona lifestyle. In the past, when he was working for the *Ministerium fur Staatssicherheit* or the Stasi, he played multiple roles both in the German Democratic Republic and West Germany. Most of

them required him to take on the cover of some member of the pro-
letariat. He wore shabby clothes and worked construction jobs just
long enough for him to identify a target. Those jobs typically ended
with the arrest or kidnap or death of the target.

After 1989, he worked multiple clerical jobs until approached
by former colleagues from the GRU. They were starting a private
security firm and needed citizens of the new Europe to help build
their network. By that time, Chesnik was a German citizen with an
EU passport. He was happy to return to clandestine work. And so,
SWORDFISH and Chesnik created a "flock of birds" or *vogelschwarm*
for SWORDFISH. The first step was the creation of the man, Friedrich Altmayer. A wealthy, cultured man with no past and a promising
future. A little seed money, a few Russian icons and other artifacts
from the collapsing USSR, and a few of his old contacts for the office
and the transformation was complete.

His new shop just down the street from the Spanish Riding School
on Michaelerplatz in Vienna became well known to the wealthy of
Vienna and their friends throughout Europe. After that, it was a short
step to open the shop in Sachsenhausen on the south bank of the
Main, and soon the wealthy burghers of Frankfurt were coming to
call. SWORDFISH had the means to deliver art looted first by the
Nazis and then by the occupying Soviet Army. It took no time at all
for Altmayer Kunst to be a self-funded arm of the SWORDFISH
smuggling and intelligence network. Now, it was all turning to dust.

Chesnik was an intelligence officer through and through: a *Chekist*
in Russian slang. He had traveled for SWORDFISH to accomplish
many different tasks in Europe. He designed operations that served
as his flock of birds like the German name of the operation. Those
sometimes included a bit of wet work. It wasn't all that hard, given
the fact that the police were always looking for the usual suspects
rather than a cultured man. A Russian dissident here, a Balkan crime
boss there. It was simply too easy to kill and escape.

And he set up the intelligence network that sold information to various terrorist groups. The Americans and the NATO allies working

the terrorist target assumed the only threat was from the dangerous, but disorganized terrorists. They never realized that their reporting networks could be penetrated by outsiders willing to sell this information to the highest bidders. Indeed, there was enough Arab and Iranian money out there that SWORDFISH made a profit on that network as well.

Chesnik was most proud of his North American successes. He provided the money for an angry, retired US soldier to start a small security firm to join his flock. He sent them leads to countries and criminal networks that needed specialized military training. Their clients paid well and SWORDFISH took a small percentage. When the soldier reported that he had an active-duty officer on the books, SWORDFISH seniors sent Chesnik to the US to determine whether this Jasper Derry would be useful. Chesnik served as his recruiter and then his handler when Derry moved to Germany. Whether Derry ever realized he was a spy for a private arm of the GRU mattered little to Chesnik and even less to SWORDFISH. Derry accomplished simple jobs and was paid what he was worth.

When he was no longer useful, he was eliminated.

Unfortunately, the SWORDFISH plans in Germany had been frustrated by the American special services. Chesnik knew that no operation ran forever, and now his flock was falling to pieces. Still, he was disappointed. Before leaving Germany, the GRU manager of SWORDFISH, Colonel Michel Istorik, called Chesnik on his sterile emergency phone. Istorik said one word in German — *Rabe* — and then hung up. Like the raven mentioned in the call, it was time for Chesnik to fly.

He checked the office and then rechecked the old-style briefcase that he had used when he worked for the Stasi. All was in order. Everything associated with poor Friedrich Altmayer was in the weighted briefcase including the revolver that he used for wet work. It was a French Manurhin, chambered in caliber .38. Considered by the French police to be a superior firearm, it was virtually unknown in Germany. He had chosen it less for its qualities than for what it wasn't: it wasn't a German pistol and it didn't eject spent cartridges. Any European service tracing the bullets from the pistol would have to assume it was a French police revolver lost, stolen, or sold years ago. That made it a very deniable weapon if/when he needed it. Chesnik would drop it along with the briefcase in the Main River. If the briefcase ever came to the surface, the assumption would be that Altmayer was the victim of a violent crime and was somewhere in the river. Frankfurt authorities would look for a body for a short time and then give up.

Chesnik's right hand touched his suit. His next identity including passport and a wallet full of identification and Euros sat comfortably in the interior pocket. He focused his attention on the new identity: Georg Messer. Out of vanity, he kept his real first name for this identity. And, there were many families in Germany that carried the name Messer just as there were many in England that carried the name Cooper or Smith. It was an easy name to remember and only a little ironic. Knife. Well, that was what he had been and would be again when SWORDFISH asked him to be so. He looked at his Swiss gold watch. It was 1600hrs. Just dark enough for him to walk to the river and drop his briefcase into the water. Then, take a taxi to the train station and the ICE train to Vienna. He turned one last time to look at the oak desk where so much had been accomplished and he spun around to leave. However, he wasn't the one to turn off the lights in the office.

In the dark, he never saw the fist. The punch hit him squarely in the nose and the pain blinded him for a moment as he fell back against the desk. When his eyes finally focused, he saw a small figure dressed entirely in black. A black hood and a black scarf obscured the face. Yellow shooting glasses protected the eyes. A strange thought ran through his brain as he regained his composure: were the eyes blue, green or grey? Certainly light. Not brown. Why did he care? It was just something that came to mind.

Next came a slap across the face. Not a woman's angry slap. Rather, an interrogator's slap. Full hand and with the full force of arm and shoulder. Early in his days with the Stasi, he had watched one of the interrogators work a prisoner. At first, he thought a slap was too gentle. Then he realized that the interrogator's slap had broken the prisoner's cheekbone. This slap wasn't that hard. Chesnik's memory was enough that he knew this was only the beginning. He needed to get out of the way of this attacker.

Chesnik stayed fit through all these years of living well. He trained in one of the most prestigious gymnasiums in Frankfurt, focusing on balance and strength using rings, pommel horse and parallel bars. He knew in his trade an unfit man was a dead man. He pressed his hands behind him and used the oak desk as leverage to vault over the desk. This wouldn't protect him from a pistol, but he knew that if his attacker had a pistol, he would already be dead. Now the desk was between them.

He knew a moment was all he had. Unfortunately, his pistol was in the briefcase with his Altmayer identity. He looked in the darkness for the briefcase. He wasn't sure, but he thought it might be to the left of the desk. He thought about what else he could use as a weapon. The long letter opener? The paperweight?

Before Chesnik could decide, another masked attacker appeared out of the darkness. The two attackers reached for the edge of the desk and shoved it. The heavy desk accelerated and pinned Chesnik against the wall. The attackers heard the crack of Chesnik's broken femur. The first attacker reached down with a gloved hand and grabbed the handle of the briefcase and moved it just out of reach of Chesnik.

Chesnik had heard the crack of the broken leg. He hadn't felt any pain yet, but he knew it would come soon enough. The shock of the injury prevented the nerves from registering pain. He was pinned to the wall. Whether it was a compound fracture or a simple fracture was not important. He expected the next thing to happen was a bullet to the brain. Just SWORDFISH cleaning up another loose end. When it didn't happen, he was puzzled. The only thing he knew for certain was Georg Messer wasn't going to be taking the night train to Vienna.

The two attackers slipped out the back of *Altmayer Kunst*. The sound of the German police cruisers' sirens echoed in the narrow streets of Sachsenhausen, warning citizens to stay clear. Two cruisers and a van, all in the green and white livery of the police, pulled up in front of the antique store. The rear doors of the van opened and men in black jumpsuits, helmets and gas masks jumped out carrying MP5 machine pistols. The last man out transitioned to the lead of the squad. He was carrying a black bulletproof shield. They waited at the door in stack formation as two policemen from one of the cruisers walked up to the door. One shouted, *"POLIZEI!"* The second one used a two-handed grip door ram against the lock, shattering the door. The men in black raced inside.

Barbara O'Connell and Jake Longstreet walked to the BMW i3 waiting two streets over from the antique shop. They had already pocketed their balaclavas and just looked like a couple at the end of the day walking toward their car on their way home. Longstreet was carrying a leather suitcase, little more than an overnight bag. As they drove across the bridge into Frankfurt, Jake looked over at Barbara. "Traffic is terrible this time of day."

Barbara smiled. She had a brown leather coat covering her black slacks and black hooded sweatshirt. She said, "Luckily we got started before the traffic really jammed up in Sachsenhausen."

"True."

When they walked into the safe house in Frankfurt, Patty Dentmann was waiting for them. "I thought I told you to stay put."

Jake shrugged. "We weren't out for long. We just needed to stretch our legs. It gets stuffy being kept inside all the time."

"Exercise?"

Barbara said, "Well, we only did a little bit of harm."

"Well, then that's ok, is it?"

Barbara nodded as she unzipped the black hooded sweatshirt. "I thought so."

Jake said, "I thought you might want to see what Chesnik was taking on his trip."

"Secrets?"

Jake shook his head. "Nope, just diamonds. Lots and lots of diamonds."

Beth, Mutt and Mark came into the room. Beth said, "Did we miss something?"

Mark squeaked, "I always miss the good stuff."

RETURN TO CONUS

Jamie walked into Sue's hospital room. She was sitting in a chair next to the hospital bed. There was a drip attached to her arm and an IV bag hanging from a hook behind the chair. She had a pulsometer on her right hand and an electronic tablet in her left hand.

"What are you reading?"

"News."

"Good news?"

"Not exactly. It looks like there is trouble in Syria. And, trouble in Ukraine." She shook her head. It was clearly a Russian-planned program to create some new sort of crisis in Europe.

"Just like Dentmann said."

"How did Dentmann know?"

"Your mom."

"Mom?"

"She found a SWORDFISH memory stick hidden behind a piece of Nazi-looted art."

"And?"

"It was a warning order for SWORDFISH to prepare for action in both countries. I guess their GRU contacts wanted the SWORD-FISH team in Germany to know ahead of time." Jamie paused. He sat down in the chair in the room that was clearly for visitors. "Let's talk about you and me."

"You and me? As in a couple?"

Jamie laughed long and hard. "No, silly. I am old enough to be your... well at least your older brother. Of course, I know you find me startlingly attractive."

Sue laughed so hard her shoulder hurt. "So, what are we talking about?"

"Dentmann wants to add a SOF operator to her team."

Sue shook her head. "Headquarters duty?"

"Not exactly. You would join yours truly and a guy named Richard and a tech guru. We would be focusing on SWORDFISH operations in Europe. It means leaving HICU, but Massoni and Flash are leaving anyhow to join Smith in the PANOPTICON."

"I thought that was your gig."

"Only for the length of GINGERHAWK. It was a decent place to run that operation. As you know, that operation is finished."

Sue winced at the word. "Finished is an understatement."

"Hey, you did everything you could do to make that right. Now, I would like you to at least consider returning to CONUS and joining my team working in an offsite. I will even sweeten the deal. I will try to find an offsite location near your house on the Potomac."

For the first time in months, Sue thought about the house on the Potomac. Her grandfather's house and now her house. She wouldn't be living in a BOQ. She would be back driving her vintage Thunderbird. She would have a new life. She said, "That sounds pretty good."

Jamie nodded. "I'm glad to hear that because whether you wanted to or not, those are your orders from the SOF commander. The commander wants to expand relations with the Agency. And, what the commander wants..."

Sue knew the rest. "The commander gets. Well, working with you would be a real treat." She didn't disguise the sarcasm.

"Sue, that's just what I said when Dentmann told me her plan." Jamie stood up and walked toward the door. "See you in CONUS in a few weeks. Give me a call at this number." He pointed to the card he had left on the table next to her chair. It had a picture of the knight chess piece and a number starting with the area code of 571. Nothing else. By the time she looked up, he was gone.

Sue had just finished her afternoon physical therapy and was back sitting in her chair drinking a hospital energy drink that looked and tasted like blended grass clippings. Her mother walked in holding two steel travel mugs.

"I'm sure you would prefer your green slime, but I have a mug of Earl Grey tea with honey to offer."

Sue carefully dropped the energy drink into the garbage bin next to her and said, "Thanks, Mom."

Sue had to admit her mother looked good given the fact that she had been attacked just a few weeks ago. It occurred to Sue that resilience was part of her mother's DNA — which meant that quality had to be in her own DNA as well.

"How are you, dear?"

Sue would normally have shrugged and avoided the subject but shrugging hurt. She said, "This is like the bullet wound that Wild Bill got back in DC. It will heal in a bit and then I will start serious PT."

"Except Bill's wound was a .22 and I understand you were hit by a Russian sniper round."

"Yup. A little bigger hole in my shoulder."

"When will you transfer back to the US?"

Long ago, Sue accepted the fact that her mother had a well-established intelligence network that rivaled many formal services. She referred to it as "the sisterhood." In this case, Sue assumed she heard the news directly from Patty Dentmann. "Well, Smith told me that they had already packed my household effects from the BOQ at Camp Ederle and sent them back to CONUS. I have to get cleared for travel. I might catch a Nightingale flight out of Ramstein back to Bragg or just wait a bit and catch a commercial flight back to DC."

"Take your time. I understand that Patty thinks you can use the Potomac River house as your base for a bit. I met Jamie and he likes that idea. Working for Headquarters but not working in Headquarters. He said he will find a small office nearby. He is a nice man."

"You don't know him, Mom. Nice is not exactly how I would describe Jamie."

Barbara laughed. "Well, I just wanted to tell you I'm heading home tomorrow."

"Done with your work?"

"Yes. I don't know if you knew I was working with Beth on a case of recovered Nazi loot. It turns out we were able to recover some valuable 1920s and 1930s art for the family while helping Patty just a bit. All in all, as good a result as you could expect given the circumstances."

Sue nearly teared up. She said, "I'm sorry that Jasper ended up such a creep. I heard he tried to do you harm."

"I'm not exactly sure that's what happened, dear. The creeps who tried to do us harm were amateurs. I'm not saying they didn't intend to do harm. I'm just saying they picked the wrong room to try."

"Always a mistake to mess with O'Connells."

This time it was Barbara who teared up. She took an aged Bulova on a leather strap off her wrist and handed it to Sue. "I heard you lost your watch in the gunfight. This was your grandfather's watch, Sue. It seems to bring good luck. I think it's time you got some."

J.R. SEEGER is a western New York native who served as a US Army paratrooper and as a CIA case officer for a total of 27 years of federal service. In October 2001, Mr. Seeger led a CIA paramilitary team into Afghanistan. He splits his time between western New York and Central New Mexico.